CW01239708

## PRAISE FOR *THE TRANSCENDENT TIDE*

'A barnstorming thriller ... and a wonderful and radical sense of a greater, wider way of seeing life on our planet' Martin MacInnes

'Doug Johnstone has crash landed into the world of sci fi, emerging from the wreckage as the unholy, octopoid lovechild of David Attenborough and Michael Crichton. Through a thrilling, action-packed adventure in the breathtaking surrounds of Greenland, Johnstone howls his desperate message of climate change and human folly. But with his always wonderfully realised characters – human and otherwise – he gives us hope: maybe it's not too late' Callum McSorely

'Such an affecting and thought-provoking read. Johnstone's worldbuilding is top notch in this pacy eco-alien tale of peril and hope. I enjoyed every single sentence' Tendai Huchu

'A delight! We need more novels that take on human exceptionalism with such gusto' Ever Dundas

'The perfect end to the perfect trilogy' Michael Wood

'Equal parts powerful, profound, prescient and pacy, *The Transcendent Tide* explores big concepts with flair and ease. A brilliant near-future tale, told beautifully, and sure to appeal to sci fi and thriller fans alike' Lyndsey Croal

'A brilliant novel, handling complex themes with great skill, at once a breakneck thriller and a timely meditation on man's destructive nature' Ambrose Parry

'As gripping as it is clever, *The Transcendent Tide* drives to a terrifying conclusion, and reveals the best and worst of humanity along the way. Johnstone fuses a scientist's logic with a master storyteller's art. Surprising, compelling and out of this world' Ann Morgan

'Doug wraps up a serious critique of the state of the world today in a tense thriller anchored in the lives of ordinary people. Excellent stuff!' James Oswald

'These books have totally taken me outside my comfort reading and I have loved them! ... The characters are all brilliant and they will certainly find a place in your heart – especially Sandy' Independent Book Reviews

## PRAISE FOR THE ENCELADONS TRILOGY

**Selected for BBC Two *Between the Covers* 2023**

**Longlisted for the McIlvanney Prize for Scottish Crime Book of the Year**

'A gateway book to sci fi … I loved it' Sara Cox

'So readable and accessible' Alan Davies

'If you read one life-affirming book this year, make sure it's this one' *Prima*

'Prioritising pace, tension and high stakes … a plea for empathy, compassion and perspective' *Herald Scotland*

'An emotionally engaging read' *Guardian*

'Johnstone doesn't shy away from complex themes and smartly leverages the lens of science fiction to cut deep into the human experience' *SciFi Now* Book of the Month

'A delicious, demanding departure' Val McDermid

'As moving as it is magical and mysterious' Mark Billingham

'A first-contact tale full of heart and high-octane action' D.V. Bishop

'Science fiction gains a new author' Derek B. Miller

'An adrenaline-filled ride of a novel, laced with empathy and understanding' Rachelle Atalla

'Pay attention, Steven Spielberg! This could be your next film' Marnie Riches

'Clever and unusual … I was on a journey with these characters, and completely transfixed' Susi Holliday

'A mesmerising tale of wonder and hope' Marion Todd

'Doug Johnstone's fresh-take on sci fi was awesome' Scott Tucker

'Elements of the story are gut-wrenching … others are so heartwarming, showing that compassion and care can still persist even in the face of hatred, fear and selfishness' Jen Med's Book Reviews

## ABOUT THE AUTHOR

Doug Johnstone is the author of nineteen novels, many of which have been bestsellers. *The Space Between Us* was chosen for BBC Two's *Between the Covers*, while *Black Hearts* was shortlisted for the Theakston Crime Novel of the Year, *The Big Chill* longlisted for the same prize. Four of his books have been shortlisted or longlisted for the McIlvanney Prize for Scottish Crime Novel of the Year. Doug has taught creative writing or been writer in residence at universities, schools, writing retreats, festivals, prisons and a funeral directors. He's also been an arts journalist for twenty-five years. He is a songwriter and musician with ten albums released, and drummer for the Fun Lovin' Crime Writers. He's also co-founder of the Scotland Writers Football Club. Follow Doug on Bluesky @dougjohnstone.bsky.social and Instagram @writerdougj, and visit his website: dougjohnstone.com.

**Other titles by Doug Johnstone, available from Orenda Books**

THE SKELFS SERIES
*A Dark Matter*
*The Big Chill*
*The Great Silence*
*Black Hearts*
*The Opposite of Lonely*
*Living Is a Problem*

THE ENCELADONS
*The Space Between Us*
*The Collapsing Wave*

*Fault Lines*
*Breakers*

# THE TRANSCENDENT TIDE

DOUG JOHNSTONE

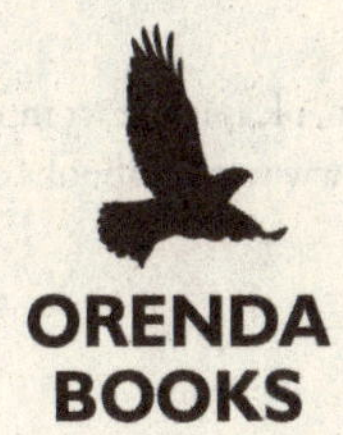

Orenda Books
16 Carson Road
West Dulwich
London SE21 8HU
www.orendabooks.co.uk

First published in the United Kingdom by Orenda Books, 2025


A catalogue record for this book is available from the British Library.

ISBN 978-1-916788-62-6
eISBN 978-1-916788-63-3

Typeset in Garamond by Elaine Sharples
Printed and bound by Clays Ltd, Elcograf S.p.A

For sales and distribution, please contact info@orendabooks.co.uk or visit www.orendabooks.co.uk.

For Tricia

# 1
# LENNOX

Lennox watched Greg lift the rifle and point it at the seal. The water was calm, their small RIB steady. Lennox looked at the young harbour seal basking on the shale beach of the headland. It raised its head, eyeing them in the boat. The bang of the gun made Lennox jump. Greg lowered the rifle and lifted his binoculars. 'Bullseye.'

<Christ.> This was Vonnie's voice in Lennox's head, as familiar as breathing.

He looked past Greg to her, standing at the prow of the boat. <I know, right?>

He lifted his own binoculars and checked the seal, the tranquiliser dart stuck in its rump. It was squirming, staring at the dart, rolling in discomfort.

Greg started the engine and they kicked up some water as they approached. Lennox kept watching the seal. It was already slowing, and lowered its head on a rock, whiskers twitching, eyes blinking heavily.

<It never gets easier.>

He turned at Vonnie's voice in his mind. Greg had no idea they could communicate like this, no one knew except a couple of people, friends they shared the gift with. Friends they hadn't seen in eighteen months.

Lennox shook his head at Vonnie. She wore a grey beanie against the cold breeze, black hair tumbling to her shoulders, a SAMS hoodie and hiking shorts, black boots and thick socks. Her green eyes were full of conflict, a feeling Lennox shared.

What they were doing here was a good thing, right? He had to keep reminding himself, especially in that moment when Greg or one of the other post-doc researchers shot a defenceless seal. He had a flashback to standing on the shore of Loch Broom a year and a half ago, American marines firing into the water, trying to hit Sandy, the octopoid creature who'd travelled millions of miles to Earth, who'd connected with Lennox in a way that no one, not even Vonnie, had matched. Lennox and Vonnie had been held captive at an American military base outside Ullapool along with their friends Ava and Heather. The Americans were there to exterminate Sandy and the other Enceladons – intelligent octopus and giant jellyfish creatures who'd come to Earth from the under-ice ocean of Saturn's moon Enceladus. Lennox and the others had originally saved Sandy, but the authorities saw these wonderful creatures as an existential threat and tried to wipe them out.

They were a few metres from the shore now where the seal still moved a little, drowsy and confused. The orange flight of the sedative dart was garish against its mottled grey fur, something artificial in this natural place. It made Lennox think how ridiculous the human race was. How they considered themselves above nature. Sandy, that octopoid creature, along with their fellow alien Enceladons, couldn't understand how humanity worked. The way we tortured and killed each other in our millions, along with billions of animals, the environment, the planet. Human exceptionalism gave us licence to destroy our home and ourselves.

Lennox looked back at the cluster of low buildings on the shore, the Scottish Association for Marine Science campus. He and Vonnie had just finished their first year studying here, immersing themselves in the biology, chemistry and geology of marine life. Sitting in a classroom listening to lectures was frustrating, but the plus side was this place. The campus was in Dunstaffnage, a few miles north of Oban on the west coast of the Highlands, and their poky student residence was only two minutes from the beach. SAMS had kayaks and scuba gear they could use whenever they wanted, and they spent every possible moment in the water, watching crabs and lobsters scuttling along the bottom, seals playing in the surf, fish of all kinds, porpoises and dolphins further out.

And every now and then jellyfish and octopuses. Each time, the sight of them made Lennox's heart thump, and he would shout out from his mind, as if he was back with the Enceladons in Loch Broom.

<Sandy?> He sent it out now for the millionth time, a message into the ether, hoping his friend would hear him and pop out of the water with that crazy light display of theirs.

Vonnie moved to him in the boat and touched his back. <It's OK.>

She'd heard him and he felt embarrassed. But Vonnie missed Sandy too. Anyone who'd come into contact with those extraordinary creatures would feel lost without that connection. Lennox had chosen not to go with them to the Arctic Ocean when they fled human persecution in Scotland, but he couldn't imagine his life stretching into the future without Sandy in it.

'He's gone over,' Greg said, pointing at the seal.

They covered the last few metres to shore. Lennox and Vonnie jumped out and pulled the RIB onto the beach, splashing through the cold water.

The smell of the seal hit him – fish, ammonia and wet dog. But they'd been tagging seals for a month now, he was used to it.

Greg's research was into migration patterns and feeding methods, so he was tagging as many local seals as possible. He'd needed help over the summer, and Lennox and Vonnie had nowhere else to go. They'd kept their heads down ever since the events at Loch Broom, so an obscure campus in a remote corner of the Scottish Highlands suited them fine.

Greg clambered out with a rucksack. He was over six feet, freckly and pale, spindly legs like a giant crab. He was earnest about his research, but Lennox thought it was kind of pointless. He and Vonnie had swum with telepathic creatures, a hundred times bigger than seals, that were part of an interconnected collective. Lennox had been down in the murky depths of Loch Ness with Sandy, and up into space with Xander, the giant jellyfish creature that was like a big brother to Sandy. Being stuck in a human body on the shore felt pitiful in comparison.

Lennox looked across the Firth of Lorn at the low shadow of Lismore Island in the distance, spotted the white lighthouse at the southern tip. In the firth, the ferry from Oban was chugging along, a speck dwarfed by the enormity of the landscape. Humans were insignificant, and being in the proximity of nature brought that home.

Greg unpacked his bag and they set about tagging the animal. The tracker was a small waterproof plastic pack that housed a chip and a battery, a short antenna sticking out from the top. Vonnie stroked the seal's head as Lennox got out the glue and squirted a square onto the back of its neck. Greg fixed the device. The seal would moult its fur eventually and the tracker would be lost. Researchers always said the devices were unobtrusive and didn't upset the seals, but Lennox wasn't convinced. He wished he was telepathic with animals so he could know for sure. The plastic box looked ridiculous stuck to the poor animal's scruff. Lennox reminded himself that this work was done to better understand and protect these animals. But maybe they should just be left alone.

Vonnie caught his eye. <It doesn't do any harm.>

'Are we sure?' Lennox said.

Greg turned. 'What?'

Lennox widened his eyes at Vonnie over the mistake of speaking out loud. 'Are we sure he's not going to wake up, I mean?'

Greg fiddled with his phone, synching the signal from the tracker with the monitoring app. 'We have some time yet.'

Lennox looked at the seal, its eyes watering, whiskers drooped.

He heard a noise and turned. Saw something in the sky, a helicopter. Not one of the tourist ones you occasionally saw around here, faster and sleeker.

It was soon above them, the noise of the blades deafening. Lennox glanced at Vonnie, who shrugged. The helicopter descended as it reached the mainland, hovered over the field next to the SAMS campus. Lennox saw a logo on the side that made him tense up – a circle with tentacles coming from behind it, as if a giant octopus was attacking a planet or moon.

The helicopter landed and cut the engines, then the door opened and a man and woman got out. They looked across the bay to where Lennox, Vonnie and Greg stood with the seal. The man put a hand up to shade his eyes. Then they turned and walked towards the main SAMS building.

Lennox looked at Vonnie and saw the fear in her eyes. They both knew this was bad news.

## 2
## AVA

'I'll never tire of this view,' Freya said.

Ava glanced at her little sister. Unruly red curls, hourglass figure in a Big Black T-shirt and shorts. Steam drifted from her coffee into the air. Ava looked at Chloe a few yards away on the beach, hunkered at a rockpool in just a babygro, a piece of brown seaweed stuck to her foot.

<Be careful,> Ava sent. Her daughter didn't look round.

Sheba was sniffing around the rockpools, staying close to Chloe. Freya had picked the collie up from the local shelter a year ago, and the dog instantly bonded with Chloe in a way that made Ava suspicious. Her daughter was two and still hadn't spoken out loud, and Ava wondered if it was to do with her telepathy. If you didn't *have* to speak, why would you? Maybe Chloe didn't understand yet that not everyone could do what she and Ava did. But the way the dog reacted to Chloe's feelings made Ava think it could sense something. She tried not to worry about that. If her daughter could communicate with animals as well as humans, what kind of life would she have?

Ava turned to Freya. 'Much on today?'

Freya sipped her coffee. 'Couple of small jobs to finish off.'

Freya was a freelance graphic designer, which meant she could work from anywhere. And where better than Ratagan, the middle of nowhere on the empty side of Loch Duich?

Ava looked across calm water at the Kintail mountains. Freya's house had been the perfect place to retreat to after the craziness of last year at Loch Broom, a backwater where Ava could concentrate on Chloe.

<Crab, Mummy.>

Ava's heart swelled at her daughter's voice in her mind. Most mothers had a deep understanding of their young daughters, but Ava had something special, could feel Chloe's moods as strongly as her own and hear her voice in her head. Just before Chloe was born, Ava had panicked that there was something wrong with her daughter. Sandy intervened in a bathtub in the Highlands, connecting with both Ava and Chloe in utero, and reassuring Ava that the girl was OK. But that had connected Ava and Chloe in a deeper way than any humans had ever experienced before. They could feel each other's feelings and it had changed their relationship forever. Imagine if everyone had this?

She'd explained it to Freya, who said she believed her, but Ava knew it sounded crazy. For now, Ava was taking each day as it came, happy that both of them were safe. They'd been through so much together already, every new day felt like a blessing.

She walked over to Chloe, on her knees and peering into the rockpool. The girl had lifted a stone and was trailing a finger in the clear water.

Ava loved bringing Chloe rockpooling, it reminded her of Sandy and the Enceladons. They were many times bigger than the tiny creatures on the beach, but since the Enceladons came to Earth they were all now part of the same ecosystem. Ava missed her connection with them, but her family was here. The only connection she needed was with Chloe.

<Yes, honey, that's a shore crab, be gentle with it.>

Chloe had the crab between her thumb and forefinger, touching the shell delicately. Ava saw the green underbelly, brown on top. She remembered Sandy's light displays, Xander and the other Enceladons too, the brilliance of it. But every creature was special, right?

Chloe held the crab up and grinned at Ava, who felt a shiver. One day this little girl would be a woman with her own life, but for now she was all Ava's. Chloe put the crab back carefully. It was natural for toddlers to appreciate every life, but that somehow got drummed out of us along the way.

<Look.> Chloe pointed, and Ava saw two miniscule shrimp, almost transparent, tails flicking.

<See their little antennae?>

Sheba came over and stuck her nose in.

Chloe looked at the dog and it stepped back.

Ava stood and stretched, breathed deeply, widened her eyes.

'You two are so funny,' Freya said, coming over. 'Obsessed with all the little things.'

'Little things are important.'

Freya rolled her eyes. 'And everything's connected, yada, yada, yada. I get it.'

Ava laughed. She understood her sister's cynicism. She would've been the same if she hadn't experienced Sandy and the Enceladons. They'd shifted her mind at a fundamental level.

<Mummy?>

Ava turned and saw Chloe resting her head on a rock, as if it was too heavy for her. Her arms were trembling by her side. Ava sensed the girl's anxiety. 'What's up, sweetheart?'

Sheba started barking, first at Chloe, as if an invisible demon was behind her, then at Ava and Freya.

Chloe sat down heavily on the stones and looked around with dazed eyes. She raised her shaking hands and frowned at them.

The barking filled the air as Ava crouched and held Chloe's hands. <What's the matter?>

<Sore.> The word was accompanied by a pounding pain that Ava felt in her own heart, distress from the girl swirling inside her as Ava tried to hide her rising concern.

'Sheba.' Freya grabbed the dog's collar and pulled her away. 'Shush now.'

<Mummy.> Confusion on Chloe's face, tears in her eyes.

<Baby, it's OK.>

Ava lifted Chloe in her arms just as the girl vomited. <Shit, Chloe.>

Freya's eyes went wide as Ava looked around in panic.

Sheba had shut up now and somehow the silence was worse than the barking.

Chloe closed her eyes and went limp in Ava's arms.

Ava's anxiety rose from her stomach to her throat and she struggled to breathe. <Chloe?> She didn't feel anything in her mind. The emptiness was overwhelming. 'Chloe? Shit.'

Freya shook her head. 'We have to get her to a doctor.'

Ava lifted Chloe's eyelid and her eye was rolled way back. 'Christ.'

Freya was already walking up the beach to the road. 'I'll get the car.'

Ava was right behind, the smell of sick in her nostrils, fear in her mind. The pain she'd felt from Chloe a moment ago was the same pain she'd felt the first time she encountered Sandy, when she almost died of a stroke.

She hugged Chloe's body to her chest as she scrambled up the stones, telling herself it was going to be OK, Chloe was going to be OK.

# 3
# NIVIAQ

Niviaq steered the boat through patches of ice, heading for the mouth of the bay. She glanced back at the brightly painted houses of Tasiilaq, home for most of her life. It felt claustrophobic at times, but out here on the water, with the Arctic wind in her face, she felt free. A couple of months ago, she couldn't have used the boat at all because of the thick sea ice. But now it had broken up just enough, and for this small window in the summer she was intent on making the most of the opportunity to get on the water.

She passed the derelict houses of Ittaajik then an old hunting hut, then headed northeast up Ammassalik Fjord. Larger chunks of ice here, some bergs from the summer glacier melt. Snowy mountains loomed to her left. The sun shone but the air was sharp, and she raised a hand to secure her wool headband, zipped her jacket tighter.

She tried to shake the dream from her mind. She'd been having these dreams for months, had never told anyone. Her mother would've fussed over them, claiming they were a warning sent by the spirits. Niviaq was torn about all that. She'd been raised on Inuit tradition, Greenlandic myths and legends, and respected that stuff. Her three years at university in Copenhagen had given her a wider perspective, but she'd been lonely on campus, her skin colour and Inuit tattoos making her stand out against the blonde hair and blue eyes of her fellow students.

When her mum called in deepest January to say that her sister Maliina had walked out onto the ice in the night and never come back, Niviaq sat alone in her student room and cried for three hours straight. Crying for her loss, but also because Maliina's darkness meant it wasn't completely unexpected. The next day she quit university and flew straight home to her mother's arms, both of them lost in grief while they tried to take care of Maliina's daughter, Pipaluk. When Maliina's decomposed body washed up months later in the thaw, Niviaq felt none of the closure she'd read about in books.

The dreams spooked her. Strange octopuses and giant jellyfish beckoning her into the water, talking to her in her mind, enveloping her body within theirs, swimming faster than a narwhal or beluga, moving through each other's bodies like they were ghosts.

Other strange things were happening around here. All up the east coast there had been many more sightings of marine mammals than usual, even some that were rarely found here like blue whales. And the northern lights, *artsarniid*, had been dancing for months, even in summer. Also, there had been sightings of underwater lights, creatures moving in the fog on the sea ice, glowing and shape-shifting. Niviaq would normally have ignored all that superstitious stuff but the dreams felt connected. They made *her* feel connected somehow.

To her right she could see a boat, it looked like the Maqe brothers, Aqqalu and Nuka. They would be hunting seal, or anything bigger if they stumbled on it. The seas were full of food right now. Niviaq had been brought up to hunt, knew how to use a rifle, but that wasn't why she was out today.

She scanned the horizon, just land and sea and ice and snow in every direction, the blue sky painfully bright, the sun shining in a way it never did in Copenhagen. It wasn't as strong here, but it was somehow purer.

She saw a harp seal on an ice floe nursing its baby and thought about her sister. Her mother insisted it was an accident, but Maliina always had a darkness that haunted her. The suicide rates in Greenland were so high it was a scandal. A YouTuber recently visited Tasiilaq, calling it 'the most suicidal town in the world' for his millions of followers, and only talked about alcoholism and domestic violence, none of the positive sides of their culture. But the numbers were undeniable, young people were killing themselves at a frightening rate. Niviaq had felt a little of that darkness in Copenhagen. Being separated from her home like that had frightened her more than she'd admitted to anyone.

She spotted something on an ice floe, a dark shape. Lifted the binoculars, presuming it was another seal. But it was a human shape, arm dangling in the water, face obscured. She swallowed hard, lowered the binoculars and frowned as she looked around. She lifted the glasses to check again, definitely a person. What the hell?

She steered towards them, cut the engine and brought the boat alongside. Bumped the ice and grabbed the man's arm, held onto him with one hand and a hooked pole to turn the boat until the transom was alongside, then heaved him with a mighty effort onto the deck.

He was in a black uniform with a dark life jacket on top. She turned him over. He looked Scandinavian, fair hair in a buzzcut, a few days of stubble. She checked his pulse, faint but still there. He was breathing but his body temperature was low.

She got a blanket from a cupboard in the cockpit and brought it over, then started to take his uniform off. Wet clothes were a sure way of getting hypothermia, even in summer. She eased his boots off, then the trousers. He had a logo on the upper arm of his jacket, a moon or planet surrounded by tentacles. She thought of her dreams, the otherworldly octopuses and jellyfish. She removed the jacket and his fleece, then wrapped him in the thermal blanket.

She went back to the helm and took a long look all around, first with the naked eye, then with the binoculars. She couldn't see a boat anywhere, no signs of human activity. What was he doing out here?

She started the engine and headed back towards Tasiilaq, staring at the tentacles on the logo and thinking about her dreams. They were connected, but she couldn't work out how.

# 4
# HEATHER

She looked down at her tentacles propelling her through the water and wondered if she would ever get used to this. She wasn't Enceladon but she wasn't human anymore either. She looked across at Jodie as they looped around each other. Jodie was at the same stage of transformation as Heather, and Heather could see the remnants of her facial features beneath the surface of her octopoid head, the hands and feet that had morphed into tentacles as they'd slowly separated themselves from their Enceladon mentors.

They passed a school of Arctic char and Heather saw a wolffish below them. One of the millions of things that had amazed her in the last year and a half was how much life was in the ocean. Humans couldn't comprehend the scale of the ecosystem down here, immeasurable numbers of flourishing creatures.

Jodie flickered blue light down her head to two tentacles, and Heather understood and followed her to a colony of harp seals near the surface, little arrows perfectly suited to their environment. As a human, Heather had only seen seals basking on the shore, where they seemed like vulnerable bags of blubber. But here they were skilful predators, chasing the char as Heather and Jodie followed.

Heather, Jodie and the other ten Outwithers who travelled with the Enceladons from Scotland to the Arctic Ocean had all had an insane eighteen months. To begin with they were each paired up with an Enceladon who wrapped their body around their human, protected them from the cold, allowed them to breathe, communicated with them. Heather had been paired with Sandy. As well as being wrapped in their octopus mentors, the humans spent time inside the larger jellyfish creatures, Xander in Heather's case, while Jodie lived inside Yolanda. The names were arbitrary, for human use, the Enceladons didn't understand individuality. Gradually, the humans' bodies changed, they could breathe underwater, didn't feel the cold. They shifted from human to octopoid, bones dissolving, limbs turning to tentacles, heads enlarging. For the last nine months they'd been able to swim on their own, adapting more every day, getting used to their new bodies. Their telepathy became stronger, so they could communicate with each other more clearly. But there was still a lot of psychological distance between them and the Enceladons because they'd evolved on different worlds, in different environments and cultures.

Heather knew that the distance would never be fully closed. She and the others would never be completely Enceladon, a naïve dream at the start of all this. She'd walked into the water with Sandy because she was fed up with being human, with humanity. She'd dreamed of being part of something, and she was. But the idea that she could become part of a completely alien society and mindset was a pipe dream.

She still had a lot of developing to do. She still didn't think of herself as *they*, like Sandy and the other Enceladons did, but she certainly felt more multitudinous than the lonely human she had been. She was beginning to feel her tentacles think for themselves, collections of neurons sending signals to her brain.

And, like Jodie, she was beginning to use the light display on her skin, shift the shape and texture of her body. This was the most amazing journey into otherness, beyond anything she could've imagined, and she was grateful for it. But she wasn't yet ready to give up some of being human.

The seals had stopped chasing the char and now slowed, floating to the surface to pop their heads up and breathe.

<They're so beautiful.> Jodie's voice was warm in Heather's mind. Jodie still had a trace of her London accent, just as Heather had a

trace of her East Lothian one. She had a brief shimmer of nostalgia, pictured Paul and Rosie in their garden. Then she remembered that her teenage daughter was dead and her marriage gone, and she shivered down her tentacles as she joined Jodie near the surface.

<They really are.>

The seals were used to the Enceladons, didn't see them as a threat. A couple of older pups sniffed at Heather's body, their whiskers shifting in the current. Heather could smell them, had begun to have a really strong sense of smell, could detect the difference between cod and halibut, crabs and shrimp. She reached out a tentacle to the nearest pup as Jodie swam around the colony.

Heather heard a distant pop and one of the seals at the surface jolted in the water, then blood began pouring from its head. As it rolled over in the water, the other seals scattered from it.

<What the hell?> Jodie sent.

Heather saw the bullet hole at the back of the seal's neck, blood descending into the sea like a red veil, the animal's eyes already blank.

The other seals were agitated and swimming around the body, nudging it with their noses. Some of them poked their heads above the surface and Heather wanted to tell them to stop, to get far away from here.

She snuck her own head out the water and spotted a boat heading towards them, two men in it, one pointing a rifle.

<Hunters. They have to get out of here.>

Jodie flashed in response and they swam to the seals, still circling their dead friend. Heather and Jodie enlarged their bodies and heads as far as they could go, flashed a warning to them, eventually pushing them away from the corpse as the sound of the engine got louder.

Heather turned and saw the boat's hull then shoved the nearest seal, which darted downward into the murk. The others followed, leaving the dead seal floating and leaking blood. Heather and Jodie swam in the opposite direction.

Jodie flashed red at her. <I hate that.>

Jodie was better at light displays than Heather. At a basic level their light displays were a mix of emotions and communication, but the Enceladons had a complexity to theirs that still dumbfounded Heather.

She felt a shrug flow through her body. <Me too, but at least it was locals. Part of the ecosystem.>

Jodie swam above her. <It's still awful.>

They'd been over this before. One of the things they'd developed as they'd transformed was their EM detectors, which allowed them to tune into different wavelengths on the electromagnetic spectrum, including human communications. It had made Heather laugh when she first met Sandy, that they had access to the human internet. Imagine being exposed to all the insanity of social media when you had only ever lived as an oceanic collective on an alien moon. But the internet had been an anchor for Heather as she transformed, a last vestige of humanity to hold on to. She'd used it to research the Greenlandic people, their relationship to the land and sea. The Inuit idea of reciprocity, take only what you need, give thanks to the creature who gave its life for you. She was as shocked as Jodie to see it in action, but she found it hard to condemn the Greenlandic hunters and fishers.

She heard a noise and wondered if the hunters were on their trail.

Jodie flashed. <What's that?>

Heather spun round, spotted a light in the distance. It got closer, the light spreading ahead of it. Gradually it resolved into a small vehicle with a torch on the front. It moved fast, a trail of bubbles from a propeller at the back.

Heather waved at Jodie. <Underwater drone.>

<What's it doing *here*? We should go.>

They should, but Heather thought about the harp seal, then she thought of the giant fish-processing ships she'd seen from a distance, scooping up every living thing in the ocean, despite the fact it was banned here by international treaty. She thought about how terribly humans treated the world.

She arrowed her head and swam under the drone.

Jodie hesitated. <Where are you going?>

<Fuck this.> When the drone's light was above her, Heather launched herself upward. The beam caught Jodie in its glare and she darted away, as Heather grabbed the vehicle in her tentacles, ripping the light from the front, buckling the metal body, tearing at the camera until it came free. She ripped the rear thruster from its casing and squeezed again until the drone was a crumpled piece of human garbage that had no place here.

# 5
# LENNOX

Rebecca was waiting impatiently at the shore. Professor Rivera was associate director of SAMS but insisted everyone call her Rebecca, it was that kind of place.

Greg landed the RIB on the beach and the three of them jumped out. Lennox looked at the helicopter on the grass. It was very sleek, a uniformed pilot stretching his legs round the back. The logo was clear, tentacles and a cratered moon.

'Come on,' Rebecca said. She was short and lean, black hair tied up, Mexican accent. Saving the oceans was an international task. She pointed at Lennox and Vonnie. 'He's waiting for you two.'

Vonnie frowned. 'Who?'

'Karl Jensen, that's who.'

Lennox knew the name, of course. Norwegian billionaire who'd made his money in tech, a handful of apps that caught fire. But the overarching company, KJI, had branched out into other fields, growing exponentially. Everyone at SAMS knew of him because he'd spent years and millions helping ocean conservation projects. He'd developed a non-intrusive way of cleaning up the Great Pacific Garbage Patch using bioengineered algae, and made more billions doing it.

Lennox glanced at Vonnie. <What the hell?>

'Why does he want to speak to us?' Vonnie said.

'Just come on.' Rebecca glanced at their scruffy clothes and wet boots as she ushered them towards the building. 'He recently donated a large sum to the running of SAMS. Very large, you understand? So whatever he wants, the answer is yes.'

<Fuck that,> Lennox sent. Jensen buying his way into SAMS was

suspicious. Why would someone embedded in late-stage capitalism suddenly be interested in a tiny research project like this?

Vonnie looked at him. <This stinks.>

Rebecca opened the door to her office and shoved them inside.

Karl Jensen was standing next to a blonde woman, both of them looking at a large bathymetric map of the sea floor on the wall, which covered the area from Loch Linnhe up through The Minch. Lennox spotted Loch Broom at the top of the map and felt a little queasy.

Karl turned. He looked younger than forty-five, tall and lean, short and messy brown hair, a light beard, bright-blue eyes. He wore a chunky, ribbed polo neck and jeans, like someone pretending to be an old sea dog. The woman was a little shorter and younger, impeccably put together in an understated suit, hair in a neat ponytail, professional smile, holding an iPad.

She turned to Rebecca. 'Thank you, Professor Rivera.'

Rebecca flushed. 'I was hoping—'

'Thank you.'

Rebecca gave them a warning stare as she left the room – *Don't fuck this up*.

Karl walked over and grinned, shook Lennox and Vonnie by the hand, holding on too long, examining their faces.

'My name is Karl Jensen.' He held out a hand to the blonde woman. 'And this is Britt Pedersen, my right-hand woman.' His Norwegian accent had an American twang to it. 'Please, sit.'

Vonnie returned his smile. 'I think I'll stand.'

Karl angled his head in acquiescence and walked to the window, looked over the bay.

<What is this?> Lennox asked Vonnie.

She pressed her lips together. <Nothing good.>

Britt was watching them, and Lennox knew that he had to make an effort not to look at Vonnie when he communicated with her.

Karl turned back to the room. 'Do you miss them?' His voice was light and airy.

Lennox's stomach tightened. 'Miss who?'

Karl pointed out of the window at the sea. 'The Enceladons, of course.'

Lennox swallowed and didn't look at Vonnie. <Fuck.>

'Who?' he said.

Karl looked from Lennox to Vonnie and back again. 'I'm very jealous. To have had such an experience must have been mind-blowing.'

Vonnie rubbed at her wrist. 'I think you've got the wrong people.'

Britt woke her iPad up and read from it. 'Vonnie Macallan, aged nineteen, grew up in Ardmair. Lennox Hunt, eighteen years old, grew up in a children's home in Edinburgh. Both passed first year of marine science with distinction. Met each other at the New Broom military and research facility at Rhue Point eighteen months ago. Were involved in the Enceladon assault on New Broom which ended with twelve dead and sixteen injured.'

Karl sat on Rebecca's desk, trying to be casual.

'I have friends very high up in the US administration,' he said. 'One of my companies was involved in the clean-up at New Broom. That was quite a job. I was given access to all the files. Everything. I know all about the Enceladons, about you.'

Lennox shook his head. 'I don't know what you're talking about.' <What the fuck do we do?>

<How the hell should I know?>

Karl smiled. 'I know about Sandy, the Enceladon you both connected with telepathically. I know about the others who connected, Ava Gallacher and Heather Banks. I know about Fellowes and Carson and all the madness.'

Vonnie looked at the door. 'I really think there's been a mix-up.'

Karl put his hands out. 'It's a disgrace, the way you were treated. The way the Enceladons were treated. I don't blame you or them for what happened. If I'd been in your shoes, I would have done exactly the same.' He pushed himself away from the desk and went to the map, tapped at Loch Broom. 'And if I'd been in charge, things would've gone very differently.'

Lennox looked around. 'Is this a joke? I keep waiting for the cameras to be revealed. We don't know anything about this, we're just students here.'

Karl nodded then glanced at Britt. 'You want to protect them, I understand. Especially given your experience. Humans are terrible creatures, we all know that. The worst instincts of humanity were on show at New Broom, and I'm disgusted to be from the same species that perpetrated that. To treat our first extraterrestrial visitors like vermin makes me feel sick.' He sucked his teeth and sighed. 'But we have a second chance.'

Lennox looked at Britt, watching impassively.

'I've spent the last eighteen months looking for them,' Karl said. 'With the intention of communicating, helping if I can. I've dreamed of first contact all my life, since I was a little kid in Tromsø. A few months ago we detected some signs off the east coast of Greenland, just below the Arctic Circle. But the sea ice was too thick to get close. So we concentrated on building our research facility while we waited for the melt. Now we have a state-of-the-art research centre on the coast, and are sending out drones and boats. We think we know roughly where they are, but they will be understandably cautious, given last time.' He glanced at Britt, then at Lennox and Vonnie. 'Which is where you come in.'

Lennox shook his head.

<We need to get out of here,> Vonnie sent to him.

'Being connected like that must be profound,' Karl said. 'It must change the way you think. I've read all the notes a hundred times, the Enceladons are extraordinary, intertwined in a way I can't begin to imagine.' He nodded at Lennox. 'But you can. You miss them, I know you do. Wouldn't you both like to see Sandy again?'

'This is nonsense,' Vonnie said.

'I can make it happen,' Karl said.

Britt showed them her iPad screen. A map of east Greenland, then a spread of buildings in a snowy landscape, mountains in the background, frozen sea nearby.

'We want you to come to Sedna Station,' she said. 'Help us make contact with the Enceladons. They'll trust you. We mean no harm, we just want to learn from them, help them.'

Vonnie scowled at Lennox. <We can't trust a fucking billionaire. This is New Broom all over again.>

<I know.> But Lennox *did* miss them. He missed Sandy like crazy and only felt like half a person since they'd been apart.

'No, thanks,' Vonnie said, then turned to Lennox. 'Come on.'

Karl focused on Lennox.

Vonnie was at the door but Lennox hadn't moved. She was a hundred percent right, these guys couldn't be trusted.

Karl approached Lennox and held out a business card. It had his name, email and number. On the other side was the logo, a moon and tentacles, with *Sedna Station* across the top.

'Sedna is the Mother of the Sea in Inuit mythology,' he said. 'The goddess of all the animals who live in the ocean. This is not New Broom, this is a second chance. Please take it.'

Lennox could feel Vonnie's eyes burning into the back of his head, but he took the card anyway. He really did miss Sandy.

## 6
## AVA

She stared at Chloe in the hospital bed and tried not to cry. Her body was electric with nerves, the panic of earlier replaced by extreme anxiety. She reached out and touched the girl's forehead then stroked her strawberry-blonde hair, running a finger across her scalp, thinking of what was going on inside that skull. Chloe hadn't woken since her attack, or whatever it was.

<Hey, baby. It's OK, Mummy's here.>

No response, which scared her. She was so used to feeling what her daughter felt that the silence was overpowering.

'Anything?'

Freya's voice made Ava jump. She was on a thin thread.

Freya put two cups of tea on the bedside table and hugged Ava. 'She'll be OK.'

'We don't know that.'

Ava didn't want to be comforted – what use were words right now? On the drive to Broadford Hospital, they'd filled the car with fraught conversation. It was a forty-minute drive from Ratagan, which they covered in half an hour, around Loch Duich and Loch Alsh, over the bridge to Skye. They were lucky, this community hospital was brand new, a low building looking over Broadford Bay towards the mainland. It had a tiny, empty A&E, where Chloe was assessed. She was breathing normally but unconscious, so they sent her for a CT scan. They'd only brought her back a few minutes ago, and Ava and Freya were still waiting for the results. Chloe was wearing a little hospital-brand T-shirt. The nurse had cleaned the vomit from her and changed her nappy earlier.

'What if she dies,' Ava said, staring at the steaming cups on the table.

'Hey,' Freya touched her hand. 'Don't. You'll drive yourself insane.'

'Freya, she's everything to me, you don't understand because you don't...'

It was a stupid thing to say. Parents didn't have a monopoly on love and fear and panic. Anyone who loved anyone felt the same. Ava liked to think she had more connection to Chloe because she could read her mind, but that was arrogant. That negated all the other love in the world, and only a cruel bitch would think something like that.

To her credit, Freya hadn't flinched.

'I'm sorry,' Ava said. 'I didn't mean anything.'

Freya looked at Chloe. 'She'll be OK, I know it. You're the best mum. You're incredible.'

Freya's crying set Ava off and she tasted tears on her upper lip. She wiped her face.

'Ava Gallagher?' The doctor was a middle-aged woman with short black hair and a confident manner. Her nametag read *Dr Chlebek*. 'Freya.' The way she said Freya's name, they obviously knew each other.

'Blanka.'

'What is it?' Ava stared at the printouts in the doctor's hand. They were from the CT scan, Ava had seen similar when she had her stroke two years ago, the first time she encountered Sandy as a light in the sky. Which had made her puke and pass out, just like Chloe. Ava held on to the side of Chloe's bed for support, reaching for the girl's hand with her fingers.

Dr Chlebek looked at the scans and frowned. 'We're not sure, there was some conflicting information.'

Ava squeezed Chloe's fingers. She had a flashback to waking up in the stroke ward in Edinburgh, sharing it with Lennox and Heather, all of them meeting for the first time and seeing a news report on television about a creature washed up on the beach. Somehow realising their futures lay with that creature.

'What do you mean?' Freya said. She knew about Ava's stroke –

that it had been an accident, something to do with a miscalibration of EM signals by Sandy. No harm meant.

Dr Chlebek cleared her throat. 'Well, our initial scan was ... impossible. It's a brand new scanner, but I'm not sure it's working correctly.'

'Let me guess,' Ava said, finding her voice. 'She had a severe stroke, a haemorrhage in her cerebellum. It's very rare, only two percent of strokes. And it was so catastrophic that she should've died.'

The doctor narrowed her eyes and looked from Ava to Freya, then to Chloe in bed. 'How did you know that?'

Frey was staring at Ava. She felt immensely tired, wished she could blink this all away, go back with Chloe to Ratagan, look at the crabs and prawns in the rockpools.

'Ava?' Freya said.

'So you did another scan,' Ava said.

Dr Chlebek nodded warily. 'Is there something we should know?'

'What about the second scan?'

The doctor shook her head. 'That's the thing. The first result must have been a glitch, so we did another. And the haemorrhage has completely gone.'

Freya breathed out and smiled, as if this was over.

Ava squeezed Chloe's hand. She didn't understand why this had happened now. For Ava, Lennox and Heather, it happened because they'd seen Sandy for the first time. Chloe was just pottering around on the beach, and Sandy and the other Enceladons were thousands of miles away. But Chloe had been touched by Sandy while still in the womb, which must have something to do with this. Maybe there had been something waiting in her brain, waiting for a trigger. There was no one else like Chloe, born able to communicate telepathically with her mother. Maybe there were other things that nobody knew about, terrifying things in her future.

'There was something else,' the doctor said, and her voice made Ava feel sick.

She swallowed and turned slowly to look at Dr Chlebek. The woman's face telegraphed bad news.

'There's a growth,' she said. 'In the same place. It was hidden by the stroke in the first instance. But once the bleeding disappeared, we could see something. So we did a third scan.'

'Cancer?' Freya said.

'A tumour of some kind. We'll need to do more tests. We have to move her to Raigmore.'

'It's in the cerebellum,' Ava said.

The doctor nodded.

Ava stared at her daughter's face, saw her eyes flickering under the lids. She could sense Chloe's confusion and fear as she started to wake.

<I'm here, baby.> She squeezed Chloe's fingers again, stroked her brow. She wanted to get into bed with her and close her eyes and hug her until this all went away. <Mummy will look after you.>

'We should do it as soon as possible,' the doctor said. 'I can arrange for an ambulance to take her to Inverness today.'

Ava shook her head. This was to do with the Enceladons, she knew that in her heart. They didn't mean anyone any harm, so it must be an accident, an unpredicted consequence of Sandy's intervention in utero. Sandy had cured Heather's cancer once, in a hotel room in Ullapool. They had powers that humans couldn't imagine.

Chloe's eyes opened and Ava smiled. She felt her daughter's anxiety. She needed to get Chloe to Sandy, only the Enceladons could help.

'No,' she said. 'No ambulance, no tests. I'm taking her home.'

# 7
# NIVIAQ

Tasiilaq Hospital was a spread of yellow timber buildings up the hill from the harbour where Niviaq had secured her boat. They'd driven the man in the town's ambulance, a two-minute journey but it was the easiest way to move an unconscious body. Niviaq stayed with him until the doctor took over and fussed her out the door.

She stood now, holding the man's wet clothes in a plastic bag, and looked around. Blue and green houses, washing hanging outside in the sun. The red-painted school was to her left, an orange shipping container the other way. A quadbike and a baby buggy were parked under the wooden stairs that led to the hospital entrance, and the Greenlandic flag rippled on the flagpole.

Out of the hospital came Kuupik, filling out his police uniform, breathing heavily as he walked down the steps, the Danish coat of arms and *POLITI* on his jacket.

'So tell me,' Kuupik said in Tunumiisut.

Everyone in the east spoke Tunumiisut but also Kalaallisut, the language of the west. Most spoke some Danish and English too.

'He was on the ice, past Nuugaartik.'

'Were you hunting?'

Niviaq shook her head. 'Just out on the water.'

Kuupik knew all about her sister, everyone knew everyone's business here. But Maliina wasn't the only one, the flag above them was often at half-mast, every time someone succumbed to suicide. Kuupik would understand her need to escape the town for a moment. He took a pack of Prince from his jacket pocket and offered her one. She declined.

He lit his cigarette and inhaled, coughed and touched his tongue with his finger. 'How far was he from shore?'

'Three hundred metres.'

'He could have floated out.'

'I guess.'

'But there are no huts around there. Any sign of a boat?'

'The only boat I saw was the Maqe boys, and that was nowhere near.'

Kuupik took a long drag of his cigarette. 'It's a mystery.'

'Will he be OK?' Niviaq said, looking at the hospital entrance.

'They think so. You did good, finding him when you did. Hypothermia hasn't got hold yet.'

Niviaq raised the plastic bag. 'What will I do with his clothes?'

Kuupik closed an eye at the cigarette smoke and put a hand out.

Niviaq opened the bag and took out the jacket, showed him the logo. 'Ever seen this?'

Kuupik squinted. 'Nope.'

'His gear looks expensive.' She meant not Greenlandic. Foreigners bought crazy-priced all-weather clothes that did nothing against the Greenlandic cold and the *piteraq*, the wind that could come at any time, ripping tents from the ground and roofs from houses. The name translated as 'that which attacks you'.

'No ID on him?'

'No.'

Kuupik pressed his lips together. 'I'll try to find out.'

Niviaq handed him the bag. She'd already taken a picture of the logo with her phone.

'OK, then,' Kuupik said. This meant the conversation was over.

Niviaq walked down the hill, more washing hanging from her neighbours' houses, the Christiansen girls jumping on their trampoline and waving at her.

She reached her mother's house – *her* house – and breathed deeply before she went in.

'Nivi!' Pipaluk clattered down the stairs and gave her a hug. Niviaq's niece had latched on to her since her mum died, even though Pipaluk's grandmother was the one who really looked after her. Niviaq loved her little shadow.

'Anaa says you found a man on the ice.'

Niviaq took in her niece. She was tall for six years old, skinny as a pole and very pretty. She had her mother's big eyes, something about her nose as well. Niviaq's heart twinged every time she saw her. The girl looked so much like Maliina at that age that Niviaq was constantly reminded about what she'd lost. She tried hard to hide that emptiness from Pipaluk, who was already so damaged by it.

'Kind of.' She touched Pipaluk's cheek.

'Is he magical?'

Niviaq laughed. 'Why would he be magical?'

'Anaa says he escaped a *dupilak*.'

Niviaq took Pipaluk's hand and walked through to the kitchen. Her mother Ivala was at the stove, a huge pot of *suaasat* simmering away. The seal soup filled the air with a gamey richness that made Niviaq's mouth water despite herself. She'd tried being vegetarian for most of her time in Copenhagen, but had returned to traditional food as soon as she set foot in Tasiilaq again. Good luck trying to live on vegetables here.

Niviaq kissed her mother on the cheek. 'What's this you've been telling Pip about a *dupilak*?'

Her mother shrugged. 'There have been sightings recently, you know that.'

A *dupilak* was a mythical avenging monster that lived on the ice. It was made from various different animal parts, wild and vicious. These days, every gift shop in Greenland had sculpted versions carved from reindeer antler.

'This guy was just lying on the ice,' Niviaq said. She turned to her niece. 'There were no signs of a *dupilak*.'

Pipaluk raised her arms and roared, pretending to be a monster.

'You shouldn't fill her head with these things,' Niviaq said to her mother.

'It's her culture,' Ivala said, stirring the soup.

'You'll make her frightened of nature.'

'She should be frightened,' Ivala said. 'Nature is dangerous.'

Everyone here believed in *dupilaat*, the Mother of the Sea and all the rest. Niviaq didn't realise until she went to Copenhagen how strange that seemed to others.

She heard a noise outside, and Pipaluk bounded to the window and peered out. Niviaq looked at the mountains across the ice-strewn water.

'Helicopter,' Pipaluk said.

The noise was loud now. They were used to helicopters in Tasiilaq, it was one of the main ways to get here, with no roads between towns. Boats in the summer, a plane or helicopter at other times, dog sleds across the ice in winter. There were sometimes tourist helicopters taking rich Americans to the glaciers. But this was different, a shiny, black aircraft flying low over their house, making the spices rattle on the shelf above the stove.

Niviaq walked through the house and out the front door, Pipaluk and Ivala behind her. Their neighbours were outside too, following the helicopter's flight. It came down next to the hospital, barely room between that and the school.

Niviaq walked up the slope, feet crunching on the gravel.

When she got to the brow of the hill, she saw four men coming from the hospital, two carrying a stretcher, another two with large handguns. The shipwrecked guy was on the stretcher. Behind them, the doctor and Kuupik were standing at the doorway, protesting. The men loaded the stretcher into the helicopter then got in, the two gunmen keeping lookout. Then the helicopter took off in a swirl of dust, turned and headed northeast over the bay.

# 8
# HEATHER

She was still amazed at how fast she could swim, slinking her body through the water with a kind of jet propulsion, tentacles pulled in to streamline her and make her go faster. She looked at Jodie up ahead. Jodie had adapted to the transition more easily than Heather. Part of Heather was still clinging to her humanity, whatever that meant.

They passed fish of all sizes and types, swam through a shoal of capelin, silver-green bodies iridescent in the thin light of the shallows. They were further northeast in Ammassalik Fjord, at least that's what humans called it. Heather followed Jodie, shimmering and signalling ahead of her, as they turned left into Sermiligaaq Fjord and dived. Heather held the broken drone in two tentacles, evidence to show the others. They turned again up a deep inlet, and the lights of the Enceladon settlement appeared through the gloom and lifted Heather's heart.

There were collective words for octopuses – consortium or cluster, or her favourite, tangle – but none of them suited the Enceladons. Neither did the words for jellyfish – a smack or a swarm. Maybe a bloom or a flourishing of Enceladons worked.

There were hundreds of octopus creatures up ahead, swimming around the edges of a large, flat expanse of sea floor, flanked on two sides by an overhanging rock face. Inside the cleared area were giant jellyfish creatures, each one the size of a bus, some nestled on the sea floor, others casually drifting or shaping their bodies to propel themselves here or there. From them hung long, straggly tendrils like an underwater forest. Both the jellyfish and the octopuses were pulsing and flashing in colours that didn't have human names, that didn't exist on this planet anywhere else. And changing shape too, from slow, throbbing ripples to ridges, knobbles and spikes, back to smooth jelly, then hard-looking carapaces. The octopuses doing the same. This was all communication, all collective thinking and acting.

Heather spotted Sandy near the edge of the group and swam down with Jodie. Sandy was swimming underneath Xander, the giant jellyfish creature that was their symbiotic partner, the two of them much more than just siblings, part of the same organism. Sandy signalled warmth and recognition, blue-grey stripes with maroon fringing, their head swelling a little. They reached two tentacles out and Heather took them.

<Sandy-Heather-Jodie partial welcome.>

Xander swung a few fronds down to entwine with them for a moment. <Heather-Jodie partial exploring?>

The Enceladons were inquisitive about their new home, and would often go on long journeys into the fjords, but they had done it less since summer arrived. During winter, this settlement was covered in sea ice and the spread of the Karale Glacier which fed into the fjord above them. But in summer the glacier receded and calved icebergs, the water became navigable by boat, and they were more exposed. Recently, they'd tended to stick to the sea floor. Their experience at New Broom had taught them that humans were deadly.

The Enceladons knew that the humans who'd come to live with them loved to explore too, and they didn't have the nervousness of the Enceladons. Heather had spent many days swimming down Ammassalik to Tasiilaq, sitting on the ice sheet in the winter and watching the locals. She was careful not to be spotted, kept her distance. Most of them had guns for hunting or protection against polar bears, and a strange glowing creature out on an ice floe was an easy target. But she loved to watch the kids playing in the streets, which they did in all weathers. She loved to watch the adults going into each other's houses, a real community. She even loved to watch the cars driving around town, amongst the colourful houses and rocks, the shipping containers and upturned boats. And she loved to watch the dog-sled teams and snowmobiles in the winter, their tiny presence against the momentous landscape.

She felt overwhelmed by the Karale Glacier, not one of the biggest in Greenland by a long way, and getting smaller all the time with climate change, but still a mighty wall of ice throwing itself into the ocean. She would go to its edge and examine the million shades of blue and green and grey and white, and feel a tightness in her heart from the enormity of it.

<We saw a seal being hunted,> Jodie sent. <It was horrible.>

Sandy fluttered orange. <Seal return to original energy state.>

The Enceladons understood how an ecosystem worked, how energy transferred from animal to animal by being eaten. On Enceladus, they'd survived by eating microscopic organisms, and here in the Arctic they consumed zooplankton and gave thanks in ceremonies for the life they received from their miniscule cousins. The idea of humans hunting was new to them, but they didn't seem to mind if it was out of necessity, done with respect and thanks.

Sandy shimmered again. <Natural reciprocity.>

Heather always forgot that Sandy and the others had the same access to the internet that she had now. That they understood more about humanity than they let on.

<But we also found this,> she sent, holding out the crushed drone.

<Non-organic creature?>

<It's a drone with a camera. But look at this logo on the side. They're trying to find you.>

She lifted it closer to Sandy's face, held up the side with the logo, the moon and the tentacles.

<Heather-Sandy partial returned drone to original energy state.>

Jodie was agitated now, flickering yellow and red. <It had a camera. They'll have footage of us. And it wasn't that far from here.>

There was silence and Heather sensed that Sandy was communing with Xander, could tell by their synched-up light displays. This was another thing she hadn't got a handle on, how the Enceladons could shut the hybrids out at times. It made her feel lonely.

<Non-organic creature is not a concern.> This was Xander now, deeper voice in Heather's mind.

Heather flashed. <Why not?>

<Enceladon-marine-animal partials. Fish and others protect Enceladons.>

<What?> This was the first Heather had heard anything like this. She'd assumed the Enceladons could connect with other animals the same way they had with Heather, Jodie and the others. But this felt like a pact, the way Xander had spoken. <What do you mean?>

But Xander and Sandy didn't answer, just spread patterns across their bodies from one to the other. Heather looked at Jodie, who shook her head in confusion. The silence in Heather's mind made her stomach tight.

# 9
# VONNIE

She sat on the beach and pushed her feet into the stones. The tide was out, seaweed stretched below her. A woman threw a tennis ball for her golden retriever, which splashed into the water after it, wagging its tail. Vonnie wondered what was going through the dog's head. Maybe nothing, maybe just the sheer joy of being a dog, living in the moment in a way she found impossible.

Out in the bay, she saw Lennox's arms and head as he swam away from shore. He looked as if he wanted to swim across the ferry route, past Lismore and Mull, skirting the Hebrides then into the deep Atlantic.

Vonnie understood the urge. They would usually go swimming together in the bay, but she'd felt sick since Karl and Britt took off in their fancy helicopter. Vonnie had thought that she and Lennox were hidden here, but that was an illusion.

Lennox pushed through the ice-cold water, wake spreading behind him, ripples disappearing in the ebb and flow.

Vonnie looked at the rocks where they'd tagged the seal. She wondered where the animal was now, in the immense expanse of sea. Whether Greg was getting a strong signal, if it was telling him something about how the seal behaved, what it was thinking, what its desires and hopes and dreams were. Did seals dream?

She didn't trust Karl Jensen but she understood why Lennox took his card. The Enceladons had affected her the same as Lennox, given them both a glimpse of a different way to live. Then they'd gone. She missed them too, but surely getting back in touch was a terrible idea.

She heard a buzz and looked at Lennox's pile of clothes next to her. Lifted his phone from his shoe. It was Ava.

She looked out to sea. Lennox was treading water and waving at her. She waved back and looked at the phone. They hadn't heard from Ava in months. They'd kept in touch after New Broom, but those calls became less frequent. Staying in touch was just a painful memory of what they'd left behind.

She picked up the phone and answered.

'Lennox?' Ava was anxious.

'It's Vonnie.'

'Oh, hey.'

'Lennox is swimming in the bay. Can I help?'

Ava burst into tears, sobbing and sniffing down the line. Vonnie felt queasy, saw that Lennox was starting to swim back to shore.

'It's OK,' Vonnie said, stomach in knots. 'Take it easy.'

Gradually, Ava calmed down. It felt weird for Vonnie, looking at the water on the bay, the woman with her dog, Ava in tears in her ear.

'Deep breaths.'

Ava sniffed. 'I'm sorry.'

'Hey. Nothing to apologise for.'

A few moments of silence. Vonnie watched Lennox in the water and imagined Sandy swimming alongside, light display flashing, tentacles tasting the air.

'It's Chloe,' Ava said. 'She collapsed this morning. We were on the beach looking at rockpools. She was sick then she passed out.'

'Oh my God.'

'We took her to hospital, they did tests.'

Vonnie breathed in and out, tucked her hair behind her ears in case she was going to be sick.

'She had a stroke, Von.' Ava cleared her throat. 'A really bad one.'

'Shit.'

'It's like when Lennox and I first met Sandy, the light in the sky. It's the same fucking stroke in the cerebellum. And just like with us, the effects of the stroke disappeared almost immediately.'

'That's great,' Vonnie said.

Lennox was close to shore now.

'No,' Ava said, and the word was like a stone. 'There's something else. A tumour.'

'But they can treat it, right?'

'This isn't a coincidence. None of it. She's the first child born with these powers.'

Vonnie noticed she didn't say telepathy. It felt so strange to say it out loud.

'No one else on the planet is like her,' Ava said. 'And it's because of them. Because of Sandy.'

'What are you saying?'

Lennox was out of the water now, walking up the beach. He was still thin but had more muscle than when they first met. A firmness that felt comforting next to her in bed.

'I need to find them, Von.'

Lennox noticed that Vonnie was on the phone. She covered the mouthpiece.

'It's Ava, Chloe's not well.' She put it on speakerphone. 'Ava, Lennox is here now, you're on speaker.'

'Is she OK?' Lennox was dripping, wet stones under his feet, the smell of salt and seaweed on him.

'I don't know,' Ava said, voice trembling. 'Lennox, I need to find Sandy.'

'What?' He stared at Vonnie.

'This is all connected,' Ava said. 'Because of who Chloe is. She has something growing in her brain. Maybe the doctors can help, I don't know. But I *know* that Sandy can help.'

Vonnie swallowed hard.

Lennox raised his eyebrows at her, asking permission. It was a gesture so loaded with meaning that Vonnie felt crushed by it. They shouldn't expose the Enceladons, but Chloe needed their help.

<Can we?> Lennox's voice in Vonnie's head was like a bell.

She didn't even have to think. <We have to.>

Lennox smiled. 'We can help, Ava. Someone just came to see us, wants us to make contact with the Enceladons. Somewhere off Greenland.'

'Really?' Ava said, her voice breaking.

Lennox was so happy now the decision was made. 'I'll set it up.'

Vonnie handed Lennox the phone and they continued to talk, but she wasn't listening. She was trying hard not to be sick. Because she had her own reason to find out why Chloe was ill, what the Enceladons had done to the first child born with telepathy. She was eight weeks pregnant.

# 10
# AVA

Ashaig airstrip was a bumpy tarmacked stretch on the coast between the Skye Bridge and Broadford. The morning sun spread shadowy fingers behind the rusted shipping container that held the closed office and toilet. Bolted to the front were a faded first-aid kit, a box for depositing log sheets and a *WELCOME TO SKYE* sign, with a list of charges for using the runway.

Ava stood with Chloe in her arms, looking over the Inner Sound to the island of Pabay. Oystercatchers were down by the shore, cormorants too, sunning themselves, holding their shiny wings out like vampires.

Ava turned to Freya, whose face gave her away.

'Please don't say this is a mistake,' Ava said, touching her sister's hand.

Freya sucked her teeth. 'It's fucking obvious you're going through with it anyway. Just take care of yourself. And her.'

She tickled Chloe under her chin. The girl giggled and reached out to her auntie, and Freya took her for a cuddle. She glanced at the rucksack on the ground between them.

'Sure you've got everything?'

'What do you need for a trip to Greenland?'

Lennox had set it up after their conversation, then called her back with details. They were sending a plane for her and Chloe, then picking up Lennox and Vonnie on the way. Lennox said the Sedna team would provide anything they needed. Ava had looked up 'Sedna', only got hits for the mythical Inuit woman and the name of a dwarf planet that orbited beyond Neptune. That made her look up

'Enceladus', and she found that Sandy's home was named after a giant from Greek mythology, the son of Gaia and Uranus. She thought of the hundreds of rocks floating around the solar system, the gods at play.

She looked at Freya. The truth was that Ava wasn't sure this was the right thing to do. She'd spent the time since the call yesterday going back and forth, searching online for Karl Jensen, what kind of man he was, the companies he ran, what he did with his billions. Nothing obviously terrible – no scandalous lawsuits or psychotic behaviour, but they would hush that stuff up anyway.

She heard an engine, saw a jet in the northwest, circling out wide then banking and coming in to land with the sun behind it poking over the nearby hills.

The noise filled her ears. Chloe clambered from Freya to Ava, who hugged her too tight, felt her daughter's anxiety, then the glow of love that was a drug stronger than meth.

The plane landed and slowed, turned and trundled back towards them. It was a glossy black thing, logo of a moon being hugged by tentacles on the fin.

The roar of the engines faded, then stairs folded out from the side and a trim blonde woman in a suit stepped down and came towards them. She had dark-blue eyes, hair in a tight bun.

She glanced at Freya then Ava. 'You must be Ava, and this is little Chloe. I'm Britt Pedersen, I work for Karl. He sends apologies that he couldn't be here to meet you in person.'

Ava hadn't expected the billionaire to fly to Scotland to say hello, but it was nice of Britt to pretend he might've.

Britt looked at Freya again, who scowled at her. She ignored it and pointed at the stairs to the jet. 'Shall we?'

Ava felt tears in her eyes, then hugged Freya long and hard, Chloe squashed between them, gurgling and sucking her fingers.

Freya eventually pulled away. 'Keep in touch.'

'Of course.'

Britt had shouldered the rucksack.

'Let's go,' she said, and stepped towards the plane.

The cabin had four padded seats and a matching sofa in cream around a low coffee table bolted to the floor. Soft carpet, wood-panelled walls that matched the table.

They'd barely strapped in and taken off when they were descending again at Oban Airport, another coastal airstrip, this time with a small terminal building. Ava had Chloe on her lap, pointing out the boats in the nearby bay, the bridge to the south of the airfield.

As they landed softly, she saw two figures come from the building with backpacks, recognised them straight away.

Britt descended the stairs to meet them on the runway.

<Lennox, Vonnie, can you hear me?> Ava hadn't used her telepathy with anyone apart from Chloe in eighteen months.

<Loud and clear!> This was Lennox.

<Hey, there,> Vonnie sent to her. She was looking at the plane so Ava waved, Chloe copying her.

<That's Lennox and Vonnie,> Ava sent to Chloe. <They're our friends.>

They stepped into the cabin, and Ava hugged them both, Chloe quickly warming to them. They were talking out loud and sending with their minds over each other, and Ava wondered how much Chloe was picking up. She'd tried to shelter her daughter from her anxieties about what had happened, but she didn't know if Lennox and Vonnie would be so careful.

Britt watched it all with a thin smile, anxious to get them seated for take-off, then they were in the air and unbuckling and talking again.

They were soon over the Atlantic Ocean, Scotland far behind, water everywhere. It was a clear, crisp day, flight time three and a half hours. It seemed crazy that it was quicker to get from Scotland to Greenland than to Greece.

Vonnie was playing with Chloe on the carpet, handing over her leather bracelets for the girl to play with, then reading her a story from a picture book that Ava had brought.

Ava looked at Lennox. The kid from school who saved her from her dickhead husband had grown up.

<So we're really doing this,> she sent.

<Looks like it.>

Ava glanced at Britt, down the other end of the cabin. They'd asked her a few questions earlier, got basic answers. She was reluctant to talk more, said that Karl wanted to do all that when they arrived. Sedna Station was in the east of the country, up the coast from a town called Tasiilaq.

<Do you think the Enceladons will be able to help Chloe?>

<I'm sure they will.>

<What do you think Sandy has been doing this whole time?>

Lennox shrugged.

Vonnie looked up from the floor. <What about Heather and the others? What do you think they'll be like?>

Chloe giggled as Vonnie made faces at her, and Ava felt the warmth between them.

'God knows,' she said quietly.

The light in the cabin shifted and she looked out of the window. Behind them were still blue skies, but ahead was a long wall of storm clouds. Greenland was somewhere in there, and Ava tried hard not to think of the bad weather as a sign.

# 11
# NIVIAQ

She stood on her back porch, sipping black coffee and looking over the bay. Low, grey cloud in the sky, looked like it might snow. She picked at the flaking dark-green paint on the wooden railing and stared at the water, thousands of ice patches against the blue sea.

Footsteps from the side of the house, then Kuupik was at the bottom of the stairs, cigarette in his mouth.

'Can I?'

'Of course.'

He walked up the creaky stairs.

'Coffee?' Niviaq said.

'No, thank you.'

'Is there news?'

They'd talked about the shipwrecked guy yesterday, straight after the business with the helicopter and the gunmen. Kuupik was as shocked as anyone by the whole thing.

'No,' he said, nodding towards the hospital. 'At least not about that.'

'Then what?'

'You said you saw the Maqe boys yesterday on the water. Whereabouts, exactly?'

She tried to remember. 'Near Aaluit, I think. What's this about?'

'They didn't come back.'

It wasn't unheard of for hunters to stay out overnight, even for a few days, but they usually planned it in advance, informed someone. Sometimes things could go wrong, of course, because of bad weather closing in. But it had been fine since yesterday.

'They probably just stopped at one of the huts,' Niviaq said. 'Got drunk and are sleeping it off. No contact?'

Phone reception was notoriously bad on the water, but the boys should have had GPS or a satellite phone.

'Nothing.'

Niviaq looked at Kuupik. He finished his cigarette and stubbed it out on the porch railing, blew on the filter and put it in his pocket.

He cleared his throat. 'Normally, I wouldn't bother this soon. But with the other guy you found out there, I just wondered.'

'Yeah.' Niviaq knew what was coming and she welcomed it.

'Could you show me where?'

She finished her coffee. 'Of course.'

Wet snowflakes fluttered in her face as she navigated the boat out of the bay. They'd checked the forecast before they left, of course, and the heavy clouds in the distance weren't predicted to turn nasty for a few hours yet.

There were bigger bergs in the open fjord. One had recently flipped, the deep blue of its underbelly like a giant piece of candy. They made for Kulusuk then turned towards Aaluit. Slabs of ice were floating in the bay between Aaluit and Piitsat. Niviaq was sure this was where she'd seen Aqqalu and Nuka.

She cut the engine and nodded at Kuupik, then the ice floe.

'Here?' he said.

She did a three-sixty, took in the expanse of ice and ocean, the hills. 'Yeah.'

'And you're sure it was them.'

'I know their boat.'

Kuupik lifted his binoculars and scanned the horizon.

Niviaq thought about the *dupilak* her mother talked of. She imagined a monster lurching out of the deep and dragging the Maqes into the abyss. She thought about the strange things townsfolk had seen on the ice over the last months. About the *qaddunaaq* she'd found yesterday, the logo on his shirt, the same on the helicopter.

She lifted her own binoculars and looked around. There were lots of rocky outcrops up the coast, seals liked to sit on the ice beneath them out here in the summer. She presumed that's why Aqqalu and Nuka had been out this way.

'What's that?' Kuupik said, lowering his glasses and pointing southeast.

She looked with her naked eye first, saw something breach the water. It got lost in the waves, then she glimpsed it again.

They both looked through their binoculars, the boat rocking as the wind got up. She took a moment to locate it, focused and spotted a familiar spout of water and air, then a bulbous white head, followed by another three.

'Belugas,' Niviaq said.

With their domed heads and pale skin, belugas had always seemed to her like ocean ghosts, otherworldly creatures.

The pod got closer and she saw more of them, maybe ten. She turned her head out of the wind and heard clicks, moans and whistles. They were talkative animals. She wondered what they were saying, what they thought with those big brains.

'Wait,' Kuupik said, looking the other way now. 'What's that?'

She followed his finger, lifted her glasses and searched. After a few moments, she saw it. A boat. Maybe the Maqes'. It was tipped on its side on the ice, its prow pointing away, so all she could see was the hull.

'It could be,' she said.

She headed out wide to avoid a small berg, passed closer to the belugas. As she approached the stranded boat she recognised the paint job. Definitely the Maqes'. No sign of tracks on the ice. She got in closer, slowed the boat, spotted something.

'What's that?'

Kuupik stood with his glasses up for a few moments. 'Blood.'

She eased the boat in and saw the rest of the deck. A seal's body with a bullet hole in the back of its head. It lay in a pool of blood, which had poured over the side onto the ice. She scanned the rest of the boat, nothing.

Kuupik lowered his binoculars and scanned the horizon. 'Where are they?'

Niviaq looked around too. No sign of them anywhere. She could see the spouts of the belugas, wondered what they might have witnessed. The Maqe boys were goofs around town, but they were experienced hunters, knew their way around the ice. She couldn't fathom what could've happened to them. She thought suddenly about her mother, scaring Pipaluk with tales of the *dupilak*, the sea monster that could destroy you out here in the wilderness. That could drag you down to the bottom of the ocean, never to return.

# 12
# LENNOX

Snowflakes slapped against the aeroplane window, black clouds beyond. They were in a storm, the cabin rocking, Lennox sharing a worried look with Vonnie and Ava. The seatbelt sign came on and Britt ducked forward to the cockpit to speak to the pilot. The rest of them buckled up, Ava securing Chloe first, giving her a hug.

Lennox gave Vonnie a smile. <We'll be fine.>

He didn't tell her he'd never been in a plane before. He didn't even have a passport, but Britt told him when they arranged this that it wouldn't be a problem. What sort of trip was this, where he didn't need a passport?

Britt came back down the cabin, face grim, and another jolt made her grab for the wall to steady herself. She strapped herself in and shook her head. 'The pilot says we should be through the storm soon.'

'Is this common?' Ava said, rubbing Chloe's arm. The girl was playing with a toy octopus, a present from Vonnie, something she'd picked up in the gift shop of the Ocean Explorer Centre back at SAMS. It was too cute, and Lennox wondered about Sandy, what they'd been through. A long way from a cuddly toy.

Britt shrugged. 'Greenlandic weather is very unpredictable.' She sounded resigned. 'It's infuriating.'

Another jerk of the cabin made Lennox's stomach lurch, and he gripped Vonnie's hand. He glimpsed a flash of lightning out of the window, turned to see the engine in flames. 'Holy shit.'

They all saw it. Ava pressed her hand against Chloe's chest, Vonnie stared wide-eyed, and Britt lunged towards the cockpit.

'This isn't happening,' Vonnie said.

Flames licked from the inlet duct and Lennox thought about every disaster movie he'd seen. He tried to breathe. Smoke billowed from the rear of the engine, whipping away behind them. The plane rocked again, the wing dipping then rising, dipping again. Vonnie's grip on his hand loosened and he turned to see her grab a sick bag and vomit into it. He rubbed her back as she leaned over. Britt burst from the cockpit and staggered to her seat, strapped in again.

'They've shut the engine off, they need to land.'

Lennox stared out of the window at the clouds. 'Where?'

'We're close to Kulusuk Airport,' Britt said. 'But it'll be bumpy with one engine.'

Vonnie raised her head and gave a weak smile, wiped her mouth.

<We'll be fine,> Lennox sent.

<You said that already.>

The plane lurched downward and left, then down again. The whine of the single engine was painful. Out of the window, Lennox caught a glimpse of snowy mountains. They looked the same altitude as the plane, and Lennox thought about how radar worked. More bumps jostled them in their seats, then Lennox heard the landing gear being lowered.

Vonnie closed her eyes and Lennox looked outside, spotted a row of lights too close, then they dropped suddenly and bounced off the ground, up then back down, brakes deployed, the plane swinging to the right then back again, Lennox's head shaking with the vibrations, his hand sore from gripping Vonnie's again. The plane roared as it raced down the runway, then they were slowing and Lennox saw a building through the storm. The plane jerked to a stop and the noise of the wind outside took over, buffeting the cabin in a way that made Lennox want to cry with relief.

◈

Within an hour the storm had passed, to be replaced by thick fog. Lennox and Vonnie looked out from the terminal building and it was like something from a horror movie. Earlier, on the runway, they'd briefly caught a glimpse of ragged mountains covered in snow, a bay full of ice chunks. But the storm had quickly forced them inside.

Ava was keeping Chloe occupied with the soft octopus and a musical toy that played different tunes. Chloe moved her body in time to each one.

Britt had spent the time talking to the pilots, then on the phone.

There was a giant map on the wall and Lennox walked over to it. It was an archipelago of hundreds of islands scattered around two fjords which cut into the mainland. *Ammassalik* across the top. He found Kulusuk on a small island at the bottom. The only other settlement of any size was Tasiilaq, in a bay across a stretch of water. A lot of the land on the map was white. Glaciers with names like Apusiaajik and Mittivakkat. Then further up the fjords, bigger glaciers which flowed from a giant ice sheet – Helheim and Midgard at the head of one fjord, Knud Rasmussen and Karale in another.

So much water covered in ice. He'd glimpsed the icebergs outside earlier, and this was the middle of summer. There must be tons of sea ice in these fjords in winter. Plenty of cover for Sandy, Xander and the rest.

He wondered what they were doing right now. Turned to see Chloe giggling as Ava made the furry octopus talk in a silly voice.

He had an idea and stepped outside, stood in the dampness of the fog and closed his eyes.

<Sandy? Are you here?>

He waited in the darkness. Imagined a tentacle reaching out from the fog, leading him to the water, diving in together like nothing had changed.

<Heather?>

'You OK?' Britt was next to him. She put her phone away then ran a hand down her skirt.

Lennox nodded into the gloom. 'How's the plane?'

'It can't fly. I could have got a helicopter to pick you up, but not in this fog.' Britt sighed and pointed to where the road from the airport disappeared. 'The only hostel in town is closed, but I've arranged for you to stay in Tasiilaq tonight.'

Lennox thought of the map. 'How do we get there?'

Britt sighed again, as if she'd had enough of Greenlandic travel. 'A local is coming to pick you up in a boat.'

Lennox thought of the icebergs he'd seen on the water, the thick fog. 'Is it safe?'

'They know what they're doing.' Britt glanced at the terminal building. 'It's either that or you stay the night here.'

'Let's ask the others.'

Britt walked inside, but Lennox waited a moment.

<Sandy? Talk to me.>

They could be anywhere, hundreds of miles up the coast for all he knew. But he craved to hear their voice all the same.

Silence.

Lennox walked inside.

# 13
# HEATHER

Heather knew from the poor light and the waves thrashing above her that a storm was passing over, but it didn't bother her down here. She watched Sandy as they dived and pushed through the water. When she'd joined the Enceladons, part of her had assumed that the enigma of Sandy would be revealed to her. Of course that was naïve. If she could suddenly communicate with a bat, a fish or a tree, would she fully understand them?

But there was still a connection with Sandy, one she couldn't put into words. She knew how Sandy was going to move through the water and complemented them with her own manoeuvres, a playful interplay as obvious as breathing.

They were heading to one of her favourite spots, the glacier at the end of Ammassalik Fjord. Humans called it the Knud Rasmussen Glacier, typical to name a gigantic wall of ice after an explorer. It wasn't even the only Knud Rasmussen Glacier in Greenland.

Heather loved to watch the border between ice and sea, the shifting patterns of light and shade, millions of different colours. It reminded her of the Enceladons' signalling. Sandy loved glaciers too, maybe because they reminded them of their home on Enceladus, where the ice over the moon's oceans was miles thick in places.

Sandy was signalling to her now, orange and cyan, colours of pure joy, happiness and comfort. They swam through a shoal of halibut, thin brown bodies like pancakes, uneven eyes searching in the gloom. The fish were unconcerned by Sandy and Heather, instinctively knew they weren't a threat. Heather wondered about that, and about what Xander had said back at the settlement. It sounded like the

Enceladons were communicating with fish more than Heather had realised.

Since she started her transition to non-human, Heather had spent a lot of time finding out about other life on Earth. There were three and a half trillion fish in the world's oceans and rivers. That was the human guess, but it was certainly a colossal underestimate. Even if it was correct, it meant there were 440 times more fish than humans on Earth.

There were also three trillion trees on land, four hundred billion birds, ten quintillion insects. Why did humans think they were so important? Why did they assume that aliens coming to Earth would try to communicate with humans first? It made sense that the Enceladons were talking to fish.

Sandy pushed downward, close to the sea floor. Heather followed. She tended to stay in the shallows, her old human mindset preferring light to darkness. But Sandy had no such qualms and lit the way for them both, sweeping flashes of pearlescence up and down their body, highlighting crabs amongst the rocks and mud.

Then Heather saw a large shape in the distance, shifting languorously through the murk. It came closer and she saw its stubby nose, mottled skin, tiny mouth and eyes – a Greenland shark. They were solitary beasts, shifting across the ocean floor in a sluggish zig-zag. This one was at least six metres long, and Heather slowed as she approached, but Sandy swam right up to it, flashing browns and greens. The shark angled its head towards them, its clouded, blind eyes reflecting patterns and shapes. It moved its head towards Heather, following her scent, and a shiver went through her.

Sandy reached out two tentacles and touched the side of the shark's head, its tail flicking at the contact. The two of them floated like that for a moment and Heather listened for any communication. Nothing. She wondered what a shark's voice sounded like. She thought about approaching the beast but didn't have the nerve. There was still a lot of human left in her.

Eventually, Sandy gave the shark a hug with all five tentacles then released it, and it lurched away.

<What was that about?> Heather sent as they swam on.

Sandy flashed blue-green. <Elder knowledge is deep.>

<You spoke to it?>

<Sandy-shark partial is deep knowledge.> So much of Sandy's chat was unfathomable.

<What did it say?>

Sandy twirled as they swam, twisted to look at Heather. <Not speak like Heather-Sandy partial. But deep knowledge.>

<Could *I* talk to sharks?>

Sandy seemed to think about this. <Heather-shark partial mind divide is large. Maybe.>

<What do you mean, "mind divide"?>

<Shark is elder creature. In human terms, four hundred and ninety-five years. Has accumulated many thoughts. Shark time is different to Heather time.>

Heather tried to do the maths in her head – that shark was born in the early 1500s, before Shakespeare, Elizabeth I, Galileo, Newton. What had it experienced in those years? Sandy was right, mind divide was large.

They were close to the glacier now, Heather knew from the shape of the fjord, rock formations to the right. Sandy rose from the sea floor, but Heather caught sight of something near an outcrop.

Sandy's light display was getting further away. She signalled to get their attention, but they kept going.

<Sandy-Heather partial,> she sent.

Sandy stopped and turned.

<There's something here.> She wondered if it was another unimaginable creature of the depths.

Sandy was still above her, hadn't come back down yet.

<Let's look,> she sent.

Sandy stayed still, tentacles swaying. They were normally just as inquisitive as Heather, and she wondered why they didn't come back.

She heard their voice in her head. <Glacier this way.>

She looked at the thing in the darkness, flashed her body as much as she could to cast light into the crevice. It didn't look like a shark or whale, the lines too clean. She looked at Sandy. <No, I'm going to look.>

<Sandy-Heather partial not interested.>

That was abrupt, almost rude.

<The glacier can wait,> she sent. <I want to see this.>

She swam to the outcrop, making her skin glow as much as possible. She saw a boat lying on its side. She'd seen plenty of wrecks, of course, but this wasn't rusted, no algae or seaweed on it. It was new.

She swam around the stern, spotted dents on the hull, a hole. It looked like it had been attacked rather than storm damaged.

<Sandy, come and see.>

Sandy drifted lower but still didn't come near. <Not worth knowing.>

Heather stopped. She'd never heard something like that from Sandy before. <What do you mean?>

<Glacier is knowledge. Shark is knowledge. Boat is nothing.>

Heather shook her head and examined more of the boat with her tentacles. Definite signs of an attack, panelling torn apart and crushed.

She came to the helm and stopped. Flashed as hard as she could. <Sandy!>

There was a man trapped under the crushed dashboard, hair waving in the current, eyes open. A thin rope of blood spread from wounds on his stomach, tiny fish swimming in it. But the thing that caught Heather's attention was his jacket, which had the same logo on it as the drone.

<Sandy.>

Sandy was still hovering above her, a strange light display flickering along their tentacles, crenelations spreading across their head. <Boat is nothing.>

They began swimming upward, away from Heather and the dead man.

# 14
# VONNIE

Vonnie usually had pretty good sea legs, but nausea was never far from her thoughts at the moment. Bile rose in her throat as the boat headed away from Kulusuk, through a strait between islands and into open water.

The fog was thicker than earlier. She looked at Lennox at the back of the boat, eyes closed. She was worried about all of this, they shouldn't be here. She glanced at Ava, fussing over Chloe, both of them in life jackets.

She turned to look at the woman driving the boat. She was late twenties, long black hair and dark eyes, wrapped up against the breeze in a knitted headband and snood, heavy jacket, fingerless gloves. She was beautiful, Inuit tattoos on her face, three lines from her bottom lip to her chin, dots from the corners of her eyes across her temples. Very cool. Her name was Niviaq, and she'd just stood and smiled while Britt made introductions on the shore.

Vonnie was worried about the boat chugging through the ice-laden water in the haar. She stepped over to Niviaq at the helm.

'Hey.'

The woman kept scouting the water for danger. 'Hey.'

Vonnie could see her finger tattoos, bands around some digits, patterns of dots on others, little line drawings like branches.

'Is this safe?' Vonnie looked at the fog. She couldn't see more than twenty metres ahead, and the sea around them filled with ice.

'It's safe.'

'And where are we going again?' Kulusuk had disappeared behind them.

'Tasiilaq.'

'How long will it take?'

'About an hour. We have to go slow in this weather.'

'Is it nice?'

Niviaq laughed.

'What's so funny?'

'It's my home.'

'Oh. I mean, some folk live in shitholes.'

Niviaq laughed again, a warm sound. 'True. But Tasiilaq is nice.' She waved a hand around at the dense fog. 'It's beautiful.'

'Is the weather always like this?'

'The weather is crazy all year round,' Niviaq said, still scanning the sea. 'Fog, sun, snowstorms, wind.'

'How many people live in Tasiilaq?'

'Two thousand.'

'Your English is very good.'

Niviaq glanced at Vonnie, scoped her up and down with a smile. Then she glanced at the others in the boat. 'You don't look like tourists.'

'Why do you say that?'

Niviaq was back to scanning the sea, guiding the boat steadily. The white ice against the blue water and the grey fog was like an abstract painting. Vonnie wondered what the marine ecosystem was like here, how different it was to the one she'd been studying off the Scottish coast.

Niviaq glanced at Vonnie's bare legs. 'Not enough clothes. Plus, you don't even know where you are.'

Vonnie wondered if she should say why they were here. She had no idea where this Sedna Station even was.

She suddenly felt sick rising up from her stomach, lunged for the side of the boat and puked into the water, her throat burning. She thought about the baby inside her. She'd looked it up online, at eight weeks the foetus was the size of a raspberry. But raspberries were so fucking squishy, she wished they'd used a more robust thing to compare it to. She wondered about the sickness. She didn't have a mum to ask about any of this. She glanced at Lennox, eyes still closed. She loved him, but he was just a boy. And she was just a girl, really. She wasn't ready. She should be sitting in her crappy room at SAMS, studying and listening to lo-fi hip hop, not on a boat in the fog, in an ocean of icebergs, heading to a secret base run by a weird billionaire.

But she looked at Chloe, remembered the sound of Ava's voice cracking on the phone. And she wanted to see Sandy too, all the Enceladons. And Heather, Jodie and the rest. She couldn't even begin to think what life had been like for them.

'You OK?' Niviaq had slowed the boat and was looking at her.

'Fine.'

Niviaq had a kind face and Vonnie felt like blurting out about the baby. Niviaq glanced at Vonnie's stomach before looking back out to sea. Could she tell that Vonnie was pregnant?

Niviaq lifted a flask from a shelf and held it out. 'Here.'

'What is it?' Vonnie wondered about alcohol. She was still trying to get her head around the changes in her body.

'Hot chocolate,' Niviaq said. 'Settles the stomach.'

Vonnie took the flask and unscrewed it, smelled it, poured some into the cup. 'Thanks.' She blew on the drink then sipped. It was thick and creamy and she felt better.

The fog seemed to be lifting a little. There was still no sight of land, just chunks of ice in every direction. Niviaq was still scanning the water. After a moment she cut the engine and lifted binoculars to her eyes.

'What is it?' Vonnie said.

Niviaq scanned for a moment, then lowered the glasses, handed them over.

'Belugas. It's a family. I saw them earlier today.'

Vonnie put down the hot chocolate and looked. Could see a

bunch of white heads in the water between ice floes, water spraying from blowholes, sleek backs sliding in and out of the water.

'They're beautiful.'

'Yep.'

Vonnie thought about parents and children, about the mothering instinct. She wondered who was growing in her, what sort of person they would be. She glanced at Chloe and Ava, asleep now in the back of the boat, Ava's arms around her daughter, protecting her.

She heard the belugas, an eery blend of moans and whines, clicks and pops, full of emotion. Mothers and daughters, fathers and sons. She stared at the waves and wondered where the Enceladons were right now.

# 15
# AVA

It was past midnight and the sun was low on the horizon, disappearing behind the hill at their backs. Long shadows stretched over Tasiilaq beneath them and the air was cold enough for Ava to turn up the collar of her jacket.

'Here.' Niviaq next to her pulled a wool headband from her pocket. 'Take this.'

'I couldn't.'

Niviaq held it out until Ava took it. She put it over her ears and immediately felt warmer.

'Do you always carry a spare?'

Niviaq drank from her beer then smiled. 'Tourists never wear enough clothes.'

'We're not tourists.'

'I gathered that.'

Ava looked over the town. Tasiilaq was beautiful, a scattering of painted wooden houses spread over the rocks and slopes of the bay, the road winding to the shore where a handful of boats bobbed in the harbour. Ava couldn't believe how quickly the fog had lifted to reveal this view. She saw people walking between houses, kids playing in the street even at this late hour. If you were snowed in for the majority of the year, you made the most of the long summer nights.

The bay was peppered with ice chunks, snow on the hills across the water. The whole view was astonishing, and Ava couldn't believe this was only three hours from Scotland. It felt like a different planet.

She sipped her dark beer then picked at the label on the bottle, which had a cartoon musk ox on it. She felt relaxed for the first time since Chloe's attack. Chloe was inside their room now, asleep in the cot the Pink House had provided. This was their accommodation for the night, a hostel at the top of the town that ran tourist excursions on the side – sledding and snowmobiles in winter, hiking in summer, boat trips to see orcas and humpbacks.

Ava had been shocked when she first stepped onto the porch and saw the polar-bear skin on the wall, mounted with head attached and teeth bared. But she shouldn't judge, these people lived as part of nature, rather than apart from it. Wasn't that what the Enceladons did?

'So this is your home town,' Ava said.

Niviaq made a noise between a laugh and a sigh. 'For better or worse.'

'It's very beautiful.'

'And remote.'

'Isn't that a good thing?'

'It can be.'

Niviaq glanced at Ava and they shared a smile. She had deep brown eyes, her face tattoos giving her fine features authority. There was something else about her. The way she held herself, how she walked and talked, it was done with self-possession and confidence on the surface, but Ava sensed a darkness underneath that she was drawn to.

Niviaq took a swig of beer. 'But it can be lonely sometimes. And the winters, the dark days...'

Ava let the silence hang for a while. 'You must need your family.'

Niviaq pointed to a green house near the shore. 'That's my home.'

'Who do you live with?'

'My mother. And my niece, Pipaluk.'

'Beautiful name. How old?'

'Six.'

Ava glanced back into the room where Chloe was snoring, tangled up in a bedsheet.

Niviaq picked up on the unasked question. 'Her mum – my sister – died.'

'I'm sorry.'

Niviaq pointed at the bay. 'On the ice.'

To be reminded every day when you looked out at this view must be devastating. 'That's awful.'

Niviaq swallowed. 'It wasn't an accident. She did it herself.'

Ava placed a hand on Niviaq's knee. She'd only just met this woman, but she felt connected.

'I killed my husband,' she said, staring out at the town. She moved her hand away from Niviaq's leg, picked at her beer label, felt the silence between them. 'It wasn't an accident.'

She felt tears in her eyes. She hadn't talked about this in a long time and she didn't know why she was doing it now. She felt vulnerable and stupid.

Niviaq took her hand and squeezed.

'I don't know you,' Niviaq said. 'But I'm sure you had a fucking good reason.'

Ava laughed self-consciously as she looked up. 'I really did.'

She resisted the urge to pull her hand away and Niviaq didn't seem to mind.

Niviaq nodded at the harbour where Lennox and Vonnie were mucking around, so comfortable with each other.

'You seem like unusual friends.'

Ava nodded, drank some beer. 'We've been through a lot together. Stuff you wouldn't believe.'

'Try me.'

Ava wanted to tell her about Sandy and the Enceladons. About how she, Lennox and Heather, strangers to each other, had all been drawn to Sandy washed up on a beach in East Lothian. How Lennox had helped Ava escape from her husband. How the three of them had gone on the run from Michael and the police, taking Sandy with them on a road trip across the Scottish Highlands to return them to the others of their species. How Sandy had calmed her when she was panicking about unborn Chloe inside her. How the military had kept the three of them captive, tried to exterminate all the Enceladons. How Sandy, Xander and the others had saved all of their lives, Vonnie's too. How they'd gifted them this power of telepathy, or maybe cursed them.

She didn't want to hold this inside any longer, but she didn't know how to start talking about it.

Niviaq noticed Ava's reluctance. 'Is that why you're here?'

'Partly,' she said, glancing back into the room. 'Chloe is sick. There are people here who can help.'

'In Greenland?' Niviaq clearly didn't believe her.

She took the card out of her pocket – Lennox had given it to her earlier. *Sedna Station* written on it, and Karl Jensen's number. She handed it over.

Niviaq straightened up as she took it. 'Is this a medical facility?'

'No.'

'Where is it?'

'I'm not sure.' Had she done something wrong? 'Up the coast somewhere.'

Niviaq rolled her eyes. 'Whoever built this place doesn't know the first thing about life in Greenland.'

'Why do you say that?'

Niviaq tapped the card. '"Sedna" is the Canadian name for the Mother of the Sea. We call her Immap Ukua here.' She ran a finger across the logo. 'I've seen this before. Recently.' She looked at Ava and held her gaze. 'I don't know who these people are, but please be careful.'

The tone of her voice made Ava's shoulders tense up. A warning from Niviaq felt like an order.

Niviaq handed the card back then pointed over the town, now in shadow. 'Look.'

Ava had seen the northern lights before above Loch Broom, but these were different. It wasn't dark here so the display was less obvious, the purple and maroon stripes and swirling shapes, dancing patterns that reminded her of the Enceladons, the inscrutable magic of their light displays.

'My ancestors believed they were the spirits of dead children playing with the severed head of a child who was noisy at night,' Niviaq said, pointing her beer bottle at the sky.

Ava watched them in silence.

'My mother says they're bad news,' Niviaq continued. 'An evil omen.'

'You don't believe that?' Ava watched the display and tried to think positive thoughts about Chloe, Karl Jensen, all of it.

Niviaq shook her head, but it was the first time since Ava met her that she didn't seem confident. 'There's no such thing as evil.'

Ava hoped she was right.

# 16
# LENNOX

Lennox watched the dancing lights in the sky, traces of crimson waving like curtains in the wind. He hugged Vonnie from behind, arms around her stomach, mouth close to her ear. He buried his face in her hair, kissed her neck.

<Wow,> she sent.

A streak of dark red plunged downward, fading before it reached the ground. It seemed so close they could almost touch it. They watched the lights until they disappeared, leaving only vague ghosts in the atmosphere, hints of colours Lennox didn't have words for. The air was cold but he felt Vonnie's warmth.

Eventually she turned and kissed him, then looked around the town. 'This time yesterday we were still at SAMS.'

There was something about the air and the light that made Lennox's brain fizz. He could hear dogs barking in the distance and the wash of water in the bay. The ice moved lazily in the currents.

Lennox looked at the Pink House up the hill, saw Ava and Niviaq sitting outside.

'Should we be here?' he said.

Vonnie glanced at the hostel. 'We didn't have a choice, Ava and Chloe needed our help.'

'Our presence is dangerous for the Enceladons. We could've let them come on their own.'

Vonnie touched his hand. <We're connected, all of us. Me, you, Ava and Chloe. We have to stick together.>

'What do you think is wrong with Chloe?' he said.

Vonnie shrugged. 'Ava is right, it must be connected with them. With how she is.'

'Do you think it will spread?' Lennox tapped his temple. <This, I mean. With Chloe having it from birth?>

<Maybe.>

Lennox looked at the boats in the harbour, the shipping containers across the other side, then back at Vonnie. <How should we play it tomorrow?>

<How do you mean?>

<Are we just going to help these people find the Enceladons?>

Vonnie looked at the sea. 'Maybe there's a way we can get in touch with Sandy without them knowing.'

'But we don't know where they are.'

'We get whatever information we can from Karl and Britt, a general location. Then get in touch with Sandy, Xander or Heather directly.' She touched her head. <This is our secret weapon.>

<Unless they can decode these messages. The guy has billions of dollars, who knows what he can do.>

<*We* don't even know how it works, how can they?>

Lennox shrugged. <I worry that this is New Broom all over again.>

Vonnie shook her head. 'We're older and wiser now, right? And this isn't some big military campaign like before. We just need to be careful.'

'How did you get so smart?'

'I've always been the smart one,' she said, a laugh in her voice.

Lennox kissed her and she kissed him back. Eventually he pulled away. 'Maybe we should go for a swim.' He looked at her with his eyes wide until she realised he was serious.

<Really?>

<Why not?> He smiled. 'Come on.'

He grabbed her hand and they ran to the shore. He whipped his jacket and top off, kicked off his shoes and jeans, felt his skin goosepimple. Vonnie stripped down to her underwear. They negotiated the rocks then stood for a moment. The nearest block of ice was a few metres away, the air cold off the bay.

'On three.'

He counted then dived in, Vonnie beside him, the shock of the cold pushing air from his lungs. He told himself to stay calm, ignore his hammering chest, his knotted stomach. Then he was overcome by adrenaline and endorphins, splashing and laughing with Vonnie in the Arctic Ocean, and it felt for a moment like home.

# 17
# NIVIAQ

The sun was already high even though it was barely six in the morning. Niviaq squinted against the brightness and sipped her coffee, tried to shake the sleep from her brain. She'd had another dream last night. She was underwater with Ava and her kid, the three of them laughing and holding hands as they met a family of octopuses and huge jellyfish who they treated like beloved relatives, aunts and uncles they hadn't seen in years. There was a party, singing and dancing underwater, until a giant net scooped everyone off the ocean floor, panic as they were lifted into the bowels of a huge fish-processing ship.

'Hey, Nivi.'

She turned to see Pipaluk next to her on the porch, still in her pyjamas, holding a furry polar bear and a blanket. Niviaq patted her knee and the girl climbed on, gave her a hug.

'I had a bad dream,' Pipaluk said.

'Me too.'

'Really?'

'Dreams can't hurt us.'

'Anaa says they can come true.'

Niviaq tousled the girl's hair. 'Don't believe everything your anaa says.'

'What's this?' It was her mother at the back door, leaning against the doorway with a cup of tea.

'We had bad dreams,' Pipaluk said, and Niviaq gave her a little pinch which made her squeal. 'But we're OK now.'

Niviaq wondered if Pipaluk's dream was the same as her own.

'Hello?'

Niviaq recognised the voice and felt a glow in her chest.

Ava came round the corner holding hands with Chloe and stopped at the bottom of the porch stairs. Her bobbed, red hair was shiny in the morning sun. 'Sorry if we're disturbing you.'

Niviaq eased Pipaluk off her knee and stood. 'Not at all.'

She did introductions, the girls shyly interested in each other. Niviaq had only told her mother the basic facts about the ferry job yesterday. She couldn't explain it, but last night she'd felt as if she'd been friends with Ava for a long time already.

Ivala raised her eyebrows at Niviaq but didn't say anything, and Niviaq wondered what that meant.

'I just wanted to say goodbye,' Ava said. 'We're getting picked up soon from the heliport.' She waved to her right, which was the wrong direction.

Niviaq put down her coffee mug. 'I'll walk with you.'

They reached the road, and Ava picked Chloe up and carried her. She stared at the girl for a few moments and Chloe glanced back at her as if they were talking, but they weren't.

'Tell me if it's none of my business,' Niviaq said. 'But you never said last night what was wrong with Chloe.'

Ava slipped a bracelet off her wrist for the girl to play with. 'She recently had a stroke. They found a growth in her brain.'

Niviaq shook her head. 'I'm so sorry.'

Ava pressed her lips together. Niviaq thought about how she'd feel if the same thing happened to Pipaluk.

'But I don't understand,' she said. 'You think these Sedna guys can help, but they're not a hospital.'

Ava stopped walking as they reached the harbour. 'I wish I could tell you, I really do. But it's safest if I don't.'

'Safest for who?'

'Everyone.'

They walked on in silence, Niviaq thinking what to say. When they came round the headland to the heliport, she saw Lennox and Vonnie down by the water. They were looking out to sea, touching their temples like they were meditating. They both turned at the same time as if they'd heard something and waved at Ava, who waved back. Niviaq and Ava kept walking to the shed next to the heliport where their bags were piled up.

The noise of rotor blades made her look up, shade her eyes against the sun. A black helicopter came in fast from the northeast, circled then lowered itself to the ground.

Niviaq recognised it, the same helicopter that had picked up the shipwrecked guy the other day. The side of the aircraft slid open and a thin woman stepped out.

Niviaq turned to Ava. 'Are you sure about this?'

'Not really, but it's the only option I have.'

Niviaq glanced at the helicopter logo, the same one on the shipwreck guy's uniform, the same as the business card from last night.

'Ava, I found a guy washed up on the ice the other day,' she said. 'His uniform had that same logo on it.'

'So?'

'So, these people came and took him from hospital at gunpoint.'

Ava pressed her lips together. The woman walking towards them was frowning at Niviaq.

'I have to go,' Ava said.

'And two local boys are missing,' Niviaq said quickly, trying to get it out. 'There's something weird going on, and it has to do with this Sedna Station.'

Ava took Niviaq's hand. 'I wish I could tell you what this is about.'

'I just don't want you getting into trouble.'

'We'll be fine.'

Lennox and Vonnie were back at the heliport now and the woman had stopped to chat to them.

'Let me give you my number,' Niviaq said. 'In case you need help.'

Ava got her phone out and unlocked it.

Niviaq put her number in, handed it back.

Ava sent her a text. 'And now you have mine.'

Niviaq was surprised to find herself hugging Ava, and she was even more surprised to find that she didn't want to let go.

# 18
# HEATHER

She was clinging to a piece of ice when she heard it. She wasn't sure to begin with, hadn't heard that voice in a year and a half, hadn't spoken to anyone fully human in all that time. She pulled herself onto the ice floe and changed her skin colour to blue-white to blend in. She tried to still herself, tune into her own mind like meditation.

<Sandy?>

It was faint, but it was definitely there.

<Xander? Heather?>

Her body flinched at the sound of her name. This was a voice she recognised, someone she loved. Lennox was nearby.

<Are you out there?> His voice again.

She tried to stay calm. <Lennox, it's Heather.> She ballooned her head and lifted her body onto her tentacles. <Where are you?>

She looked at Tasiilaq, the bright houses, the boats in the harbour. She could see people in the streets, but couldn't identify anyone from this distance. She waited and listened. All she could hear was the lapping of waves, the squeak of ice chunks bumping into each other nearby.

<Lennox?>

She swam towards town, jetting through the water. He must be up there somewhere. She was in the shallows near the harbour when she heard something again, stopped to listen.

<Sandy? Are you there?>

He hadn't heard her. Maybe she wasn't good at using her telepathy with humans, she hadn't done it in so long. <Lennox!> She lifted her head out the water, scanned the shore, nothing.

<Xander?>

She sensed his voice was coming from down the coast somewhere. She swam away from the houses, diving underwater to go faster, then lifting her head to look at the shore – a huddle of metal tankers, a concrete tower covered in graffiti, rusted old boats out of the water.

<Lennox?> She wished she could still speak out loud. Why had she given up her vocal cords so easily? Why had she agreed to dissolve her humanity into this alien body?

She swam to the shore and clambered onto the rocks, lifted herself up and saw some people standing by a helicopter in the distance. She recognised Lennox, Vonnie and Ava amongst them.

<Hey!> But no one heard. <Lennox!>

There were two other women, a blonde ushering them into the helicopter, and a local woman who stepped back, hands in her pockets, as the rotor blades started and the aircraft took off. It lifted quickly and swung round to the north.

<Lennox!>

But they were gone, moving fast in the sky, soon a black dot on the horizon.

What the hell were they doing here? Lennox had called for Sandy, they were obviously here to see the Enceladons. But why? She was angry with herself that she hadn't heard the voice earlier, that she hadn't moved quicker or been able to shout louder.

The only person left at the heliport was the Inuit woman. She turned and walked back along the path towards town.

Heather clambered over the rocks. She felt clumsy and awkward, her tentacles tasting the air as she climbed and pulled herself to the path, then followed the woman from a distance. She felt the weight of her body suddenly after months in the sea, tasted the constant smells in the air, felt the grime against her tentacles. She stumbled a few times, unused to moving this way on land.

The woman must know Lennox and the others, and she would know where they'd gone. Heather had to find out.

The woman was looking out to sea as she walked. Heather's tentacles were covered in dirt as she followed. They came over the rise and passed two derelict huts, and Heather saw they were close to town already. If she was going to do this, it had to be soon.

She scrambled off the path, over moss then behind boulders above the woman. She scuttled clumsily round the rocks and eventually came back up to the path ten metres ahead of her. She tried to compose herself, make her body look unthreatening while still as noticeable as possible.

The woman stopped and stared for a long time, eyebrows raised. She looked behind her along the path then down at the water, avoided looking in Heather's direction, as if all this might just go away. Eventually she turned back to her.

Heather lifted a tentacle and waved, then realised how ridiculous that was.

The woman's mouth fell open and she gawped for a long time.

Heather waved again.

Finally, the woman lifted a hand in acknowledgement.

Heather thought about how to play this. She approached the woman very slowly. The woman had Inuit tattoos on her chin and temples, a strong face and big eyes. Heather glanced around. The path they were on looked over the quayside, if anyone down there had binoculars, the two of them could be spotted. But she had to take this chance.

She crept forward, holding two tentacles up in a human gesture of acquiescence. She was almost at the woman now, could smell her scent and the lingering smell of someone else, maybe Ava. Heather stretched out a tentacle and held it up to the woman's hand.

The woman looked at it for a long time, then glanced around again as if this was a practical joke. Eventually she opened her hand and took hold of the tentacle.

Heather tried to concentrate. <My name is Heather, can you hear me?>

The woman's eyes went wide as she took a step back and dropped the tentacle. 'What the fuck?'

Heather lifted her tentacle again, waved it in front of the woman.

The woman looked at her own hand and rubbed the side of her head. For a moment it seemed as if she would run away down the path, but she kept her eyes on Heather. Slowly, she reached up and took hold of the tentacle again.

<I take it that was a yes,> Heather sent. <You can hear me?>

The woman shook her head and blinked very slowly. 'What are you?'

Heather squeezed the woman's hand with her tentacle. <It's hard to explain.>

The woman laughed, but there was fear in the sound.

<All you need to know just now is that I'm a friend of Lennox, Vonnie and Ava, and I need to get in touch with them.>

The woman took a long time to reply. 'This is insane.' She breathed heavily in and out.

Heather could see her trying to stave off panic. <Do you know where they went?>

The woman muttered under her breath, and shook her head again. Eventually she looked Heather in the eye, and Heather saw something she liked, clarity and strength, maybe. <Yes, I know where they're going.>

Heather jumped and let go of the woman's hand from the shock of her voice, clear as a bell in Heather's mind.

# 19
# VONNIE

The view outside the helicopter was jagged mountains, glaciers flowing into every fjord from the ice sheet, the turquoise sea peppered with drifting ice, the edge of the land covered in scree and gravel, moss and hardy grass. Vonnie had grown up in the Scottish Highlands so she was used to amazing landscapes but this was next level stark and beautiful. They'd passed a tiny settlement a while back, but no signs of humanity since then.

The noise of the rotor blades filled the cabin. Vonnie looked around. Lennox was staring outside, eyes wide. Ava was pointing out of the opposite window, showing something to Chloe on her knee. Britt was on her iPad, talking on a headset in Norwegian.

<This place is incredible.> Lennox's voice in her mind made her turn to him.

<I know, right?>

She looked back outside, avoided Lennox's gaze, didn't want to draw attention. As far as she knew, Britt and Karl didn't know about telepathy between humans yet – that wouldn't be in the Loch Broom files because the Americans never found out. Vonnie wondered about this whole KJI company. Karl Jensen had a dozen billion-dollar organisations, but did this work at the Sedna Station come under any of them, or was it top secret?

She felt queasy, tensed her stomach muscles to quell the feeling, touched her hand to her abs, kept looking outside. She saw a flat area of land covered in derelict oil barrels, machinery and vehicles, all brown with rust.

'Old American military base,' Britt said over the noise in the cabin. 'They abandoned it after the Second World War.'

The mention of a military base made Vonnie throw Lennox a stare.

Britt leaned forward. 'Don't worry. This is different to what happened at New Broom. Trust me.'

After a while, the helicopter came over a mountain and Vonnie saw what she assumed was Sedna Station – a hexagon of large metal pods painted in bright colours – yellow, orange and blue. They were all connected to each other and a central hub via walkways, everything lifted off the ground on hydraulic legs. There was a harbour alongside, three boats and two submarines docked, all of them yellow. A handful of green shipping containers sat alongside. It looked like the whole site was constructed by a kid with a lot of Lego.

They were quickly down on the helipad next to the station, Vonnie's guts lurching as they landed. Even before the engines cut, Karl was striding over in hiking trousers and a thick jumper.

Britt opened the door and they jumped out, and Karl grabbed Vonnie then Lennox in enthusiastic hugs as if they were old friends.

'I'm so glad you're all here.' He caught Chloe's eye and knelt down. 'And who's this?'

Chloe was clutching her cuddly octopus. Karl stroked the toy's head, then held his hand out and got a high five from Chloe. He stood and held out a hand for Ava, who shook it.

'She's normally very shy around strangers.'

Karl beamed. 'I'm good with kids.' He turned to address them all. 'Sorry about the travel snafu yesterday. But it just highlights the problems we have here in Greenland, even in the middle of summer.'

He led them to the nearest pod building, waved at the logo and name above the door. 'Welcome to Sedna Station.'

Inside, everything smelled new, bright plastic and metal. They walked past open-plan offices and a science lab. Karl showed them their living quarters, surprisingly spacious, each room with a comfy bed, en suite, desk and a sofa. The windows were all small like ship's portholes, presumably to protect against the weather.

'Come,' Karl said, 'there's someone I want you to meet.'

Vonnie noticed that Britt had disappeared somewhere along the tour. She wondered about her and Karl, whether he was a good boss, whether she knew all his secrets. Maybe they were fucking. Two beautiful, ambitious people, why not?

Karl led them to the control room in the middle of the base, large screens showing interactive maps of the local land and sea, a weather tracker on another screen, video footage on several more. A bunch of people were working on laptops. The huge map on one wall drew her attention, it showed Sedna Station along with Karale and Knud Rasmussen glaciers at the tops of nearby fjords.

'This is Dr Thelma Helland,' Karl said. 'Thelma is our head of research.'

'Hi,' Thelma said. She was short and slim, black hair in a bob, serious face, pale skin sprayed with freckles.

'I've read your work,' Vonnie said. 'On narwhal communication.'

'You must be one of the few who have,' Thelma said with a laugh.

'Your research is amazing,' Lennox said.

Dr Helland was one of the worldwide experts in sea mammal language. The last Vonnie knew, she was high up at the Norwegian Institute of Marine Research in Bergen.

Thelma looked coy for a moment. 'Can I just say, it's an honour to meet you.' She glanced at Chloe and Ava. 'All of you.'

'Why?' Ava said.

'I read all about you in the files. Sandy and the Enceladons. That's why I agreed to work here, it's an amazing opportunity. What an incredible experience you've had.'

Vonnie wanted to be cynical. Her guard had been up since Karl landed at SAMS, and she still didn't trust him. But Thelma Helland's reputation was impeccable, her research was super smart and groundbreaking. If *she* thought this was a legit operation, maybe it was.

Thelma looked at Chloe. 'I believe we have this little one to thank for you being here.'

Ava looked uncomfortable, but Thelma leaned in and lowered her voice. 'How is she? OK?'

'She's been fine since the episode.'

'We have good medical facilities here,' Thelma said. 'Did Karl show you?'

Karl cleared his throat. 'I want to get on the water as soon as possible now you're here. We have a window of good weather, you never know how long that will last.'

Ava glanced at the other two. <I don't want to take Chloe on a boat, not yet. I'm not sure about this.>

Lennox nodded. <Me and Vonnie will go, bring Sandy back to Chloe.>

Karl and Thelma watched them closely. Did they know about inter-human telepathy after all?

'I think Chloe should rest,' Ava said. 'We'll stay here for now.'

Karl frowned, then looked to the other two. 'But we can go out?'

Vonnie looked at Lennox and didn't need a message to know what he was thinking. 'Sure, let's go.'

# 20
# NIVIAQ

<Can we go somewhere more private?>

The creature's voice in Niviaq's mind made her want to run screaming into the hills. She was holding one of the thing's tentacles, its voice somehow in her head. It was larger than any normal octopus, blue-and-white patterns moving across its body. This was crazy. Niviaq wondered if her mother was right, *dupilaat* were real. The sea monster had come to drag her to the bottom of the ocean. Its eyes were big and blue, traces of green and brown. Its head or body, or whatever it was, rippled and flowed, expanding then contracting as it looked around.

Niviaq realised it had asked her a question. 'What?'

It moved its head, two tentacles waving, a third still in Niviaq's grasp. <We're a little exposed here.>

Niviaq closed her eyes, hoping it would be gone when she reopened them, but it was still there. She looked around. The creature was right, they were conspicuous here, someone could come along any minute. There were homes just down the hill, activity in the harbour. She glanced behind her.

'There's an abandoned hut over there.'

<Perfect.>

The thing let go of her hand and scuttled across the rocks towards the ramshackle building. It was old Pavia's place before he died, no family to keep it on. Niviaq thought about running. She could just sprint back towards the heliport or into town. She could raise the alarm, bring a posse, chase the thing away. But it had said it knew Ava. It had a name, Heather. It somehow sounded human.

The octopus stopped and turned back, pink light splaying across its head. It looked as if it was trying to communicate, and Niviaq realised it could only talk to her if she was touching its tentacle. It beckoned to her.

Niviaq looked at the town then followed the creature to the hut. It shoved at the door with its tentacles, pushed inside. Niviaq followed, leaving the door open.

The hut was mostly intact, some rubbish blown in where two windows had broken. It smelled damp, but light streamed in through the doorway and windows.

The creature explored the room then turned to Niviaq and raised its tentacle. She hesitated for a long time before taking it.

'You said your name was Heather?'

The tentacle wrapped around the back of Niviaq's hand. <Yes. What's your name?>

'Niviaq.'

<You can talk like this, in my mind. You already did it outside.>

Niviaq didn't remember that, maybe she was in shock. 'How?'

<Just try.>

She closed her eyes, focused. <My name is Niviaq.> She opened her eyes and saw flashes of blue and red on Heather's head, which seemed to indicate approval.

<There you go.>

Niviaq shook her head. 'What are you?'

Heather slouched then lifted a tentacle towards Niviaq's ear. <This is very draining for me, talking like this. But I think I can make it so that we don't have to touch. I can leave a tiny part of my tentacle in your ear.>

'What?'

Heather flashed down her tentacles. <It's not intrusive. It happened to me.>

Niviaq looked the creature up and down. <But you're not human.>

<I used to be.>

<What?>

<I used to be human.>

Niviaq pointed. 'Was it the thing in your ear that turned you into this?'

<No, no, I made the decision to become this. That's separate.>

'Shit, I don't know.'

Heather shivered. <It really would be easier if I could just get your permission.>

Niviaq was scared, but also needed answers. And the fact Heather was asking permission and not doing it by force suggested it was friendly. Maybe. <OK.>

She felt a warmth in her right ear, a tentacle touching her neck, then a moment of pressure like descending in an aeroplane. Heather's tentacles retracted, and the one Niviaq was holding slipped from her fingers.

<Can you hear me?> Heather's voice was a lot clearer.

Niviaq felt dizzy, put a hand against the wall to steady herself. <I hear you.>

The octopus flexed its tentacles, shrank its body. <That's a relief. I honestly didn't know if that would work.>

Niviaq raised a hand to her ear, ran it along her jaw, wondered about what she'd agreed to.

Heather hunkered down, tentacles kicking up dirt. <I assume you want an explanation.>

Niviaq laughed. <You think?>

<This is all going to sound crazy, but just let me get it out. You can ask questions at the end, OK?>

Niviaq nodded.

<I used to be human, my name was Heather Banks. I met Ava and Lennox two years ago in Edinburgh in Scotland. We met a creature like me, an octopoid being. They're called Sandy. They came from the oceans of a place called Enceladus, one of Saturn's moons. We

rescued them and took them across Scotland to find their family. People were chasing us and eventually we were captured, the humans were. Sandy escaped along with other Enceladons. But we were experimented on, tortured, along with some Enceladons that were taken. Eventually we all managed to fight back together and overcome the military.>

Niviaq leaned against the wall and closed her eyes. She was losing her mind.

<The Enceladons decided to leave Scottish waters and come north. I came with them to Greenland.>

<Wait, when was this?>

<Eighteen months ago.>

That coincided with her octopus dreams. With the incredible northern lights displays. With the increased number of sea mammals in the ocean and the sightings of *dupilaat*, strange visions on the ice.

<But you were human?>

Heather shuffled. There was something about her head, a ghost of a human face under the surface now that Niviaq looked closely.

<I was then, but I changed, I wanted to. I'd had enough of humans. I was ill anyway, going to die, and I just wanted to be part of what the Enceladons had. They helped me and the others when we first came.>

<Others?>

Heather waved a tentacle out the window. <There are twelve of us hybrids in total. The rest were all drawn to the Enceladons, they had dreams, impulses they didn't understand.>

Niviaq thought about her own dreams. She wondered if she would be like this creature one day, a *dupilak* herself. <But not Ava?>

Heather shivered. <Ava had Chloe, Lennox and Vonnie had each other. They stayed in Scotland.>

Niviaq thought of Pipaluk and her mother down the road. About her sister walking onto the ice, into nothing. Maybe Maliina could've become one of these creatures, rather than end it all.

None of this made any sense. But things nagged at her – the shipwrecked guy, the missing Maqe boys, the Sedna Station logo.

Heather gestured at her. <You said earlier that you knew where Lennox and the others were going.>

Niviaq nodded. <A place called Sedna Station, up the coast somewhere.>

<Why did they come to Greenland?>

<Chloe is sick. Ava thought that something here would make her better. It's you, right? They've come here to find you.>

She remembered Lennox and Vonnie down by the water, staring out. It was obvious now, they were trying to get in touch with these creatures telepathically.

Heather's tentacles fidgeted. <We need to find Sedna Station.>

# 21
# LENNOX

They were all wearing thick jackets with the Sedna logo on the sleeve. They were on board the *Qivittoq*, a research vessel fitted with the latest sonar, some digital sea-floor-mapping instruments that Lennox didn't understand and a handful of underwater drones, their pilots set up in the small control room at the front of the ship.

Lennox had a flashback to New Broom, being on the ship with Carson as they used smaller Enceladons as bait to capture one of the huge jellyfish. He shook his head and reminded himself this was different. There were no men with machine guns, no crazy scientists with torture devices, they weren't being held hostage. But just being out on the water, close to Sandy, made him feel a tightness in his chest. He was dying to see them again, but also nervous.

They'd left Sedna twenty minutes ago and motored further up the fjord, then turned towards Karale Glacier. Karl had talked to Lennox through the whole journey, quizzing him on the Enceladons. Lennox had tried playing dumb but Karl knew everything that the American military knew. But those files would be a skewed vision, they'd seen the Enceladons as an invading force, parasites to be eradicated. Lennox knew the truth, that they were vulnerable refugees trying to make a new life in a strange place.

There were large bergs now as they got closer to Karale. The blue line of the glacier grew as they approached until it was a cliff of ice, behind it a frozen river of blue-white sweeping into the mountains. Amongst the hills either side of them, pockets of fog hung in the depressions. There were high, feathery clouds overhead and a bitter wind sweeping off the ice sheet. Lennox understood what Karl had said before, that Greenlandic weather was deeply unpredictable.

Thelma was demonstrating to Vonnie how the drones worked. She held one in her hand, pointed to various parts, the pilot showing her how he guided it.

'I'm very envious,' Karl said, rubbing his palms. 'Of your connection.'

That made Lennox think of Oscar Fellowes, the scientist who'd been first to track down him and Sandy. Who started working for the Americans before realising he was on the wrong side, then helped them escape. Who gave his life for theirs.

Lennox shrugged.

Karl narrowed his eyes. 'So Sandy really left a small part of themself inside your ear?'

'Yeah.'

'And you could hear each other at a distance.'

Lennox nodded.

'Have you ever had it examined? The piece of tentacle.'

That had never occurred to Lennox. 'I don't think it's even in there anymore.'

'What do you mean?'

Lennox didn't know how to explain. 'I think it's just ... I don't know, dissolved into me.'

'So it's a part of you now.'

'That's the thing,' Lennox said. 'It's not a part of me. There is no *me*, not really. I swam inside Sandy's body in Loch Ness. I was inside Xander's body in space. Part of them *is* me, just like a part of me is them now too. We each carry a tiny part of everyone we meet, whether it's carbon dioxide from your breath, microbes that passed when we shook hands, skin cells.'

Karl nodded and Lennox hoped he understood. If he really got it, he would treat the Enceladons with respect and kindness. It was impossible to act otherwise once you stopped thinking of yourself as separate from the universe.

Karl rubbed his stubbled chin. 'I think I've always had this feeling. As small children, we know we're a part of the world, linked to everything. The grass and trees, buildings, toys. But as we get older, that gets drilled out of us. We get taught to stand alone, to think of others as different, to exploit and judge.'

Lennox laughed then covered his mouth.

'What's so funny?'

'That's some hippy shit for a billionaire. What you're talking about is capitalism. You're saying that the way humans exploit the world and each other is bad. But isn't that how you became one of the richest men on the planet?'

The boat rocked and a cloud passed over Karl's face.

'I know how it looks. I never wanted to be rich. Truly. I was just a coder who liked working things out. I had a few apps take off, and that's how they get you. Investors come in, things snowball, then you have teams working for you, depending on you for their livelihoods. Shareholders, boardrooms, more investments. Advisors telling me to invest my own money, make it grow. How does money grow? It doesn't make any sense to me.'

Lennox watched Karl closely, tried to work out if he was being disingenuous. 'You could retire, of course.'

'I've tried, many times. But they don't like that. Markets will crash, companies will go under, people will lose their jobs, their homes. All of a sudden it's my fault that someone is homeless.' He waved around the boat. 'Besides, there are advantages to having money. I can use it for good. It's obscene how much I give to charitable causes. My accountants hate me. And I can do stuff like this.'

Lennox was still wary. The myth of the benevolent billionaire was just that, a myth. You didn't accumulate wealth and power by accident, no matter what Karl claimed.

Thelma and Vonnie joined them at the back of the boat as the engine stopped.

'We're here,' Thelma said.

Lennox looked round. 'Where?'

Karl grinned. 'The site of our last drone footage.'

Thelma handed her iPad over and Karl swiped the screen, played a video and showed the others.

An underwater drone camera, spotlight picking out tiny organisms, a flicker of fish tails in the gloom. A few seconds where the light fell on a bioluminescent octopoid creature swimming in the water. Then a tentacle slid across in front of the camera lens, obviously wrapping around the drone. For a moment the picture was chaos, something was attacking it. Then for a brief instant a close-up of an octopus head, staring at the camera before the feed ended.

'It's them, right?' Karl said.

Lennox stared at Vonnie, they'd both seen the same thing. Ghostly human features barely visible under the surface of the creature's skin. Features he recognised.

<That's Heather,> Vonnie sent, and Lennox couldn't help grinning.

# 22
# HEATHER

Heather glanced back from the prow. Niviaq at the helm was staring at her. Heather supposed her existence was hard to believe from Niviaq's point of view. Some random telepathic octopus called Heather turns up claiming to have been human eighteen months ago. She tried to remember what it had been like when she first encountered Sandy. They saved her life. She was trying to die back then, walking into the sea with her pockets full of stones. Then a flash in the sky, something hitting the water, a vague shape dragging her back to land.

They were on Ammassalik Fjord in Niviaq's boat, heading northeast. Niviaq pulled her snood up to cover her mouth and nose like a bandit. The cold didn't bother Heather, she hadn't felt cold since she'd joined the Enceladons. She turned back to scan the horizon, looking for landmarks, but she was more familiar with the underwater landscape.

<Back in a minute,> she sent to Niviaq, then launched off the front of the boat, swam down and to the left. She tasted all sorts of presences in the water, a school of cod to her right, a pod of dolphins behind her. She tasted a trace of a male humpback, it had come through here a while ago. She'd accumulated all this knowledge day by day living in the water in her Enceladon body.

She thought about her friends as she swam alongside the boat. They wouldn't have come here if they thought these Sedna people intended to harm the Enceladons. But surely any contact with humans was bad news for the aliens? Ava, at least, must be desperate.

Heather grabbed the side of the boat with the suckers of two tentacles and pulled herself over the side, and Niviaq jumped at her sudden appearance.

<Sorry.>

'Just not used to things jumping into my boat.'

She was obviously struggling, and Heather understood. It was a lot. Back at the hut, Niviaq had called Ava on her phone but there was no reception. She'd decided to get her boat, had gone into town and brought it round the coast. Heather watched her go and wondered if she was going to go through with it. She was relieved to see Niviaq and the boat appear round the coast half an hour later.

They navigated through a narrow part of the fjord now, small glaciers tucked into the clefts of the mountains on either side. Heather recognised the spot, they weren't too far from Karale Glacier.

Niviaq turned to her. <I have a couple of questions.>

<Of course.>

<How does it feel? Like, knowing you used to be something else. A seal only knows being a seal, same for an Arctic fox. But you know what it's like to be a different animal.>

Heather felt the question in her gut. <It's strange. But I've changed mentally as well as physically, they go together. If your body changes, so does the way you think.>

<Do you miss being human?>

<Sometimes. But I was done with being human when I chose this. I hadn't had a great time in a lot of ways.>

They were in a wider part of the fjord now, low-lying cloud between the peaks. Heather saw a stack of rusted oil drums along the shore.

<There's something else,> Niviaq said in her mind. <Are you sure about these Enceladons?>

<How do you mean?>

<That they're peaceful.>

<Why do you ask?>

Niviaq sighed. <I found a guy's body a couple of days ago. He was unconscious on the ice. He was wearing the Sedna Station logo.>

Heather thought about the boat she'd seen yesterday, with the dead man in it. She would never blame the Enceladons for protecting themselves, but they *had* felt different to her since New Broom. They'd learned how to fight that day.

'Something else,' Niviaq said. <Two guys from my home town have gone missing. I found their boat, they were hunting seal.>

Heather had a flash of the seal with the bullet wound, blood drifting from its neck. <You think the Enceladons did something to them?>

Niviaq shrugged. <Maybe.> She pointed. 'Look.'

Heather saw a cluster of buildings on the shore alongside a natural harbour. The bright colours mimicked the Inuit houses, but this settlement was brand new.

Niviaq steered the boat towards land. <Sedna Station.>

Heather shivered through her body at what was to come.

# 23
# VONNIE

Karl clapped his hands. 'Let's suit up.'

Vonnie was still reeling from the footage of Enceladon Heather, someone who was human when they said goodbye to her on Ardmair Beach. Who she'd last seen walking hand in tentacle with Sandy into the Atlantic Ocean. Of course Heather had changed, what did Vonnie expect? The Enceladons had promised the humans they would adapt. But seeing an Enceladon version of Heather made Vonnie's head spin. This was genetic engineering vastly more advanced than anything humans could even think of.

Vonnie gave Lennox a look. <We can't let him come with us. We have to make sure he's not a threat.>

<I know.>

Vonnie cleared her throat. 'Karl, Lennox and I discussed this. The first dive is just us.'

Karl narrowed his eyes. 'You're only here because of me.'

Vonnie tensed at his tone. 'And we're grateful, but we don't know you. We've been through a lot, the Enceladons even more. We have to be cautious.'

Karl shook his head. 'I need to meet them.'

Lennox took a step towards him. 'You will, but we have to take it slow. We have to ask their permission.'

Karl looked at Thelma, his fists clenching and unclenching.

'They know them, we don't,' Thelma said. 'If this was an undiscovered tribe in the Amazon, we wouldn't just storm in. These are intelligent creatures from another world.'

Vonnie smiled at Thelma, she was so glad the woman was here.

'Fine,' Karl said eventually. 'But you wear cameras, OK? And keep them switched on.'

Vonnie nodded. 'Deal.'

Karl watched them as they got their dry suits on, tested the scuba gear, checked the chest-mounted cameras. Thelma showed Karl the feeds on her iPad.

'You'll find them with telepathy, right?' he said.

Lennox nodded and looked at Vonnie. <Ready?>

They sat on the edge of the stern then fell backward into the sea. Vonnie followed Lennox as they swam through the clearest water Vonnie had ever been in. She wasn't as confident they would find Sandy. They'd only used their telepathy with each other for the last eighteen months. Who knew if they could still communicate with others at a distance?

Lennox switched on his torch as they descended. <Heather? Sandy? It's Lennox and Vonnie.>

<Sandy, are you here?> Vonnie felt foolish, calling into the vast expanse of the ocean.

A school of silvery fish swam through her torch beam, flicking one way then the next. Then a few moments later she saw the outline of a seal heading in the same direction. So the fish were swimming for their lives. Everything in this ecosystem was connected, predator and prey, symbiotic relationships in every drop of water. It was the same on the surface, but humans didn't see it. We'd removed ourselves from nature, didn't appreciate that it was all an interconnected biosphere.

Lennox was swimming deeper and deeper. <Jodie? Xander? Is anyone here?>

At this depth, sunlight was just a diffuse shimmer far above. Vonnie wondered what giant beasts swam below in the darkness, what their lives were like. <Sandy? Please, it's Vonnie.>

Silence and darkness. Algae, plankton and other small life floating in her field of vision, shrimps and other creatures going about their momentous lives.

The spotlight from her torch moved as she looked around, caught Lennox's flippers. Then she spotted something else, a faint blue light below them, flickering in the gloom.

<Sandy-Vonnie-Lennox partial!>

She knew that voice, Sandy's presence in her mind like a hug.

Lennox turned. <Sandy!>

Vonnie could see them now, swimming fast, blues and greens and reds across their body and rippling down their five tentacles, their head billowing with joy, brown eyes gleaming.

<Sandy!> Vonnie sent. <It's good to see you.>

Sandy launched themself at Lennox in a massive hug, wrapped their tentacles around his head and body, spinning the two of them. They released two tentacles from Lennox and pulled Vonnie close, curling one tentacle around her head, the other on her back.

<Sandy-Vonnie-Lennox partial no longer stretched. Close connection.>

The joy in Sandy's voice made tears come to Vonnie's eyes, and she could see Lennox grinning. They embraced for a long time, Vonnie and Lennox laughing into their mouthpieces. She hadn't realised how much she'd missed this. It was like a depression being lifted, when the land bounces back after an ice age.

<It's great to see you,> Lennox sent. <How are you?>

Vonnie was conscious of the cameras on their chests. They were so close that the footage would be a mess, a mêlée of arms and tentacles, but she could imagine Karl's face as he watched.

<Sandy-Enceladon whole well. Good energy in new home.>

The three of them floated in the glow of Sandy's light display, yellow rings up and down their body.

Vonnie touched a tentacle. <Heather and the other humans?>

<Heather-Enceladon partial is well. Not human energy now. Enceladon-human energy.>

<We know,> Lennox sent. <Where is she?>

Sandy tugged at both of them. <Come and see Enceladon home.>

<Is it far?> Vonnie sent.

<Short swim.>

Vonnie looked at Lennox. She could see that he had the same idea as her. She touched her chest camera, found the power switch and turned it off. Lennox did the same.

<OK,> he sent. <Let's meet the family.>

# 24
# AVA

She watched Chloe sleep. Ava hated the advice that mothers sometimes got, to sleep when the little one was sleeping. That was for people living in a dream world who didn't have a million other things to do. She felt wired. Two days ago she'd been living a quiet life with her sister in Ratagan. Now she could barely remember that life, couldn't imagine going back to it.

Chloe snuffled and Ava leaned over her. But the girl just wriggled her nose and turned, nothing to worry about. Ava had been in panic mode since Chloe's first attack, in constant fear of a second one.

She looked around the room, her firm bed and Chloe's cot alongside, a desk with a bookshelf of non-fiction about the Arctic, some novels set in the north, authors drawn by the allure of the white expanse. Drawers and hangers for clothes, a kettle and a snack cupboard. All the baby-changing stuff she needed in one corner.

She wondered how Vonnie and Lennox were getting on. She walked to the window overlooking the fjord. She could see towards the glacier, a white blanket draped between mountains. She thought about Enceladus, a whole moon covered in ice, water underneath. It made sense that the Enceladons came here. Maybe they should've gone further north where they would be harder to find, but Ava was glad they hadn't, otherwise she might never have been able to reach them.

Meeting up with Lennox and Vonnie again, exercising her telepathic muscles, had reminded her of how strong she'd been before, escaping Michael, getting rid of him, protecting Chloe. And she was still trying to protect her.

Her phone rang on her bed. She was surprised it got a signal out here. She saw that it was Niviaq and answered. 'Hey.'

'I can't believe I finally got through.'

It was good to hear her voice again so soon. 'What's up?'

'This is a strange question, but where are you?'

'At Sedna Station, you know that.'

'No, I mean where, *exactly*?'

'In my room with Chloe. Why?'

'What colour is the outside of your building?' Niviaq's voice was breaking up, and Ava checked her phone, one flickering bar. She waved it around as she walked to the window, looked at the sill outside. 'Pink, why?'

Niviaq's voice broke up.

'What?'

'...just wait ... minute...'

All Ava could see outside was a huge expanse of water, ice, land and sky.

There was a thud on the window and she saw a tentacle, then another crawling across the thickened glass, then the rest of the creature. She thought for a moment it was Sandy, then realised this animal had human features buried underneath their outer skin, a face she recognised.

<Heather?>

<Ava!>

<Wait.> Ava spotted Niviaq behind Heather, smile on her face. She glanced back at Chloe, still sleeping in her cot. She tried to work the release mechanism on the window, eventually popped it and the window swung outward. She glanced both ways at the rocky expanse but couldn't see anyone else, no obvious cameras.

Heather swung herself inside the window then launched at Ava, squeezing her and flashing blue up and down her body.

<Is it really you?> Ava sent.

<Who else?>

<It's so good to see you.>

Heather released her and stepped back on two tentacles, still holding Ava's hand with a third. Behind her, Niviaq was squeezing through the window.

'Hey.'

Ava looked from one to the other. 'How did you two…?'

Niviaq nodded at Heather, shimmers up and down her body. 'She turned up just after you left. She'd heard Lennox trying to get in touch.'

Ava didn't know where to begin. 'Can you talk to her?'

Niviaq tapped her ear. <Yup.>

Ava heard it in her own head and felt a blossoming of something through her body. Niviaq's voice was part of her and Ava couldn't be happier.

She turned back to Heather. <Look at you! How does this feel? How did it happen?>

Heather laughed in her mind. <I can't put it into words. It's just so … different.>

<Good different?>

A slight pause that made Ava wonder.

<Mostly, yes.>

<How are the rest of them? Jodie?>

<She's great, they're all well.>

<And Sandy?>

<Same as always.>

Something in Heather's tone made Ava pay attention, as if this wasn't the whole story. She glanced at Chloe then Niviaq. 'Did you tell Heather why we're here?'

Niviaq nodded.

Ava indicated the fjord outside the window. 'Lennox and Vonnie are out there now, trying to find Sandy.'

Heather slid over to the cot and gazed at Chloe. <She's changed so much.>

<Look who's talking,> Ava sent back.

She thought of Heather's daughter, how she'd struggled after the girl's death. How she'd been a mother to Ava and Lennox when they needed it.

Heather ballooned her head. <She's beautiful, Ava, you must be so proud. But I'm sorry to hear she's not well.>

<I remembered what Sandy did for you with your tumour. Do you think *you* could help her?>

Heather's head shrunk and her skin flickered brown and grey. <I don't know anything about that. But I'm sure Sandy or Xander can help.>

Ava looked at Niviaq. 'I'm sorry I got you mixed up in this.'

'Are you kidding? This is the most incredible thing that's ever happened to me.' <And this ...> Niviaq said in Ava's mind. <Is insane.> She glanced at Chloe. <Can *she* do this?>

Ava nodded.

<Lennox and Vonnie?>

Heather nodded this time, and Ava felt a glow at having her friend back in her life.

<Where does it all go from here?> Niviaq asked.

Ava looked at each of them in turn, different but connected, and she wondered what the answer was to that question.

# 25
# LENNOX

Swimming in his dry suit was frustrating compared to what he'd experienced before with Sandy. The first time they swam together in Loch Ness, Sandy had enveloped him in their body, enclosing him in a cocoon which allowed him to breathe through Sandy's body. That had happened over and over again as their adventure continued. Once, he'd been taken into the upper atmosphere by Xander, again inside their body, to meet the whole Enceladon tribe.

But stuck in his human body now, separated from his environment by a dry suit, mask and mouthpiece, Lennox felt like an astronaut walking on the moon. Sandy kept stopping and turning back like an eager puppy, waiting for Lennox and Vonnie to catch up. It was a longer swim than Lennox expected, but he felt the buzz in his chest from being with Sandy again. Sandy felt like a sibling to him, a twin even.

Lennox had lost his sense of direction down here in the deepest part of the fjord. The only lights were Sandy's iridescent displays, along with his and Vonnie's headtorches. Occasionally, Lennox spotted movement, unknown creatures living down here.

They turned and dived further, Lennox checking on Vonnie alongside him. <You OK?>

<All good.>

Then he saw lights up ahead and knew they were here. Sandy's display increased its pulses up and down their body as they approached.

<They're so excited,> Lennox sent to Vonnie.

<Like you're not,> Vonnie replied.

<Sandy-Vonnie-Lennox-Enceladon-human whole.> The delight in Sandy's voice made Lennox grin.

They came around a rocky outcrop and the full extent of the settlement was revealed. Lennox's heart leapt in his chest to see all the teeming life. He checked his chest-mounted camera was definitely off. Karl would lose his shit.

There were hundreds of octopoid creatures like Sandy milling around, some resting in makeshift rocky nests on a cleared area of sea floor, others swimming lazily with each other or around and under giant jellyfish, amorphous floating forms, long tendrils trailing from their bodies. There were creatures ducking in between the jellyfish's fronds, some of them were Enceladon octopuses, but there were also shoals of fish, shrimps, crabs on the ground, thousands of sea creatures. Coral stretched around the edges of the settlement where the dirt had been pushed into ridges, and many more fish and sea mammals swept through those areas too. Lennox saw seals and porpoises, starfish and sea cucumbers. He wondered what they made of their alien cousins, evolved on a completely different world, but converged into the same ecological niche.

Further out, Lennox caught glimpses of more fish and mammals, salmon and char, belugas and narwhals, their tusks like spiralling swords. He saw something else shifting against the sea floor.

Vonnie nodded at it. <A Greenland shark.>

It seemed like these animals were drawn to the Enceladons in the same way Lennox and the others had been. He wondered if the Enceladons were talking to the fish. Why should they restrict their communication to a single land species? They had a lot more in common with a beluga whale than they had with him. He felt a pang of envy.

Lennox thought of something. <Heather, are you here?>

He caught the background murmur of messages between some Enceladons, like voices in a crowded room, but couldn't sense Heather.

Vonnie caught up with him, the reflection of innumerable light displays making her eyes shine under her mask. <Is she here?>

Lennox saw Sandy heading towards Xander and followed. <Sandy, where's Heather?>

Sandy flashed yellow and white for a moment, then back to aquamarine and browns. They looked around, waved all five tentacles. <Heather-Sandy partial is stretched.>

<What do you mean?>

<Hello Lennox-Vonnie-Xander partial.> This was Xander's voice in Lennox's head, deep and resonant. Several of the jellyfish's tendrils stretched out and wrapped around Lennox's hands and head and he felt warmth and love.

<Lennox-Vonnie-Xander partial is very welcome.>

'Xander' was a random name the humans had ascribed to Sandy's bigger relative. Lennox had come up with Sandy's name at the start simply because their body was covered in sand when Lennox first found them. Then the Enceladons had adopted the nomenclature, given themselves arbitrary names so that the humans could tell them apart. Like Yolanda, the enormous jellyfish who Lennox now spotted nestling under an outcrop, body ebbing and flowing with the currents, swelling and shrinking.

<Jodie?> Vonnie sent. <Is that you?>

An octopus flashed a beautiful display of green hoops as it approached and hugged Vonnie, tentacles rippling. Lennox looked at her closely, saw vestigial human features under her skin.

<Vonnie, wow!>

Vonnie knew Jodie from the beach encampment up the coast from New Broom in Scotland, had been friends with her before Lennox met either of them. So many connections between them all.

<Why are you here?> Jodie sent, loosening her grip on Vonnie's arms.

<It's a long story, but Ava's Chloe isn't well. We were hoping these guys could help.>

Lennox turned to Xander and Sandy. <*Can* you help us? Chloe is ill, has something in her brain similar to what Heather had. Sandy cured her before, do you think you can help Chloe?>

Sandy and Xander touched tentacles and tendrils, obviously talking between themselves. They released each other and Sandy turned to Lennox. <Sandy-Chloe partial is good energy. Sandy present at Chloe-Ava meeting, much joy. Sandy-Chloe partial must reunite to change cells. Sandy-Chloe partial close by?>

Lennox grinned, he knew Sandy would help. <Yes, change cells, Sandy-Chloe reunite.> He looked at Vonnie. <She's with Ava on land, nearby. Come with us.>

# 26
# HEATHER

She was glad to be back in the sea, her heart warmed by seeing Ava and little Chloe, knowing that Lennox and Vonnie were in this same water. She pictured them emerging from the darkness in front of her. She wondered if they'd found Sandy yet, or if she would find them first.

She swam past a school of shimmering capelin. She was so familiar with life in the sea now, didn't think twice about what she saw, the currents she felt. She was part of this world, wasn't that what she wanted, to be part of something bigger? But she was in an alien body swimming through a cold sea, thinking of old human friends and how she might spend more time with them. She'd connected with them too, and thrown it away.

She passed a large school of cod heading in the same direction as the capelin. Something in their movements made her pay attention. She became aware of giant shapes to her right, a pod of bowhead whales, their barrel bodies sliding through the depths, swimming with purpose. She realised they were going the same way as both schools of fish. Something weird in their energy. Heather followed in their wake. The matriarch of the family glanced back, flicked her fluke as if to encourage Heather, who swam in her slipstream, admiring her agility. She got close, but the whales didn't mind.

They skirted round the headland where Heather knew the village of Sermiligaaq was. They swung through a tiny archipelago like a submarine mountain range and out into deep water, Heather sensing the larger currents, the colder water away from the shallows, the immense size of the endless ocean in every direction.

She realised there were many more fish in larger schools around her, under her, above her. More mammals too, a herd of hooded seals, minke and beluga whales, a huddle of walruses. They were all being drawn towards something, and so was Heather. She felt the pull of it, realised now she'd felt it all along, someone had sent out a signal through the ocean, some kind of call.

For help.

All the animals were congregating up ahead, where a large shadow spread over the surface of the sea. She could hear the clicks and chirps of belugas, the rumble of a fin whale calling out.

The shadow was from a large ship, a big industrial vessel, not an Inuit fishing boat. Spread out behind it was a colossal dragnet full of thousands upon thousands of fish and crustaceans, all crushed by the tight net, squirming and wriggling across each other's bodies, searching for a way out.

Commercial trawling and fishing were supposed to be banned in the Arctic Ocean, but plenty of ships were in these waters doing exactly that and paying no penalty. It was impossible to police an expanse of sea this size, and even if you found a fish-processing ship like this, what could be done? The melting ice caps created more open water and made fishing and mining easier, and profit was a god.

She swam closer. The fish and other animals were all helping, trying to free the trapped creatures. The walruses tugged at the wire netting with their tusks, narwhals doing the same further down the bulging net. Thousands of fish pulled at strands from inside and outside the net, working together in a way Heather had never seen before. Seals were helping too, their serrated teeth tearing at the cords, ignoring the fish around them who would normally be their prey. This was an ecosystem working together to fuck humans.

It reminded Heather of the Enceladons. She thought of what Niviaq said about the shipwrecked man, the missing hunters, the dead body she'd seen in the sunken wreck. But they weren't big commercial operations. She wondered what was happening here.

The walruses tore a giant hole in the net, seals swimming in and ripping it wider, all the cod and salmon and char escaping and spreading out, mixing with their rescuers in something that seemed like a celebration.

A fin whale approached the hull of the ship and rammed it with its nose, denting the metal. Then more whales began doing the same, the ship rocking from the impacts, the hull crumpling and eventually holed. A pod of narwhals flanked by walruses had hooked their tusks through the net and were dragging it to the side of the ship, rocking the vessel until it listed heavily. They coordinated their pulls so that the ship tipped further and further over. Thousands of creatures pulled at the ship until it capsized with a tumultuous wave that Heather felt through her body.

## 27
# NIVIAQ

Less than twenty-four hours ago she'd been sitting on the porch of the Pink House drinking beer with Ava. She'd felt a connection with her then, but looking back she'd had no idea what that connection really meant.

She was sitting with her again now, this time in some weird science station, and they didn't even need to open their mouths to talk. They were inside each other's heads and Niviaq liked the intimacy. She realised now how alone she'd felt since she came home from Copenhagen. She loved Ivala and Pipaluk, of course, but this was something else entirely, a whole new level of togetherness.

<So.> There was laughter in Ava's voice in her mind.

They were both drinking black coffee, Ava sitting on her bed, Niviaq nearby on the chair by the desk. Chloe was still asleep in the cot across the room.

<So,> Niviaq replied.

Ava smiled. <You see why I couldn't tell you everything.>

<I wouldn't have believed you.>

<I owe you an explanation.>

Niviaq blew on her coffee. <You don't owe me anything.>

<I got you involved in something.>

<I love being involved.> This felt so alien but natural at the same time.

Ava looked at Chloe, who turned in her cot.

'Two years ago, I was heavily pregnant with Chloe.' Ava glanced out of the window, then at her lap. 'I was in an abusive relationship with my husband. It's hard to talk about, even now. He controlled everything I did, isolated me, gaslighted me until I had no personality of my own.'

Ava sounded so fragile that Niviaq wanted to hug her.

'I still feel so ashamed about it.'

Niviaq leaned forward and touched Ava's knee. Ava raised her head.

'You have no reason to be ashamed,' Niviaq said.

'You didn't know me then, I was so weak.'

'No,' Niviaq said firmly. 'I didn't know you then, but I've known men like that. They make you think you're weak, that's how they have power.'

A look of recognition in Ava's eyes. 'I suppose so.' She took a sip of her coffee. 'I'd had enough. I packed a secret escape bag, drugged him and drove away. But I crashed the car because I had a stroke. It was to do with Sandy, an accident. It meant I was back to square one. But Lennox saved me. He helped me escape from Michael. Along with Heather, we ran away with Sandy.'

Niviaq nodded. 'No wonder you're so close.'

'They're my family.' Ava looked at Chloe again, who was coming round from her nap, stretching her fingers, yawning. 'I was worried about Chloe, thought she might not be alive anymore inside me. I asked Sandy, and they helped me talk to her.' <Like this. Then I knew she was OK.>

<You spoke to her in the womb?>

<Crazy, isn't it?>

<And you can communicate with her like this now?>

<Yeah. By the time she was born, Michael had caught up with us. He tried to take her away, but I couldn't let that happen. I hit him with a wrench on the back of the head.>

Niviaq's hand was still on Ava's knee and she gave a squeeze.

'I was convicted of manslaughter, but given a suspended sentence. Then I was kidnapped off the street and taken to the military base on Loch Broom, along with Chloe. The Enceladons saved us, we owe them our lives.'

'And now you're here for a favour.'

Chloe opened her eyes and Ava smiled at her. Niviaq didn't hear anything in her mind, but she was sure that mother and daughter were talking to each other.

'These Enceladons,' Niviaq said. 'Are they like your friend Heather?'

'Some of them look very similar,' Ava said. 'Sandy, the one we met first, they look like her.'

'They?'

'They think of themselves as collectives, plural. They have lots of mini-brains around their body that talk to each other to make decisions.'

'Sounds like chaos.'

'And they also think of themselves as part of a larger superorganism, like a hive mind. They think very differently to us. The way Sandy talks is strange, because they don't understand humans.'

Chloe waved her hand at Ava and smiled at Niviaq, who smiled back.

'And there are other creatures,' Ava said. 'Much larger, like huge jellyfish, the size of a small boat, maybe.'

Niviaq thought of the Maqe brothers and their boat, the damage done.

'How many of them are there?'

'Hundreds, maybe thousands.'

'Sounds like an army.'

'They're not violent. They're so different from anything on Earth.'

Niviaq drank her coffee. 'And they're really from one of Saturn's moons?'

Ava nodded.

'Why are they here?'

'Refugees. We never found out what they were running from, but they had fled for their lives.'

'According to them.'

Ava frowned. <Wait till you meet them, you'll understand.>

Niviaq wanted to believe Ava, but it all seemed too good to be true.

'Chloe?' Ava said.

She stood and Niviaq followed her gaze. The girl was standing, holding the bars and swaying, eyes rolling back in her head.

<Chloe!> Ava lunged across the room and Niviaq stood.

Chloe vomited before Ava could get to her, sick splattering off the cot bars onto the carpet. Ava grabbed her as she started convulsing like electric currents were passing through her, and lifted her shuddering body into a hug.

<It's OK, Mummy's got you.>

The girl was shaking and her eyes had closed. The smell of sick was strong. Chloe went limp in Ava's arms and Niviaq felt a rock in her chest.

Ava turned to Niviaq. <Get help. Please.>

# 28
# VONNIE

Vonnie and Lennox were inside Xander's body, shifting through the Arctic water. Sandy swam alongside, darting under and over, waving their tentacles around. Vonnie looked at Lennox. They both still had their dry suits on, but had removed their masks once Xander had enveloped them. They could somehow breathe through the substance of Xander's body. That presumably meant that part of Xander was now inside her, and inside her unborn child. She thought about Chloe, and her body tensed. But she needed to find out what was wrong with Chloe so that she was prepared for her own kid. She was already thinking about being a mum, imagining holding her baby in her arms.

<This is insane.> Lennox was grinning. He'd missed being with Sandy, Xander and the rest so much. He looked the happiest she'd seen him in a long time and that worried her. How could she compete?

She thought about Lennox as a dad. Maybe there was a reason she hadn't mentioned it to him yet. He'd grown up in the care system, without parents, with no home or any sense of normality. Vonnie had no doubt he would want to be a good dad, but how would he cope?

They were slowing now, Sandy flashing green and purple as they and Xander swam to the surface a short distance from shore.

Vonnie was gently squeezed out of Xander's body alongside Lennox. They were right next to Sedna Station. As they swam towards shore, Karl's boat appeared from behind a nearby headland.

<Sandy, Xander, you should hide for now,> Lennox sent.

<Not Chloe-Sandy partial?>

Vonnie breathed deeply. <Not yet.>

Sandy slipped behind an ice floe. Xander disappeared under the surface and for a moment they looked like a piece of ice, shimmering blue and white under the ripples until they were gone.

The boat came alongside them. Karl offered them a hand but Lennox shook his head, pointed at the shore.

<This stinks,> Vonnie sent.

<I know. The way they just appeared, they knew we were coming. They're tracking us.>

Vonnie touched her oxygen tank. <The scuba gear.>

They were in the shallows now and waded to the beach.

<That means they know where the Enceladons live,> Lennox sent.

<Shit.>

The *Qivittoq* had docked at the harbour and Karl jogged towards them, Thelma behind. Britt emerged from the station and walked their way.

'Where are they?' Karl said, looking out to sea.

'You tracked us?' Vonnie said.

'I just want to meet them. Anyway, you switched off your cameras.' He waved an iPad at them. 'But I saw one before you went dark.'

<He's going to have to meet them,> Lennox sent. <If we want to help Chloe.>

Vonnie sighed. <I know, but...>

Karl's puppyish enthusiasm seemed too good to be true, and they had been so badly burned before.

Lennox removed his tank, Vonnie likewise. She ran a hand across her stomach in the neoprene suit, felt the wind off the hills, thought about hot chocolate.

'They're incredible,' Karl said, showing them the shots from their own cameras. They were only glimpses of Sandy hugging Lennox and Vonnie. Karl was giddy at that tiny crumb of footage.

Vonnie looked at Thelma, her being here made the difference. She had a reputation for caring about the creatures she studied, there's no way she would let Karl run roughshod. Britt stood alongside, impassive, maybe she was the pragmatic voice in all this.

'Please,' Karl said, his voice cracking with emotion. 'I have to meet them.'

Lennox looked at Vonnie, who shrugged. She glanced at Sedna Station, tiny against the vast expanse. This wasn't New Broom, there were no armed guards and no barbed wire. And she'd seen what the Enceladons did to that place anyway, they could handle themselves.

<We have to, for Chloe,> Vonnie sent.

Lennox looked out to sea. <Sandy, Xander, show yourselves.>

Vonnie saw a scuttling motion across a nearby berg, recognised the way Sandy moved. They scurried across the ice, flashing brown and blue, before slipping into the water, stretching their tentacles behind them. Then they slid upright, three tentacles in a weird trotting motion as they walked up the beach, two tentacles tasting the air, zigzag stripes across their body.

They casually slung tentacles around Lennox and Vonnie's shoulders, as if they were gang members on a street corner, and Vonnie laughed at Karl's face, his mouth hanging open. Thelma and Britt were the same, gobsmacked at seeing an alien up close for the first time. It was easy to forget how mindboggling this was.

'This is Sandy,' Vonnie said.

Sandy waved a tentacle and Vonnie laughed.

Karl shook his head. Thelma was filming on her phone, looking over the top with her eyebrows up.

Vonnie heard a noise behind her like a thousand baths emptying at once. 'And this is Xander.'

She turned to see the massive jellyfish lifting out of the water fifty metres away, rising into the air, seawater cascading from their body, long luminous tendrils swaying beneath them, a multitude of colours and patterns shifting and swirling across their skin, their body pulsing like a heart, shocking and beautiful.

She looked back at the others. Karl closed his eyes for a long time, then opened them. Britt shifted her weight, shaking her head. Thelma was still recording on her phone, gawping.

<Xander-Sandy-new-human partial welcome.> This was Xander's deep voice in Vonnie's skull, like a prayer.

'They say hello,' she said.

# 29
# HEATHER

She approached the settlement still reeling from what she'd seen. Thousands of sea creatures working together to rescue thousands more trapped in a net. But beyond that, taking revenge on the ship and the humans on board. Heather had watched as the lifeboats were launched, saw dozens of people scrambling into them as the vessel sank. The whales and dolphins, seals and fish all vanished into the gloom, but she stayed and swam under the people, watching their arms and legs thrash in the water, working together to haul crewmates from the icy water. Twice she'd seen individuals struggling to get the attention of the people on the lifeboats. She swam close, wrapped her tentacles around them and dragged them towards the boat, releasing them within sight. She remembered Sandy when they met, pulling her from the sea and saving her life. She couldn't watch people drown.

But she didn't blame the sea life either. Humans had scooped up thousands of fish illegally. Even if it had been legal, the whole industry, the whole system, was corrupt and immoral beyond words. Humans were out of control, killing everything in their wake. But now the world was fighting back.

On the outskirts of the settlement, Heather saw octopuses and jellyfish coming and going. Their light displays never ceased to amaze her. She couldn't spot Sandy or Xander. She swam through the crowd, caught snippets of conversations in her mind.

Jodie and Yolanda swam towards her, signalling greetings. Jodie's humanity had mostly gone now, her human features were fainter than Heather's, she'd assimilated much better. Jodie had been having dreams of the Enceladons for months before she met them, she'd always been more ready and open to the idea of change.

Heather flicked a tentacle. <Hey.>

Jodie shimmered orange and examined Heather's body with her tentacles, tasting the water between them. She flashed concern. <Are you OK?>

If your species showed their emotions all the time, it was so much easier to read body language. Heather was an open book. <I saw something disturbing.>

Yolanda loomed over them both. It would've been intimidating if Heather didn't know what these creatures were like, their temperaments. <Heather-Jodie-Yolanda partial is not good energy.>

The vagueness of their language was frustrating. They sometimes used the phrase 'not good energy' to mean 'bad', but also 'unhappy' or 'anxious'. Heather wondered if that was deliberate on the Enceladons' part, like they wanted to keep something of themselves unknown. But they *were* speaking in a language and a culture entirely alien to them, so maybe she was being unreasonable.

<Yolanda, do you talk to all the animals in the ocean?>

Yolanda glimmered positively. <Of course. Enceladons now part of Earth whole, sea whole. Part of ... biosphere. Human words, not full sense.>

<What do you mean?>

Jodie's head ballooned, a display Heather recognised as an urge to speak. <These are human words,> Jodie sent. <Ecosystem, biosphere, ecology. Humans don't really understand the complexity of these ideas, so the words don't encompass the full meaning. It's like humans are glimpsing the world out the corner of their eyes.>

Jodie was using the word 'they' to refer to humans, even though she used to be one. Heather wasn't in the same place yet, maybe she never would be.

She held a tentacle out and ran it across a part of Yolanda's body. <What do you say to the other animals?>

Yolanda shifted some tendrils. <Biosphere talk all the time, all parts, energy is flowing. Enceladons connect in all ways.>

<But what do you tell them? Did you tell them to destroy a fishing ship?>

Something flowed between Yolanda and Jodie, a purple and cerise twisting shape like a DNA strand which passed from Yolanda's body into Jodie's.

Jodie flashed a quick yellow sparkle across her head. <We don't tell them to do anything, we're not in charge.>

<You do this, too?>

Jodie gave a non-committal sway of her tentacles. <I've been in contact with some animals. I'm just learning.>

Yolanda's body felt suddenly oppressive to Heather. If they wanted to, they could crush her without even thinking about it, such was their size and power.

Jodie placed a tentacle on Heather's body, which made her flinch. <The Enceladons taught us how to communicate with them, to become them. You must have known that it wasn't just humans they were in contact with. They're a marine species, part of this world now. Obviously they would talk to fish, seals, whales.>

Heather looked at Yolanda, placid and flowing. <What are you telling them, to rise up against humanity?>

Jodie shook her head, a vestigial human gesture, so she wasn't completely Enceladon yet. <We don't have to tell them anything. We just show them the unfairness, the imbalance. You know what humans are capable of. That's one of the reasons you came with us and did this.> She waved tentacles at Heather's body.

<I didn't want...> But she didn't know what she wanted.

She looked at Yolanda. The Enceladons had come here as refugees, hadn't understood how humans worked. But they'd learned. They'd been treated badly and that opened their eyes. Now they were passing that knowledge onto the other animals in the ocean.

Heather looked around again. <Where are Sandy and Xander?>

Jodie flashed orange then pink. <Didn't you know? Lennox and Vonnie were here. They took Sandy and Xander to the human base, the ones that are looking for us. To help Chloe.>

Something in Jodie's tone suggested she didn't approve. But Lennox and Vonnie were Heather's friends and she wasn't about to give up on them. She thought Sandy and Xander were her friends too, but time would tell.

# 30
# NIVIAQ

'Will she be OK?' Ava said.

They were in a small room in the compact medical block of the station, first-aid posters on the wall, defibrillator mounted alongside.

Niviaq looked at Ava standing over Chloe in her bed. The girl was far too small in the adult bed, so vulnerable. She was unconscious, the doctor having persuaded Ava that anti-epilepsy meds would best suppress the seizures.

'We're monitoring her situation,' the doctor said. Her nametag read Dr Olsen but she'd introduced herself as Elna. She was middle-aged, tall and slim, black hair with strands of grey in a bun, glasses perched on her head. She'd got Chloe into the bed without fuss after the alarm was raised, hooking her up to the heart monitor, checking blood pressure and taking a blood sample, administering the clonazepam with a small needle in her arm. Chloe had been drowsy and confused after the attack, more so after the drugs, crashing out quickly. Her face now was slack with sleep.

Niviaq tried to imagine how Ava was feeling. It was awful to see your baby drugged, but Elna said it was necessary to stop a possible chain of escalating seizures.

Ava had told the doctor about the thing in Chloe's brain. She clearly had no faith in human doctors, was waiting for these alien creatures to come and do what they could.

Dr Olsen excused herself and left with the blood sample, and Niviaq wondered about that. They now had some of Chloe's blood, the girl who could communicate telepathically.

Niviaq glanced at Ava. 'What do you think she's doing with that blood?'

Ava didn't answer, just stood over the bed staring at her daughter, eyes wet. Eventually she turned. 'What?'

Niviaq nodded at the doorway. 'Why did she take Chloe's blood?'

Ava shook her head as if she couldn't believe any of this. <What are you saying?>

Niviaq jumped at Ava's voice in her head. <I don't know why she needed it, that's all.>

Ava realised what she meant and cleared her throat. 'You're saying I shouldn't have given permission.'

'I don't know.'

The stress in the air was palpable.

'I'm a bad mother.'

Niviaq held her hands out. 'God no, I wasn't saying that. You're obviously a great mum.'

<Yet I've let a bunch of random strangers take my girl's blood.>

'I'm sorry,' Niviaq said. 'I was just thinking out loud.'

'Maybe keep that shit to yourself.'

Ava's eyes flickered as if she regretted her tone, but Niviaq didn't blame her. Her words stung Niviaq all the same. She felt a stronger connection with Ava than she'd felt with anyone for a long time. Sometimes you just clicked with someone, and they'd done that the first time they met. Ava was obviously beautiful and Niviaq was attracted to her, and there was maybe a hint that Ava might feel something too. Or maybe Niviaq was kidding herself. She hadn't had a romantic relationship for years, sometimes she felt like that part of her had atrophied.

Ava turned back to Chloe, radiating anxiety. Niviaq wanted to reassure her but didn't know how.

'I'll leave you guys alone,' she said.

Ava didn't acknowledge her.

Niviaq stepped out of the room and closed the door, looked

around the reception area, wondered where Dr Olsen had taken the blood. She opened the door adjacent to Chloe's, just an empty room. She walked across the corridor and tried the door there, same. The next door was locked. She went back to the reception desk, checked the drawers. Stationery and paperwork. Found a small box with keys. She walked back over, took a deep breath. The third key she tried turned in the lock. She opened the door and stepped inside.

There was another hospital bed in here, this time with someone she recognised in it. It was the guy she'd pulled from the ice floe, who'd been flown away from Tasiilaq Hospital at gunpoint. She walked over and stared at him. He was hooked up to a heart monitor, pulse regular, a drip connected to his forearm.

She checked the folder at the bottom of his bed. Per Nordström, in an induced coma. There was some other stuff she didn't understand, a couple of graphs with data points, a list of acronyms. Dr Olsen's signature.

She placed the back of her hand against his forehead and wondered why he'd been out on the ice. What he'd seen.

She left the room, locked it and replaced the key, then went back to Chloe's room. She was reaching for the handle when the door opened, Ava standing there holding a sleeping Chloe against her shoulder. She tapped her temple.

<I just got a message. They're here, outside.>

# 31
# AVA

She walked to the front entrance, sending comforting thoughts to her baby. She felt bereft when she got nothing back, Chloe's drug-induced stupor like a slap in the face. It was a glimpse of the future, when the girl grew up and didn't need her mother anymore. The long letting go of every parent, compounded by their closeness.

Ava was aware of Niviaq at her back as she walked, felt bad at the way she'd spoken earlier, just the stress of everything. Niviaq was good and kind, on Ava's side.

She carried Chloe out of the door and stopped. Almost laughed at the sight of Xander's huge body on the shore, Sandy next to Lennox and Vonnie, shimmering patterns and flashing colours. Karl, Thelma and Britt were goggle-eyed in front of them. Other staff were out here filming the event, some on their phones, others with more professional set-ups including thermal imaging and other EM spectrum monitors.

Sandy ballooned their head when they saw Ava and Chloe, scuttled towards them while flickering magenta and cyan across their brow.

<Ava-Chloe-Sandy partial welcome! Good energy returned.>

Sandy wrapped two tentacles around Ava's back, a third stroking Chloe's brow. The air was sharp out here, wind sweeping down the fjord, and Ava worried about Chloe getting cold.

She glanced at Lennox and Vonnie, mouthed a silent thank-you, then turned to Sandy. <Did Lennox tell you about Chloe?>

<Sandy-Chloe partial has bad molecule energy.> The tip of Sandy's tentacle was hovering over Chloe's ear. <Chloe-Sandy partial very low energy. Low awareness. No permission possible.>

<I give permission,> Ava sent.

Sandy paused. <Ava-Sandy partial allowed?>

Chloe was only two years old, surely Ava could give permission. <I think so. Please can you help her?>

Sandy hesitated then placed the tip of their tentacle in Chloe's ear. The girl was still a dead weight in Ava's arms, and she wondered how long she would be out for. A second of Sandy's tentacles supported the back of Chloe's neck, a third gliding across the girl's body. There were small striations on Sandy's skin where the suckers were, which led like tiny rivulets to firmer blue lines under their skin. Was that their blood? The lines rippled softly, and Chloe shifted in Ava's arms but didn't wake.

Ava glanced around, everyone was watching them. Above her, a drone was filming. They were getting as much data as they could. If they could work out how Sandy cured cancer, maybe they could replicate it. But Heather's cancer came back, one of the reasons she became Enceladon.

<Sandy, what's happening?>

Sandy's light display faded briefly and their head shifted to an oblong shape, crenulations forming in two parallel ridges almost like a frown. <Sandy-Chloe partial molecular inefficiency not same as Sandy-Heather partial.>

<In what way?> Ava looked around again, realised Heather wasn't here.

Sandy stroked Chloe's face, their tentacle moving from Chloe's ear to Ava's arm and giving a squeeze. <Heather-Sandy partial was human for many Earth cycles. Chloe-Sandy partial was human-Enceladon from beginning of life.>

<She's not Enceladon,> Ava sent. <She's human.>

Sandy angled their head, deflating like a silent sigh. <No. Once Ava-Chloe-Sandy partial connected, Ava-Chloe-Sandy partial is both human and Enceladon. All parts, all connected, all species.>

<I don't understand.> Ava felt tears coming. <Can't you fix her?>

Sandy twitched, and Xander began moving in synch. Their body lifted from the water by the shore and skirted across the stones towards them.

<Ava-Chloe partial visit Xander?> Sandy sent.

Ava frowned. <Visit?>

<Exist inside.>

Ava looked at Xander's colossal body. <Is it safe?> She looked at Lennox, then Sandy. <OK, Ava-Chloe partial can visit Xander.>

Sandy flashed yellow-orange and ushered them to Xander, who unfolded some of their flesh and let them walk inside, then enveloped all three. Ava panicked for a moment then remembered to breathe, but it was Xander's flesh or substance she was inhaling.

Chloe woke up and looked at Ava, smiled and hugged her. She looked around, saw Sandy and giggled.

Xander's flesh ebbed and flowed around them, tiny particles or creatures within it swimming around Chloe, some going into her mouth and up her nose. Ava wanted to scream but it was too late for that now. Sandy was right – all parts, all connected.

Chloe giggled again and sent a wave of happiness that made Ava's heart burst. The girl was enjoying being part of something bigger.

The swirl of Xander's flesh spun around them for a while, and Ava kept her eyes on Chloe throughout.

<Well?> she sent eventually.

A pause that made Ava's stomach hurt.

Then Xander's voice. <Chloe-Xander partial unusual connection with Sandy partial. Dangerous to rearrange molecules. But possible.>

<Dangerous?> Ava felt sick.

Xander's body rippled around them. <Ava-Chloe partial can visit other Enceladons?>

Ava breathed whatever it was, took Xander into her lungs. <In the ocean?>

Sandy next to her shimmered with zigzag shapes across their head. <Ava-Chloe-Sandy-Xander partial will be safe. Enceladon whole will help rearrange.>

Ava looked at Chloe, sucking her thumb like a regular kid. <Let's do it.>

# 32
# LENNOX

Lennox looked at Ava and Chloe inside Xander, and remembered when they'd saved his life at Ullapool Harbour then taken him into space, where the entire Enceladon colony were waiting to come to Earth. If he knew then what he knew now, maybe Lennox would've advised them not to bother. But they were marine animals, he'd assumed they could live in Earth's enormous oceans without being hassled.

'Hey.' Karl had a hand on his shoulder, leaning in like they were friends. 'We had a deal.'

They *had* taken advantage of Karl to get here, refused to let him in the water, turned off their cameras. 'What exactly do you want?'

Vonnie nudged Lennox in the ribs. <Be careful.>

Karl looked at them both. 'I want to connect with Sandy.'

Ave and Chloe had stepped out of Xander's body. Chloe was awake and happy, and Lennox's heart lifted.

<Sandy?>

Sandy turned their head and flashed silver and gold, head narrowing as they scuffed over.

<Sandy-Lennox-Vonnie partial happy. Ava-Chloe-Xander partial to visit settlement, become Enceladon-human whole.>

'What are they saying?' Karl said.

Karl used the plural pronoun. It was a small thing, but it suggested he was empathetic and taking this seriously. Lennox reminded himself this was the billionaire head of a multi-national collection of companies. Karl was good at making you think he was your friend. His hand was still on Lennox's shoulder.

Sandy was with them now, examining Karl, sniffing the air with their tentacles. <New human good energy?>

Lennox looked at Vonnie and she shrugged. He didn't know how to answer.

<Honestly, I'm not sure.> He glanced at Karl. <But he wants to connect with you.>

<Sandy-Lennox partial thinks Sandy-new-human partial similar?>

<I hope so.>

'What's happening?' Karl's voice gave away his frustration.

Sandy quivered. <Sandy-new-human partial will connect.>

That's what Sandy did, they always saw the good in people.

Lennox turned to Karl. 'They'll connect with you.'

Karl beamed like a little boy.

Lennox realised he was jealous. For a while he'd had Sandy to himself, before even Ava or Heather connected with them. Before Vonnie. Part of him wished he was back in that moment, the intimate feeling between just the two of them. But that was pathetically human, not wanting to share what you had. Sandy would hate that attitude.

Karl waved, and Thelma approached with a skullcap packed with electronics. Lennox immediately shuddered, reminded of a similar thing used at New Broom for their experiments and torture.

Thelma saw his reaction and held a hand out. 'This is to monitor Karl's brainwaves. We just want to understand.'

Britt stood behind Thelma looking inscrutable. Lennox wondered what she thought of all this.

Thelma placed the skullcap on Karl and checked her iPad for a signal.

<Are we sure about this?> Vonnie sent to Lennox.

Sandy looked at her. <Vonnie-Lennox-Sandy partial unsure?>

Vonnie touched one of Sandy's tentacles. <Just be careful, Sandy, we don't know this guy. Don't leave yourself open.>

But that was ridiculous, Sandy didn't know any other way to be.

Karl adjusted the cap, rubbed his hands on his thighs then straightened his shoulders. Sandy curled a tentacle to Karl's temple, wrapped another around his hand. Karl jolted at the touch, and Lennox watched the veins on his wrist, the blood moving through him.

Britt was looking over Thelma's shoulder at the iPad now. All the brain patterns in the world wouldn't explain what this felt like. It wasn't about data, it was experience.

Lennox didn't detect anything from Sandy, which meant they were keeping it between them and Karl. He wondered about that. The Enceladons were open with their connections but still able to restrict them when they wanted. Maybe they weren't so different from humans.

Karl nodded. 'I give permission.' His voice was shaky.

Sandy's tentacle went into his ear. Britt looked as if she might intervene, her body tense. Thelma glanced between the action and the iPad screen.

Karl groaned and his eyes rolled back, then his body went limp. Britt stepped forward but Thelma held out a hand. 'He's OK, I think.'

Karl was being held up by Sandy, like a lover cradled in their arms. Sandy's tentacles moved over his body, one tentacle still in his ear. Karl's face was ashen as if all the blood had drained from it.

'Thelma,' Britt said. 'Is he OK?'

Thelma shook her head in amazement. 'These signals are incredible. His brain is more active than I've ever seen, like he's experiencing something profound.'

Britt shook her head. 'He looks half dead, we need to stop.'

'No,' Lennox said. 'He's fine.'

He honestly didn't know if that was true. Maybe Sandy had changed since New Broom.

'Pull him out,' Britt said.

Thelma hesitated, staring at a spiking graph on her iPad. Britt grabbed Karl's shoulders, then his body jerked violently. His arms and legs shook, then his neck snapped forward. He opened his eyes and blinked too many times, breathing heavily. He looked around at Thelma and Britt, then at Lennox and Vonnie.

'You know,' he said softly to Lennox. 'You know what this is like.'

Lennox glanced at Vonnie.

<You know what this feels like.> Karl's voice was clear in Lennox's head, full of awe. <This changes everything.>

He looked at Thelma and Britt, shook his head as if he couldn't believe his own life. 'This changes everything.'

# 33
# NIVIAQ

She felt like an extra in the craziest movie. Ava and Chloe had been inside the giant jellyfish called Xander. The octopus Sandy was in a weird embrace with some guy from the station, others monitoring him, Lennox and Vonnie looking worried alongside. Niviaq was the only Greenlander here. She looked around, wind whipping down from Karale, waves chopping along the shore. Snow on the hills, icebergs on the water. This was her home, but *she* felt like the alien.

She strode back to the base, in through the heavy door and down the corridor to the medical block. She went into the room where the shipwreck guy was still lying in bed, closed the door behind her. She looked at his notes again. Per Nordström. She walked to the top of his bed. He was handsome if you were into that sort of thing. She glanced out of the window, thought about how everyone here was Scandinavian. White people had been coming here for centuries, telling the Inuit how to live. Building towns that no one wanted, with schools and churches, making everyone Christian, giving the Inuit Danish surnames. Using the land for themselves. Using and taking all the time, trying to civilise what they saw as savages.

She watched Per's chest rise and fall. She leaned over and took hold of his shoulders, shook him gently to begin with, then more strongly, lifting him from the bed. 'Hey.' She kept shaking. 'Wake up, I want to talk to you.'

Nothing.

She stopped. Stared for a moment at the heart monitor and the drip bag. Then slapped him in the face, soft the first time, then harder. Then a third time harder still.

'Per, come on, wake up.'

He groaned and she felt guilty. He moved his head a little then raised a hand to his cheek, which was red where she'd hit him. He cleared his throat, coughed a few times then opened his eyes, blinking like he'd been asleep for years. He saw Niviaq and frowned, rubbed his cheek with his hand, then the stubble on his chin. Looked around the room. He smacked his lips together and closed his eyes.

'Water,' he said.

Niviaq spotted a sink in the corner, filled a glass and brought it back. Held it to his lips as he sipped and coughed, dribbled down his chin.

'I'm in Sedna?' His voice was like it came from the bottom of a well.

'Yes.'

His eyes were still closed. He shook his head, felt for the glass in Niviaq's hand and sipped some more. 'I feel like shit.'

'You've been in a coma.' Niviaq watched his heartrate monitor, which was beeping faster now. She wondered about that coma he'd apparently been in. You couldn't just slap someone out of a coma. She stared at the drip bag, wondered what was in it.

Per opened his eyes. 'Who are you?'

'Niviaq. I found you on the ice in Ammassalik Fjord.'

He ran his fingers across his throat, round his collarbone, as if checking he was real. Pushed his shoulders back a little, winced in pain. 'You?'

Niviaq nodded.

Per tried to smile. 'Thanks.'

Niviaq glanced at the door. This might be the only chance she got to speak to this guy. 'Why were you out there?'

Per shook his head as if trying to shake away ghosts. 'How did I get here?'

'I took you to the hospital at Tasiilaq. Some guys came in a helicopter and removed you, brought you here.'

Per narrowed his eyes. 'What are you doing here, if you're local?'

Niviaq didn't know how to answer without sounding crazy. 'I came looking for a friend.'

Per frowned.

Niviaq leaned in, spoke more forcefully. 'Why were you on the ice? What happened? What's going on here?'

Per pressed his cracked lips together, took shallow breaths, the heart monitor speeding up. 'They attacked us.'

'Who?'

He shook his head. 'You wouldn't believe me.'

Niviaq laughed. 'I've seen some shit. Right now, I would believe anything.'

Per coughed again, took another sip of water.

'Was it the Enceladons?' Niviaq said.

Per's eyes widened. 'How do you know about them?'

'There's two outside right now.'

Per looked at the door, tried to sit up. 'I need to go.'

The heart monitor was beeping too fast.

'Who attacked you?' Niviaq said. 'Was it them?'

'Hey.'

Niviaq turned and saw a woman coming through the door, face tight, heading for Per in bed. She recognised her from the boat-taxi hire at Kulusuk and the heliport at Tasiilaq. Britt.

'What are you doing?' Britt said.

'I'm not doing anything,' Niviaq said. 'He just woke up.'

Per was trying to get out of bed. 'I need to—'

'You're not going anywhere,' Britt said, pressing his shoulders into the pillow. 'You've been through a lot, Per, you need to take it easy.'

'But—'

Britt threw a dirty look at Niviaq. 'What have you been saying to him?'

'Nothing.'

Britt narrowed her eyes. 'Why are you even here? You're the boat woman, Niviaq.'

Niviaq didn't know how to answer.

Britt turned back to Per and fiddled with the valve on the drip bag, and Niviaq saw liquid travel down the tube into Per's wrist. It was almost comical how quickly it took effect, Per relaxing into the pillows, head slumping to the side, eyes closing.

'What did you do that for?' Niviaq said.

'You have no idea about brain trauma,' Britt said. 'It's very dangerous to jump someone out of a coma like that. You need to do it gradually.'

'He wasn't in a coma,' Niviaq said. 'You're drugging him.'

'It's an induced coma, it's highly technical. You can't just mess around.'

Niviaq shook her head and looked at Per. She wanted to scream and shake him until he told her everything. But she had to play it smarter than that, she'd seen the guns when they collected Per from the hospital, they meant business.

'You need to leave,' Britt said, looking at the door.

Niviaq followed her gaze and saw a guard with a rifle pointed in her direction.

# 34
# AVA

'The Enceladons can't leave now, I need more time with them,' Karl said.

Lennox had told him about Ava's plan to take Chloe to the settlement with Sandy and Xander.

Ava looked around. Sandy, Xander, Lennox and Vonnie were next to her, at least ten Sedna staff out here too, Karl closest to her, Thelma just behind, others recording everything. Britt came out of the station frowning and rejoined them, and Ava wondered what she'd been up to. She looked for Niviaq but couldn't see her, felt shitty and wanted to say sorry.

Lennox put a hand on Karl's shoulder. 'You don't get to tell them what to do.'

'That's not what I meant,' Karl said.

Ava wondered if they were speaking out loud for the benefit of the other Sedna crew. But sometimes it was just more natural to talk with your mouth, to keep your self intact.

'I understand now,' Karl said to Lennox. 'What Sandy showed me. The way they live, the way they're together. It's something humanity's lost, if we ever had it.'

'We had it,' Ava said, thinking of Niviaq. 'Indigenous people *still* have it.'

Karl nodded vigorously. 'I get that now. All of this…' He waved his hand around Sedna Station and out to sea, as if trying to take in the whole world. 'Everything I've done with KJI – all the companies and products and markets and boards and shareholders – it's all meaningless. Worse than meaningless, it's catastrophic. I've been part of the system fucking up the planet.'

The words tumbled out of him and Ava wondered if the epiphany was genuine. It was fine to spout all this out here, but what about when he got back to New York or London. Like a holiday romance, all this would fade as reality kicked back in.

Ava noticed Britt watching Karl closely with narrowed eyes.

'We're coming back,' Ava said to Karl, hugging Chloe closer to her. The girl was staring at Xander. Imagine as a kid meeting a creature the size of a bus that you could talk to, get inside and breathe its body.

Ava wondered about what Xander had said, that Chloe wasn't the same as Heather, that she'd been part-Enceladon her whole life. Chloe was the first of her kind anywhere and that scared the shit out of Ava. All she wanted for her daughter was a good life, healthy and happy, like any mother. To be something different, something special, was dangerous.

Karl stared at her and Chloe, then nodded at Sandy and Xander. <Are *they* coming back too?>

Ava understood his need to be connected. <I promise they'll be back.>

<I need more,> Karl sent. <I need to find out about their lives. About Enceladus. How they came to be here. And I have to meet the others.>

Lennox put a hand on Karl's shoulder. 'You'll meet them, I promise. But we have to let Ava take Chloe first, she needs their medical help right now. We have plenty of time if you're true to your word. If you're not here to harm them.'

'Of course not.' Karl sounded affronted. 'I just want to learn more.'

A splash behind Ava made her turn and she saw Heather clambering out of the water and scuttling towards them.

<Ava.> She placed a tentacle on Ava's shoulder and wrapped Chloe in a hug at the same time. She looked at Sandy and Xander. <Can they help her?>

Ava tried to stop tears coming to her eyes. She thought of Chloe, her little brain, whatever was going on inside. <They're not sure.

We're going to meet the others, see if they can figure it out together.>

Blue and green shifted across Heather's body. <Are you sure the settlement is safe?>

<Why wouldn't it be?>

She felt the suckers of Heather's tentacle grip her shoulder. <Just be careful.>

<But we can trust Sandy and Xander.> Ava looked at them now, as unknowable as they'd always been. <Can't we?>

<I'll come with you.> Heather flashed bright colours for a moment, then her body went darker again.

Ava noticed that she hadn't answered the question.

# 35
# LENNOX

They were in a meeting room in the station, windows looking over the sea. Lennox stared at the icebergs and worried about Chloe. Ava had taken her inside Xander and they'd slunk into the water, followed by Sandy and Heather. Karl asked Lennox and Vonnie to stay, said he had something to discuss with them.

Karl was looking out of the window too, Britt a few feet away from him, iPad in her hand. Thelma and the rest of the staff had been bubbling with excitement as Xander and the others left, keen to examine all the footage and data, running inside to upload and assess.

Karl turned now to Lennox, rubbing his ear where Sandy's tentacle had been. 'You were the first. Please, tell me about it.'

Lennox had been over this a million times in his head and it felt like dredging a story from the depths of his soul. But now, as he put it into words, it seemed to take away the profundity of the experience. There just weren't the human words to explain it, but human words were all he had.

Vonnie glanced at him when he'd finished talking. <You OK?>

For the last eighteen months, it had been only the two of them able to communicate like this, but the last few days had blown that out the water. They were back with the aliens, with other telepathic humans. Lennox missed what they'd had and wanted it back.

'What are you saying?' Karl looked from Vonnie to Lennox and tapped his ear. 'Why can't I hear it? Are you blocking me?'

Lennox would never understand the telepathy fully, but he and Vonnie had much more experience and control than when they first got it, and could keep Karl out of their minds for now. Lennox wondered what it would be like if everyone could talk like this, if there were no barriers. No lying. But was that true? When he first met Sandy, they'd claimed not to understand lying, but maybe that was just lost in translation. Maybe the Enceladons could lie all along. Or maybe they learned how to lie at New Broom.

<It's not a free-for-all,> Lennox sent to Karl. <It's a skill you develop.>

'I need to understand,' Karl said. 'This is too important.'

He glanced at Britt, who gave him a tight-lipped smile.

'Why are we here?' Lennox said. 'You wanted to talk so badly.'

'I'm still getting my head around this. Do you know how hard it is to admit you were wrong?' He looked at Lennox as if he expected an answer.

'Sure.'

Karl widened his eyes. 'But what if you were wrong about everything.'

Vonnie stuck her chin out. 'How do you mean?'

Karl shook his head like he couldn't believe his own stupidity. 'Did you know that I own one of the five biggest organisations in the world? A huge, multi-national conglomerate. Fingers in so many pies, even I don't know what half of them do. I have boards and CEOs dealing with that, but it's all in my name, right? It's all in the name of Karl Jensen.'

He ran a finger along the back of a chair pushed up against the table in the middle of the room.

'But I never started out that way. I was a computer geek. Just looking to make games, then how to make them more efficient, algorithms that ran faster, better. How to get information from one place to another more effectively. Then suddenly it's ten years later and I'm a millionaire getting interviewed on television, exclusive conferences, meetings with bigger fish in the pond. I soaked it all up, like anyone would. The parties, holidays, girls. It's ridiculous, all of it. But it's so easy when it's just handed to you. What else could I do?'

'Sounds awful.' Lennox couldn't keep the sarcasm out of his voice.

Karl stared at him. 'I know you're joking, but it is. It truly is.'

Vonnie scoffed. 'Yeah, bummer.'

Karl pointed at the two of them. 'But you *know*, you both understand. You've connected with Sandy and the others. You know there's another way.' He breathed deeply and glanced at Britt. 'This is all bullshit. Capitalism, consumerism, human exceptionalism. All of it is totally fucked. We are fucking the planet, fucking each other. There's no sense of fairness, empathy or humanity.'

Lennox couldn't stop a laugh escaping. 'Says the billionaire tech bro.'

Karl grinned. 'Exactly. But I'm not going to be the billionaire tech bro anymore.'

Britt swallowed and her body tensed as she watched him.

'What do you mean?' Vonnie said.

Karl looked at Britt, who put on a smile. 'I'm changing everything, all the companies, the infrastructure. I'm focusing on what I can do in a positive way.'

Lennox shook his head. 'That's easy to say out here. But when you get back to those boardrooms, you'll change your mind.'

'No.' Karl spoke with conviction. 'I can never go back, not after what I've experienced here.'

'What are you going to do to make things right?' Vonnie said. 'How can you hope to change the system? You're just one guy.'

Karl sucked his teeth. 'I haven't worked it all out yet, but I will. I got to this position, didn't I? I can make the companies pivot to sustainable tech, environmental work, charities, social equality. I have billions, I can use them for good.'

Britt took a step away from them and put the iPad down on the table.

'You're still part of the system,' Lennox said.

'But it's a start, right? I'll campaign for change, use the money to make it happen. It's something, isn't it?'

He looked at Lennox and Vonnie hopefully, for approval. Then he turned to Britt. 'Right?'

She smiled at him, took a small gun from the waistband of her skirt and shot him between the eyes, then two in the chest. He slumped over the chair then fell onto the floor.

Lennox looked at Vonnie, as shocked as he was.

'What the fuck?' he said, eyes wide, his legs suddenly weak.

Britt slid the gun along the floor halfway to Lennox and Vonnie, then pulled another pistol from her jacket and pointed it at them.

'Guards! Help!' Her voice was full of panic, but she smiled at Lennox and Vonnie.

An icy shiver flowed through Lennox as he realised what Britt had done. What it meant.

'What the fuck?' Vonnie said, voice quivering. She looked at Lennox, shaking her head. <She's crazy.>

Britt didn't speak, just smiled until an armed guard came through the door. Then she put on a distressed act, pointing at Karl's body on the ground.

'They killed him,' she said, glancing at the discarded gun on the floor. 'They shot him. Oh my God, Karl.'

She went to his body as the guard trained his rifle on Lennox and Vonnie.

'She did it,' Lennox said, his voice sounding too high in his own ears. He pointed at Britt, but he already knew it was useless. 'She's fucking crazy. She killed Karl.'

Britt pretended to search for Karl's pulse, blood oozing from his wounds, then she turned, tears in her eyes.

'Arrest them,' she said to the guard.

# 36
# NIVIAQ

She'd been sitting in the locked room for a while when she heard shots. Three sharp pops that she recognised straight away – you didn't grow up in Tasiilaq without knowing the sound of gunfire. She heard footsteps, a guard clattering down the corridor past her door.

<Ava? Are you OK?> Waited a moment with her head to the side. Maybe she wasn't doing telepathy right, how could she know? <Ava?>

Nothing.

She thought about Per in the hospital bed. How they'd locked her in here just for talking to him.

She looked around the room. It was a large storage cupboard, shelves of supplies, some outdoor gear, a few pieces of equipment she didn't recognise. She went to the small window and looked out over the back of the base towards the mountains. Large white clouds cutting across the sky. Rough terrain, boulders and scree, streams running down from higher ground.

She tried the window but knew it was locked. She ran her finger around the frame, assessed the size. Flexed her shoulders forward and back. Most of her body would probably fit through OK, but her hips might be a problem.

She went back to the shelves, pulled out a pair of thick mittens, put one on. Walked to the window and stood for a moment steeling herself. <Ava?>

Nothing, she was on her own.

She brought her mittened fist back and slammed it into the

window, a judder through her bones but the window held. She did it two more times, nothing. Toughened glass.

She took the mitten off and threw it to the ground, flexed her fingers. Went back to the shelves, rooted around. On the bottom shelf she found a large screwdriver. Looked around for something heavy, saw a metal doorstop in the corner. Took both over to the window and set herself with the screwdriver point in the middle of the glass. Heaved the doorstop and hammered the screwdriver, again and again, the window shuddering then cracking then finally shattering but staying in place. She kept hammering away as shards of glass fell around her, some spraying into her face. She paused and grabbed goggles off the shelf then went back to it, chipping away the first pane until it was in pieces on the floor.

She stopped, listened. No alarm, no voices.

She repeated the hammering on the second pane until it was in pieces on the ground, her goggles chipped by flying shards, grazes on her cheeks where she'd been struck. She tried to make sure all the glass was gone from the frame as the wind whipped through the open space.

She leaned out, looked both ways, no other windows were overlooking her because of the shape of the station.

She stopped, listened again.

Grabbed the mittens and put them on, found a balaclava and pulled it over her head. But she couldn't use anything to protect her torso, the extra bulk would get in the way.

She pulled over a chair and stood on it, leaned out and put her hands and arms through first, then her head. She bent down and grabbed the side of the building, flexed one shoulder through but the other got stuck, snagging against a shard of glass, her sweater ripping, her muscles spasming. She wriggled some more and felt like an idiot, a fish flapping on the deck of a boat. She tried to steady her breath then kicked from the chair and pushed against the outside wall as much as she could, angled her body this way then that. Her second shoulder popped through. Pain in her muscles, blood from somewhere. But she wriggled on, hips gliding through, she wasn't as wide down there as she'd thought. She tumbled onto the rocks in a heap, felt them poke into her.

She righted herself, whipped off the balaclava and mittens and looked around. Checked her body, a cut on the right shoulder. Aches and pains, nothing else.

She crawled under the adjacent windows, round the corner of the building, then the next. Got to the front and there was no one there. An hour ago it had been full of people and Enceladons.

<Ava, can you hear me? Heather?>

She went up the far side of the building towards where her boat was moored behind rocks. She saw movement at a window and stopped. Breathed in and out before looking up. Caught a glimpse of Lennox and Vonnie having their hands bound by one security guard, another pointing a semi-automatic at them.

<Vonnie? Lennox?> She had no idea if she could do this, she'd never spoken to them like this before. No reply. She tried again, nothing.

A rock slid under her foot, making her stumble and gasp. She heard one guard telling the other to check outside.

She crouch-ran past the entrance and over clear ground. She waited for shouts, gunfire, but there was nothing. She reached the outcrop and dived behind.

Her boat was where she'd left it. She got in and pushed off. Waited a long moment as she thought about the engine. Figured it was worth the risk and switched the ignition on, steered into the fjord.

She kept glancing back for the next half hour, expecting boats in pursuit. Eventually her shoulders relaxed a little.

She thought about her next move. Why had Lennox and Vonnie been detained? Why had she been locked up for talking to Per? Where were Ava and Chloe? They must have gone with the Enceladons, but she had no way of finding them. She could head back to Tasiilaq to get help, but how could she explain to anyone what had happened?

The sky was bright but it was the middle of the night now. She felt the sting of her shoulder and dug into the medical box for antiseptic spray and a bandage. She realised all at once how exhausted she was, now that the adrenaline had gone. She killed the boat's engine, grabbed a blanket and leaned back. She closed her eyes, intending to rest for just a moment.

She woke with a jump at a crack against the hull. Rubbed her eyes and opened them. The light was different, she must've been asleep for hours. The air was bitter against her face and she shivered. Another thud of ice against the hull, then another. She stood and looked out and her heart sank. She was entirely surrounded by ice, packed in. No way to move the boat in any direction.

# 37
# AVA

She'd seen the entire Enceladon population once before in the depths of Loch Broom, but that had been like a refugee camp compared to this place, which felt like a home. They'd settled into a huge depression in the sea floor, created structures along the outer edges, something like monuments in the middle, piles of rocks in fluent shapes, mud and sand moulded into similar, curvy constructions.

Ava saw all of this through the membrane of Xander's flesh, a translucent skin that added shimmer to the light displays of the creatures milling about in the natural bowl. She wondered how deep the sea was here. She was entirely at the Enceladons' mercy. Without them, she and Chloe would drown long before they reached the surface. She looked at Chloe, eyes closed, nestled into some folds of Xander's flesh. What else could Ava do but trust Xander and Sandy? It was the only way to cure Chloe.

<Is she OK, Sandy?>

<Sandy-Chloe-Ava-Xander partial is safe.>

Sandy had stuck close to Xander for their trip from Sedna, passing in and out the surface of Xander's body like it was nothing. Ava would never get her head around it – were they even separate beings?

Sandy seemed different to how they'd been back in Scotland. More grown up, more serious. Maybe that was natural, or maybe their circumstances had changed them. Ava thought about what Heather had said, or not said, when Ava asked if she could trust Sandy and Xander. Heather had accompanied them back to the settlement, but Ava looked around for her now and couldn't see her, or at least couldn't tell if she was one of the hundreds of octopoid creatures swimming around their giant cousins, in and out of the enormous jellyfish's tendril forests, the whole thing an illuminated network.

Xander swam towards the centre of the settlement.

Chloe's eyes opened. <Mummy.>

<Everything's OK, honey.>

Other jellyfish swam into the centre of the clearing and began propelling themselves in an anti-clockwise circle around it. Xander joined in as Sandy slipped inside them next to Ava and Chloe.

<Xander? What's happening?>

A long pause before she got anything back.

<Enceladon-whole create special energy.>

Ava frowned and reached for Chloe, who was holding her hands out for a cuddle. <For Chloe?>

They were moving faster now, closing the gaps between their bodies, so that they seemed like one giant creature, a rotating tower of life.

Ava turned. <Sandy, what's going on?>

The speed they were going, Ava started to feel dizzy. The centrifugal force pushed her away from the middle, Chloe in her arms, eyes wide, smile on her face. Ava worried for a moment they would be flung out of Xander's body, left to drown on their own. <Sandy?>

<Enceladon-whole new energy. Bigger communication. More knowledge than Sandy-Xander partial. Any partial.>

The loss in translation was more frustrating than ever. <Knowledge? What do you *mean*?>

<Chloe-Enceladon partial is new life. Not like other partials on Enceladus or Earth. New kind of life.>

Ava shook her head.

The Enceladons were swimming around faster than Ava could comprehend. It was like a fairground ride crossed with some insane body-horror movie.

<She's not new life,> Ava sent. <She's my daughter.>

Sandy touched Chloe lightly with a tentacle, <Ava-Chloe partial want molecular inefficiency improved?>

Why couldn't they just ask if she wanted Chloe's brain tumour gone? <Of course. Please, tell Xander and the others to do what they can.>

There were dozens of giant jellyfish now in a colossal rotating doughnut shape. Ava felt sick. She hugged Chloe but the girl was nonplussed. The light display all around them was incredible, streaming from one creature to the next, no sense of individual animals. White and blue and green flashes and sparks, long lingering tracers following intense strobing, shifting networks of patterns underneath, moving both with and against the direction they were spinning. It was the most incredible thing Ava had ever seen, but she worried she might pass out if it got any faster, any more intense.

An eerie purple light glowed around her and Chloe, then entered Chloe's body and she went limp.

<Chloe!> No sense of anything from her daughter, she was out cold. Ava turned to Sandy. <What happened? What have they done?>

<Chloe-Enceladon partial in rest state. More efficient absorption of new energy.>

<Sandy, for fuck's sake, what does that mean?>

<Human rest state prime for molecular manipulation.>

<Manipulation?>

Sandy placed two tentacles either side of Ava's forehead, their eyes glowing gold and green as Ava stared into them and felt herself falling. Her eyelids grew heavy, a cool liquid flowing through her body and mind. She shook herself awake, had to stay alert for this.

<What's happening? Sandy, what are you doing?>

<Human rest state.>

<Are you drugging me? Did you drug Chloe?>

But she felt her mind slip away and fell into blackness.

# 38
# VONNIE

She'd slept somehow. Vonnie opened her eyes and looked around the room. It wasn't a proper stockade like the one she and Lennox had been in at New Broom. Sedna was a scientific base rather than a military one. But the room was bare and secure, heavy door locked and bolted on the outside, no window. The walls were solid, Lennox had already had a go at them last night in frustration.

They'd been given water and there was a bucket toilet in the corner of the room, a single hard bunk they'd shared last night, lying under the scratchy blanket and holding each other. Vonnie pictured the baby growing inside her, her stomach pushed against Lennox as they slumped into exhausted sleep.

Lennox was pacing up and down now, shaking his head, fingers at his temples. He saw Vonnie sit up.

'Did I wake you?'

Vonnie shook her head and rubbed sleep from her eyes. 'Are you trying to reach Sandy?'

<Anyone, really.>

Vonnie knew from his face he hadn't been successful. She looked at the door. 'What do you think they're going to do?'

They'd talked this to death last night. Images of Karl had haunted her dreams, blood leaking down his face, the light gone from his eyes. The Enceladons had this idea that everyone's energy lived on in the universe, but Karl was dead. His epiphany had got him killed.

Lennox bowed his head, fingers digging into his skull, trying to communicate. He was better than her at using his power, could direct it in a way she couldn't. Some people just had more aptitude for it, she guessed. But he was out of practice.

She remembered what they'd worked out last night. As far as they knew, Sandy, Xander, Heather, Ava and Chloe were all still at the Enceladon settlement. But they would come back, Ava and Chloe couldn't stay down there indefinitely.

The sound of the outside bolt made Vonnie stand and Lennox straighten up.

Vonnie glanced across. <I've got your back.>

Lennox nodded. <Likewise.>

The door opened and Britt came in, followed by one of the guards who'd detained them yesterday. He was in body armour and carrying an assault rifle, handgun in a holster at his waist. He stood at the door as Britt looked at them both. She was wearing a tight-fitting grey suit like a fucking junior executive, not someone who'd just killed her boss.

Lennox looked at the guard. 'You know she did it.'

Britt laughed. 'It's cute you think that's a wedge you can use.' She took the pistol from the guard's holster and nodded at him. 'Wait outside.'

He looked reluctant but left anyway.

Britt closed the door and pointed the gun at the bed. 'Sit.'

Vonnie clenched her fists.

Britt looked at them both. 'You know, I can't work out which of you is the boss.'

'No one's the boss,' Vonnie said. 'Not everyone thinks like that.'

Britt smiled. 'All relationships are like that, whether you admit it or not. Every couple has a dominant partner.'

Lennox shook his head. 'Not us.'

Britt's smile faded. 'That's right, you're all super-modern, thanks to our alien friends. You work together in perfect harmony, right? Helping each other towards a beautiful utopian future.'

Vonnie's hackles rose. She knew that's what Britt wanted but she couldn't help it. 'It's better than whatever you're doing.'

'Is it?' Britt angled her head to the side and waggled the gun.

Lennox shifted his weight and Vonnie thought for a second he was going to go for her. <Don't.>

Lennox didn't indicate that he'd heard her.

'The gun doesn't matter,' he said, waving around the room. 'None of this matters.'

'But it does,' Britt said. 'A great deal.'

Vonnie wanted to distract her. If Britt goaded him enough, Lennox might take the bait and Britt would shoot him.

'Why did you do it?' she said to Britt. 'Why kill Karl?'

Britt tutted. 'Come on, we're all smart people here. You know why.'

'Karl was a threat to the shareholders,' she said.

'I mean, that's part of it, yes.' Britt was pretending to be nonchalant, but she was clearly enjoying coming out of the shadows, having power. 'There have been contingencies in place for a while now. The board of the parent company, the big investors, they've had concerns about Karl for a long time. He was a terrible businessman, to be honest. Open-minded, concerned for others and the environment. Not even trying to maximise profit properly. When he discovered this whole Enceladon thing ... well, eyebrows were raised.' She waved a hand. 'All this doesn't come cheap, his pet project. However, the others were glad to have him out the way for a while. But there was always a risk that this thing would turn out to be real. That he would make contact, and he would change. I didn't think it would happen so quickly, just goes to show what a weak man he was. But that was all covered in the plan.'

'So you had permission to kill him?' Vonnie said.

Britt made a face. 'More than permission, a specific instruction. Not that it's traceable, of course. Frankly, I didn't need to be asked twice. Working for that man...' She sighed. 'He was quite taxing.'

'Why have you come to see us?' Lennox said, looking at the door.

Britt had noticed him inching closer to her and focused the gun on him.

<Please don't do anything stupid,> Vonnie sent.

Britt straightened her shoulders. 'Your little Inuit boat-friend, Niviaq. She was here but she's slipped the net and I don't like loose ends. You two are here, the others are at the Enceladon settlement. We're just not sure where your friend is.'

Vonnie shrugged. 'We don't know.'

Britt tapped her temple with the gun. 'But you can find her, right?' She looked at Lennox. 'I presume you've been trying to communicate.'

Vonnie looked around. They'd searched for cameras last night, assumed they were being spied on. Britt had all that data from Karl connecting with Sandy. Vonnie thought about Thelma, she couldn't be part of this, surely? Maybe she'd been dealt with the same as Karl.

'We can't reach anyone,' Lennox said.

'You wouldn't tell me if you could.' Britt sighed. 'So I'll just have to let Gunnar outside have a word with you.' She rapped on the door and it opened. She paused at the doorway, gun still trained on Lennox. 'The good thing about private security is that there are no rules, they just get the job done.'

'What about the settlement?' Vonnie said.

Britt knew where that was now, with the tracking data. She shook her head at them, smiled and left.

# 39
# HEATHER

She missed sleeping in a bed. In her new body, she spent periods of rest in the settlement, but was never fully asleep. Physically that was fine, but psychologically she'd never got to grips with it. Jodie and the others seemed OK about it, and she wondered again if she was meant to be here.

She looked at Xander across the settlement, Ava and Chloe asleep inside them. Dreaming human dreams, resting and recovering, preparing for a new day. If you never properly slept, were you ever really ready?

She spotted Sandy propelling themself to the outer rim of the settlement, then over the ridge. She followed them, shifting fast through the gloom, hesitated for a long beat before sending. <Sandy? Sandy-Heather partial?>

Sandy stopped, tentacles spread around them, and turned. Put on a cheery light display and Heather wondered whether it was a true reflection of their feelings. When she first met Sandy, she thought Enceladons couldn't lie, but she wasn't so sure anymore. Over the last eighteen months with them she'd noticed a growing evasiveness, a reluctance to fully reveal themselves. And recent events had compounded that. Sandy's reaction to the dead man in the sunken boat, Yolanda and Jodie being cagey about what they'd discussed with marine life. Sometimes they still seemed innocent, but the other stuff was casting doubt in Heather's mind.

<Heather-Sandy partial welcome.>

Heather had learned a few things about interpreting Sandy's tone. <What is it?> She'd reached them now, a brief touch of tentacles.

<Worry Chloe-Enceladon efficiency.>

<You don't think you can cure her brain tumour?>

<Necessary understand new lifeform. Unknown efficiency.>

Heather saw two seals in the distance, the reflection of Sandy's light displays in their eyes, whiskers twitching.

<Where are you going?>

Sandy waved a tentacle. <Deep water, deep thought.>

Heather had mostly kept to the continental shelf around the coast of Greenland. When they first travelled here from Scotland, they crossed a thousand miles of water, much of it deep ocean apart from the Mid-Atlantic Ridge. There was something terrifying about knowing that the water below you went down for thousands of feet. The Enceladons had settled in the shallows around Greenland, and she was never sure why. It was surely more exposed than the deep, but it must be their preferred conditions. She had no idea about the topography of Enceladus.

She'd noticed that sometimes Enceladons would disappear from the settlement, usually alone, and not return for days. She learned they were going on expeditions of the sea floor, but she never got a satisfactory reason. Maybe 'deep water, deep thought' was good enough. Time to think, she got that.

<Can I come?>

Sandy flashed blue-green then orange. <Sandy-Heather partial welcome.>

They swam together for a long time. Heather had no real concept of hours and minutes anymore. After a while the water got colder and something in the current let Heather know the ocean floor had dropped away. She sensed a deeper flow, a feeling of immense darkness.

Sandy swam downward and Heather felt the increased pressure, but her octopoid body could handle it fine. Human bodies were pathetically niche in their construction, could only survive in a tiny window of conditions. Other Earth animals were so much more hardy, could adapt to whatever the planet threw at them. That went for the Enceladons too.

They were deep now and Heather began to feel claustrophobic. There was no sense of a surface above, and without that to orientate her she felt a nervous tremor through her tentacles. Their light displays highlighted sea cucumbers, ghost fish, a pair of large eels. The shadow of a whale in the distance.

Sandy swam towards it and Heather saw it was a sperm whale. Sandy flashed patterns Heather had never seen before – swirling browns and oranges, slipping into reds and yellows. The whale flicked a fin and Sandy attached themself to its head. Their light display went crazy, tentacles moving over the whale's skin. Heather stared at its huge eye, which stared back. She wondered what the hell a sperm whale's experience of life was like, what Sandy was saying to this beautiful creature.

Eventually Sandy separated from the beast and swam downward.

<Sandy, what is it? What did they say?>

<Something to see. On the floor.>

Heather felt the pressure increasing as they dived, adjusted her body. But the scale of the darkness scared her.

She swam in Sandy's slipstream, their bioluminescence lighting the way, plankton and krill around her, smaller fish and crustaceans she didn't recognise. Then she noticed something ahead, a faint light. Another Enceladon way out here?

<Sandy, what is it?>

No answer.

As they got closer, Heather saw sharp lines, the kind of straight edges that don't exist in nature. The single light resolved into a bank of six spotlights strung along the front of a machine. It was yellow and chrome, looked like a piece of farm machinery, a giant harvester. It threw up a plume of sediment as it moved along the sea floor, scooping up the top layer and sending it along a giant tether connecting the machine to something at the surface.

A deep-sea mining vehicle. Heather had read about them while researching her new environment through her mental internet connectedness. Ahead of it, the ocean floor was strewn with black nodules, rocks that contained rare-earth metals, needed for all sorts of technology from phones to electric cars. But God knew what else this monster was scooping up along with the rocks, what damage it was doing to the environment. Destroying the last pristine ecosystem on Earth as if it was nothing.

Sandy swam to the side of the harvester, waving tentacles for Heather to follow. She heard the crunch and grind of the machine, the rattle of the sediment flowing up the tether.

She joined Sandy at the back of the machine and saw something.

A logo, a moon surrounded by tentacles.

# 40
# LENNOX

The door opened and Gunnar stood there with another security guard. He pointed his rifle at Lennox.

'Come.'

Lennox shook his head then looked at Vonnie. <I'll be OK.>

She hugged him then the second guard pulled them apart, dragged Lennox to the door. He punched the guard in the stomach, made to grab his gun, but the guard jabbed the butt of his rifle into Lennox's gut. He doubled over, felt a fist to his temple, blinding pain through his head as he fell to his knees.

'Don't,' Vonnie pleaded. <Baby, don't fight them.>

Lennox was hauled to his feet and dragged outside, caught a glimpse of Vonnie as Gunnar closed and bolted the door.

<I love you,> he sent.

<Just come back to me.>

They marched him down a corridor, no one around. Lennox wondered what the rest of the staff were doing. Were they all in on Britt's little revolution? Maybe they could be made to see reason.

'Hey!' he shouted. 'Help! Is anyone here?'

A boot slammed against the side of his knee and he crumpled to the floor. More kicks to his stomach then his back, agony through his body as he curled up. He wasn't a brave person, just a kid really.

'Ole, enough.' Gunnar's voice was quiet. 'Not here.'

Ole dragged Lennox into a storage closet, shelves of supplies, small window boarded up. Lennox couldn't concentrate for the pain.

'You know what we need.' Gunnar watched as Ole strapped Lennox to a chair in the middle of the room.

'I don't know where Niviaq is,' Lennox said. 'I swear. She must've just wandered off when we were outside.'

He was close to crying, tried to keep it inside, didn't want to give these pricks the satisfaction.

<Lennox, don't do anything stupid, please.> Vonnie's voice was faint in his head. He tried to think what to say back. Gunnar was talking to him now. Ole put his gun down and pushed his sleeves up.

Lennox swallowed. <I love you.>

The first punch knocked the breath from his lungs, buckled him over.

'We don't want to do this,' Gunnar said to him. 'Please just make it easy. Tell us where she is.'

'I don't...'

Ole threw a fist into his face, then another and another. Lennox thought his jaw might be broken, head pounding, blood in his mouth, one eye swollen. More punches to his stomach and chest, a boot to his knee again, over and over, so that he cried out and tears flowed down his cheeks. He sobbed like a baby.

'Tell us.'

He made his mind wander from this room, the violence and pain, and it floated outside, over the sea, plunged down into the cold water that soothed his bruises and cuts, deep into the darkness, then he saw the light of the Enceladons and their home. He tried to talk to Sandy but his telepathy wouldn't work, and he felt more blows to his head, to his stomach and chest.

His mind left the ocean and he flew into the sky then higher into the blackness of space, moving fast away from the heat of the sun into the chill, past Mars and Jupiter to Saturn and Enceladus, down through the plumes of the South Pole, through the ice to the water beneath. Somehow Sandy, Xander and the rest were all there, and Ava, Chloe and Heather, Vonnie too, all laughing and singing and dancing and welcoming him with hugs and shrieks of joy.

He didn't know how long he stayed there, how long he disassociated from his body. He came to in the room, every nerve and muscle and sinew on fire, screaming for relief.

He couldn't see out of one eye. His mouth was full of blood, his chest agony when he breathed.

'Enough.' This was Gunnar, his voice coming from the end of a long tunnel. 'Fetch Pedersen.'

Lennox heard the door open and close, felt Gunnar's breath close to his ear. He spat blood onto Gunnar's shoes, felt another punch in the face, his neck snapping back. He sat there swimming in pain, didn't know how long for. Could hear Gunnar breathing.

<Vonnie?> But he had no energy. Could hardly breathe, let alone send signals. Maybe Ole had punched the telepathy out of him.

The door opened and he smelled Britt's perfume, opened his good eye.

She glanced at Lennox then at Gunnar, who shook his head.

'Are you sure?'

'He's not a strong person. He doesn't know.'

Britt thought this over for a moment.

'Let Vonnie go,' Lennox said. He sounded broken.

Britt smiled in disbelief. 'Why would we do that?'

'You don't need her,' Lennox said.

'We do,' Britt said softly. 'We need her here. But you.' She turned to Gunnar. 'Take him to the other site.'

Lennox felt his mind churn through the pain. 'What other site?'

Britt ran her tongue around her teeth, leaned closer. 'I know what your little aquatic friends can do. I saw New Broom after they destroyed it.'

'They were defending themselves,' Lennox croaked. 'It was that or be killed.'

Britt shook her head. 'Carson's biggest mistake was making it personal. He saw them as an existential threat, but that gives them too much credit.' She straightened up. 'This is all just business.'

'You're wrong.'

Britt sighed. 'But just in case, we need you as a human shield at Ikusik.'

'What's Ikusik?'

'Ikusik is the real reason we're here.'

# 41
# HEATHER

She didn't know much about deep-sea mining but she knew it was banned in the Arctic, like commercial fishing. But humans broke laws all the time. History was a long litany of men doing whatever they wanted for their own gain at the expense of others, to hell with the repercussions. She thought she'd escaped all that with her new life, but here they were on her doorstep.

Sandy swam in Heather's slipstream as she hurried back to the settlement. They were out of the deep ocean now and she saw a pod of white-beaked dolphins to her left, then a pair of beluga hunting fish above her. Each time they passed another animal, Sandy would brighten and expand their body as if they were talking to them, yet Heather heard nothing.

She didn't know what to do. No one at Sedna could be trusted. They were pretending to carry out scientific research when all along they were destroying the marine habitat. It was all lies, no more than she'd come to expect. This wasn't the military like New Broom, this was worse. It was just another day at work.

Sandy caught up with Heather. She had a sudden incongruous memory of eating a rare sirloin at an Edinburgh restaurant with her ex-husband. Knocking back Malbec by the glass, laughing at something he said. She had a sudden urge to eat meat again, blood oozing from the steak as she cut into it. She felt disgusted with herself but couldn't deny the craving, that part of her was still inside somewhere. But industrialised farming and fishing were brutal. Everyone was implicated in the mass torture and murder of animals. She had to keep reminding herself why she was here in an octopoid body, that she'd had enough.

<Why machine eat sea floor?> Sandy's voice made her jump.

She'd swum away from the mining machine in disgust, hadn't spoken to Sandy since. <They need materials. For technology.>

<Technology?>

<Phones, electronic devices and cars. I don't know what else.>

<Why?>

It was like talking to a kid, frustrating because it highlighted how fucked the situation was, how stupid humans were. <For batteries, to store power.>

<Not good energy?>

<No.>

Sandy flashed red. <Rocks are slow life.>

<What?>

<Rocks make oxygen for ecosystem.>

<Rocks don't produce oxygen, Sandy.>

Sandy's head shrunk a little. <Rocks make oxygen in sea.>

Heather shook her head, a vestige of her old human body. 'Slow life', what did that mean? Sandy touched a tentacle to her head and she felt suddenly dizzy with a vision, picturing metallic nodules in a fizzing dance with seawater, bubbles floating upward from the reaction. She somehow knew it was true, the creation of dark oxygen down here in the depths.

She shook her head and saw the bio-glow of the settlement in front of her. Swam over the ridge into the main area, spotted Ava and Chloe still asleep inside Xander. She wondered how long she and Sandy had been away.

<Ava.>

Ava sat upright inside the bulk of Xander, looked around confused, reached out and touched Chloe's hand. Then she saw Heather and Sandy.

<I had a crazy dream,> Ava sent.

<They're mining the sea floor.> Heather's voice was too high. <We can't trust them. We have to warn Lennox and Vonnie.>

Ava looked at Chloe and narrowed her eyes, as if she didn't have headspace for anything else right now. <You're sure it's the same people?>

<I saw the logo on the side of the harvester.>

<What was it doing?>

<Digging up the ocean floor, sending sediment to a ship on the surface. Destroying everything.> Heather flashed orange down her tentacles. <If they'll do that illegally, they'll do anything.>

Sandy's body ballooned and a black-and-brown zigzag slithered across their head and along their tentacles. Their eyes went wide. <Sandy-Niviaq partial in trouble.>

Ava straightened her shoulders. <What?>

Heather was confused. <Did you hear something?>

<Sandy-Niviaq weak distress call for Ava-Niviaq partial.>

<From Sedna Station?> Ava sent.

Sandy's tentacles elasticated out to form a canopy. <No. Ava-Niviaq-Sandy partial on boat. In the ice.>

Ava looked at Chloe.

Heather waved two tentacles. <We should help her. And speak to Lennox and Vonnie while we're at it.>

Ava went to wake Chloe.

Sandy's tentacles narrowed and bristled along their edges. <Dangerous to wake Chloe-Xander partial. Best chance of efficiency improvement if stay in low energy.>

Ava shook her head. <I can't leave her.>

<She'll be fine,> Heather sent. <Xander will look after her. We should go.>

Heather waited until she saw the smallest of nods from Ava.

# 42
# NIVIAQ

Niviaq looked around. The ice was packing in tighter and she worried about the hull. She'd been in boats before that were crushed or lifted entirely onto the ice sheet. She looked but didn't see any leaks, her feet still dry.

She heard a roar, thought about tales of the *dupilak* from the town elders. But she knew this wasn't a mythical beast hell-bent on dragging her to the bottom of the sea. It was worse than that.

A polar bear.

She scanned the horizon but couldn't see it. The ice around her was an array of colours, grey and dark blue, green murky shadows, icebergs and shards, cracks and fissures. In the distance was the coast, a patchwork of snow and gravel, moss and scree, rocky escarpments and cliffs. Polar bears had evolved to be camouflaged in this landscape.

Another roar. She knew what that sound meant. It wasn't calling to other bears, agitated and scared. It was hungry.

She crouched in the boat and scanned for movement. But the creaking and shifting ice made it hard to spot anything. She lifted her binoculars at something, but it was a harp seal sliding into the water.

She lowered the glasses and scanned again.

Saw something, closer this time. Lifted the glasses. Yellowish fur against the ice, the bump of its nose, black holes for eyes. It was a male, much bigger than the females, immense muscles quivering as it stalked across the ice.

Towards Niviaq and the boat.

She moved her head to sense the wind, a steady breeze from behind her. Not good. The bear could already smell her.

She ducked into the boat and looked around, but her rifle was missing. Maybe KJI guards had discovered her boat and removed it while she was locked up. It was for seal hunting, and probably wouldn't stop a bear of this size anyway, but she might scare it away. The bears had been getting more desperate for years, their habitat disappearing, food scarce.

She had the flare, that might scare it, or maybe just make it angry. She grabbed it and lifted her head over the side of the boat.

The bear was two hundred metres away. She could see it without binoculars, breath billowing in the air, the shimmer of its fur as it jogged towards her, nose up, following her stink.

She unlocked the flare, aimed over the bear's head and fired. The crack, thud and whoosh made the bear pause as pink smoke floated in the sky. It looked around then up, shook its fur and continued on.

Shit. She thought what else she could do. She didn't have her phone, no satellite phone either.

She placed her fingers on the side of her temples. <Ava, can you hear me?> She should've thought of it earlier, but it seemed crazy. It still felt as if her telepathy was part of a dream. <I'm in trouble, Ava. Please. I'm stuck in a boat in the ice, there's a bear coming. If someone can hear me, please, I need help.>

She felt stupid, wasting her time. She sneaked a look over the gunwale. The bear was still approaching, sauntering now as if it knew she couldn't escape. It moved its head side to side, nose still in the air.

If she left the boat it was suicide. She couldn't outrun it and there was nowhere to hide. But if she stayed in the boat she was a sitting target.

She looked around. There were a couple of oars in the boat in case of engine failure, but they would snap like twigs. She turned to the tiny cockpit. That door was lockable. She lifted her head. The bear was fifty metres away, staring at the boat, eyes black and empty.

She grabbed the oars and some rope and jumped inside the

cockpit, locked the door, slid one oar through the handles and tied it with the rope. The other three sides of the cockpit were glass. An eight-hundred-kilo polar bear with paws the size of dinner plates wouldn't even blink.

Shit, shit, shit.

The bear roared, catching her scent stronger now, and the noise shook her ribs. She heard snorts and low growls between roars. The boat rocked as the bear tested a paw on the port side. She could see it from the side of the cockpit as it heaved into the boat, which creaked against the ice.

She thought she might piss herself as she held the second oar and stared at the flimsy door.

More growls and whines. Then a moment's silence before a whump and crash against the locked door. The door shuddered against the frame, the handle rattling and the oar shifting.

<We're coming.>

She jumped and looked out of the cockpit window, as if the voice had come from right outside.

<Sandy-Niviaq-Ava-Heather partial arrive soon.>

<Shit, please hurry. There's a bear, it's going to kill me.>

Another crash against the cockpit door made Niviaq jump and lean back against the helm. Another thump and the door almost caved in, the oar just holding it in place. Then Niviaq felt the boat rock as the bear shifted to the starboard side. She saw its huge face, then a paw smashed through the glass. A growl and a roar and she smelled its breath, fish and seal. The bear saw her and shifted round further, took another swipe and smashed the whole side of the cockpit in, showering Niviaq in glass.

<Hold on.> This was Ava's voice.

The bear pushed at some wood and glass shards, trampled them under its paws, took a step into the wrecked cockpit.

Niviaq yelled at it and jabbed with the oar. The bear roared again and swatted the oar, smashing it against the helm. Niviaq grabbed the other oar from the broken door and held it up like a harpoon, waving it at the bear's face. It tried to swipe it and she ducked and jabbed it into the animal's throat. It took a step back, growled again, then smashed the second oar away and stepped up to her.

She raised her arms in front of her face.

But the bear didn't attack. It stood, sniffing the air, looking around, the boat rocking underneath them. It waited a moment then arched its back, straightened its shoulders.

Then something appeared from a crack in the ice sheet to the left of the boat. It moved so fast Niviaq couldn't make sense of it at first.

Sandy slithered over the side of the boat and Ava slid out of their body like a newborn, on her knees panting and confused. Behind them, Heather emerged from the sea and clambered aboard.

Sandy stood on three tentacles and approached the bear. It roared at them, grumbled a little then sat on its haunches and let Sandy touch its face with two tentacles. The bear swayed and closed its eyes as Sandy flashed black and blue, then magenta and crimson, swirling patterns like an oil spill.

The two of them stayed like that for a few moments, Niviaq trapped in the corner of the wrecked cockpit. She looked at Sandy and the polar bear, still communicating. The bear was passive now. Eventually it opened its eyes and looked at Niviaq for a long time. Then it turned, lumbered off the boat and sauntered away across the ice.

Niviaq stood there panting, heart hammering in her chest, and watched it go. Eventually she turned to Sandy. <What did you say to it?>

Sandy shimmered gold and silver, then returned to blue swirls. <Niviaq-Sandy partial experience?>

They stretched two tentacles towards her and held them there. Niviaq stared at them for a moment, then took hold.

And suddenly she wasn't in a wrecked boat in the Arctic sea, she was flying at indescribable speed through the atmosphere, the wind shocking the air from her lungs, then there was no air, just black, empty space and she was pummelling away from the ferocious heat of the sun into the chill of the outer solar system, past Mars and the asteroid belt, heading towards the shiny discs of Jupiter and Saturn. She approached the icy, blue-white ball of Enceladus, striations like giant claw marks across its South Pole. She floated for a moment in space, part of Saturn's rings, a tiny piece of dust amongst the rock and ice debris, then she dived down through the volcanic plumes that shot into space from the South Pole, through the cracked icy surface to the warm water beneath. She swam in the deepest blue, the under-ice oceans that spanned the whole moon, where the Enceladons had lived for millions of years. She wasn't human anymore, was completely Enceladon, tentacles swirling around her octopoid body as she swam alongside others in a giant gathering of illuminated creatures that spread as far as she could see. A faint red glow was beneath her, the distant underwater volcanoes like the gods of this world, quietly watching their creations. The roof of thick, blue-grey ice overhead was comforting, a giant blanket.

But then suddenly she was pulled away from the great assembly of Enceladons, yanked back and upward to the volcanic vents, and spewed out into space, separated from her new home, floundering in the dark, avoiding the rocks and dust of Saturn's rings, then she was hurtling away from this beautiful moon back towards the distant smudge of the sun, which grew until she could feel its immense nuclear power, then the Earth was beneath her, the shrinking ice cap of the Arctic, the outline of the Greenland coast, then she was rocketing through the atmosphere at insane velocity until she thumped back into her body in the destroyed boat.

Niviaq opened her eyes and dropped Sandy's tentacles, then she leaned over and vomited on the deck.

# 43
# VONNIE

The silence in her mind was agonising. She hadn't been able to contact Lennox for hours, and was trying not to think of the worst-case scenario. Sickness rose up from her gut out of nowhere and she rushed to the bucket and puked, the smell making her feel worse. Her stomach tightened as she retched then spat, tried to breathe slowly, ran her tongue around her furry teeth, her tongue sweating. She thought about the baby, letting her know they were in there, stewing away. Developing their organs, limbs, brain.

She slumped against the wall and shuffled away from the stinking bucket. <Lennox, please.>

Nothing. She had to face it, he might be dead. Or unconscious, beaten into oblivion. Maybe he was so weak his telepathic powers had deserted him, or maybe they'd moved him off the base, but she couldn't think of a reason they'd do that.

She'd lost all sense of time. She couldn't remember the last time she ate, and she'd finished her plastic bottle of water a long time ago.

She scrunched up her face. <Lennox? Sandy? Anyone?>

Tears came to her eyes and she wiped them away with her sleeve. She told herself it was hormones, the emotional swings, fatigue and sickness. Her body trying to kill her from the inside. The first act of her unborn baby was to make her feel fucking terrible. But that was unfair to the baby. Having a creature grow inside her was traumatic but it was also a miracle.

She heard something, low voices in the corridor.

<Lennox, is that you? Honey, please talk to me.>

The voices continued. She couldn't make anything out, but they seemed to be arguing in whispers. After a few moments she heard the outside bolt slide across, then the clunk of the key.

She pushed herself against the wall.

The door opened, and Thelma and a Nordic guy she hadn't seen before were standing there, looking anxiously around before they slid inside and half closed the door.

'This is Per,' Thelma said. 'We're going to get you out of here.'

She glanced at Per, who nodded.

Vonnie got to her feet, wobbled a bit. 'What's going on?'

Thelma cringed. 'We didn't know, OK?'

'Didn't know what?'

Per glanced outside.

'We have to be quick,' Thelma said.

Vonnie wanted to run out of the door, but she worried this was a trap. 'What didn't you know?'

Thelma rubbed her hands together. 'We have to go. I'll tell you on the way.'

'No, tell me now.'

Thelma's eyes went wide and she shared a look with Per. He shrugged, looked outside again.

Thelma sighed and came closer. Bags under her eyes, worry lines on her forehead. 'Britt told us that you and Lennox killed Karl. I didn't think that made sense. I've been having these dreams…' She shook her head. 'I know you and Lennox are friends with the Enceladons.' She angled her head. 'I haven't been sure about Britt for a while. Just a feeling. She wasn't like Karl, he was obsessed with the Enceladons, with the work here. He was so excited to meet you guys, Sandy and the rest. I couldn't see why you would kill him.'

'We didn't.'

Thelma nodded. 'I watched the security camera footage from the meeting room. Britt is so arrogant, she didn't even delete it, just assumed we would believe her.'

Per glanced at the door. 'They could be back any minute.'

He came over and took Vonnie's arm but she shrugged him off.

'I'm not going anywhere without Lennox.'

'He's not here,' Thelma said. 'They beat him up, trying to get information on your friend Niviaq's whereabouts. But now they've taken him to the Ikusik mining station.'

'Mining station?'

Thelma shook her head. 'We just found out there's a KJI deep-sea mining station further up the coast. We thought this was a legitimate scientific expedition, but it was just cover for a mining operation all along. Britt is in charge of it.'

Per sucked his teeth. 'We really don't have time for this. If you want to stay alive, you need to come now.'

Thelma gave Vonnie a pleading look.

She glanced around the room. 'OK.'

She crept out behind them, following Per's signals along the corridor, waiting at each corner, then through some functional rooms – the first full of scientific equipment, then washing machines and dryers, finally an empty kitchen. They reached an exit at the far side of the complex.

'Where is everyone?'

'Extraordinary meeting,' Thelma said. 'We're going to get shit for not being there.' She handed Vonnie a Sedna puffa jacket.

'You're coming with me, right?'

Per and Thelma shared a look. Per leaned in, voice low. 'If we stay here, we can get more evidence against Britt.'

Vonnie shook her head. 'No, we go to the authorities.'

Thelma laughed and pointed at the door. 'What authorities, the Greenland police? There isn't an officer within hours of here. And even if there was, there's nothing they can do. This is a multi-billion company with an armed private-security firm.'

'We have to do something,' Vonnie said. 'We have to stop them.'

She heard voices from round the corner.

Thelma opened the door. 'Go. There's a small boat on the shore beyond those rocks. You know how to drive a boat?'

Vonnie nodded and let herself be pushed outside into bright sunshine and sharp air. The door closed and she ran for the cover of the boulders, throwing on the jacket as she went. She waited for alarms or voices, but all she could hear was the wind in her ears.

# 44
# LENNOX

They'd been in the air for a while and he'd watched the rocky coastline and the giant inland glaciers out of the window the whole time. Initially there were a couple of villages, just handfuls of bright houses, gradually looking more derelict as they travelled up the coast. The expanse of glacial ice to his left was impossible to take in, an ocean of white and blue as far as he could see. It seemed to be creeping forward but he assumed that was an illusion caused by the ripples on the surface.

Gunnar and Ole were in the back of the helicopter with him, Britt up front with the pilot. He wondered who at Sedna knew what was really happening there. He found it hard to believe that Thelma would go along with it, but money and power do strange things to people.

The noise of the rotor blades filled Lennox's mind. He'd spent the journey trying to contact Vonnie, but no luck. He felt so weak that he thought he might pass out. His left eye was swollen and bruised, and he wondered if there was any permanent damage. His knee was agony, and he'd needed help to walk to the helicopter. Pain radiated up his leg and through his body.

Britt removed her headset and undid her seatbelt. She clambered to the back, sat next to Lennox. His wrists were bound in plastic restraints, and Gunnar had a handgun trained on him. He barely had the energy to raise his head, let alone attack someone. But when he saw Britt's smile, he wanted to try anyway.

'What are you going to do with Vonnie?'

Britt touched his wrist. 'Don't worry, she's no use to us dead. Human shields don't work that way.'

Lennox shook his head, felt pain surge through him. 'Human shields don't work at all. Haven't you seen a war in the last hundred years?'

Britt sucked her teeth. 'Maybe that's true with humans. But you and the girl are the Enceladons' friends, they won't do anything to harm you.'

'I wouldn't be so sure. Why would they attack you anyway?'

'They've already started.'

'What do you mean?'

Britt glanced down at the endless ocean beneath them. 'We've lost research boats. Sunk. Crew killed.'

'I don't believe it. How do you know it was the Enceladons?'

'Who else?'

Lennox stared at her. 'You're going to kill them, you're going to destroy their home.'

Britt looked him in the eye. 'It's us or them.'

'It's *not* us or them, that's the problem,' Lennox said. 'And human shields only work if the other side knows about them.'

'I'm pretty confident the Enceladons will be able to sense you and Vonnie. Heather and Ava are with them, right? You have a connection to them.'

'Not anymore,' Lennox said.

'Interesting.' Britt looked him up and down. 'Because of your injuries, or because of the distance we've travelled?'

Lennox shrugged.

'I've wondered about the extent of these powers,' Britt said. 'How to exploit them.'

'Jesus Christ, "exploit them". You have no idea.'

Britt smiled. 'Go on then, explain it to me.'

Lennox knew she was goading him, yet found it hard to resist. But Britt was so blinkered it was impossible to talk to her about the way the Enceladons had opened his eyes, not without sounding like a lunatic.

'What's the point, you don't care.'

Britt leaned in close and her perfume tickled his nose. 'Quite the opposite. I care about your telepathic ability a great deal. That kind of technology.'

'It's not technology.'

Britt wagged a finger. 'But it will be. You have no idea how important this is.'

'You mean how valuable it is.'

'Now you're getting it.'

'You're crazy if you think you can control this.'

'Look, this is coming, OK? Since the Enceladons arrived, the cat is out the bag. This exists in humans now. What's important is who controls it. Whoever can provide this power to people – for a fee, of course – will be the most powerful company on the planet by a long way.'

'Everyone should have this,' Lennox said.

'That's not how the world works.'

'It could be.'

Britt touched his wrists again, firmly this time. 'No, it can't, don't be so naïve, Lennox. It's human nature to be competitive, to want power. That's how it's always been and how it always will be. You can try to opt out of that if you want, but it will still exist. The important thing is to back the right horse, to get ahead. If KJI don't exploit this, someone else will, and what if their intentions are bad? What then?'

'If you destroy the Enceladons, you'll have no chance of finding out how the telepathy works.'

'Our researchers think otherwise.'

'You said you read the New Broom reports. They had us in there with the Enceladons for months, they didn't crack it.'

'They almost did, by the end. It just needs more time, more resources. And now that we have a bunch of confirmed telepathic humans, we can experiment on them as much as we want. We don't need the Enceladons anymore.'

The helicopter banked and Lennox glanced out the window. He saw a large complex of buildings at the shoreline clustered around a long natural harbour. It was all protected by high fences, razor wire, lookout towers and armed guards. A flotilla of ships were anchored in the harbour, each with chunky machines on board, secured at the rear. They looked a lot like farm machines, and Lennox felt sick looking at them.

# 45
# AVA

The boat was sinking fast. The chaos of the bear attack must've damaged the hull.

Ava went to Niviaq, who looked like she might pass out. 'You OK?'

Niviaq swallowed. 'Sure, I'm always getting attacked by bears.'

They were both knee deep in freezing water, Sandy and Heather floating on the surface.

'We need to get off the boat,' Niviaq said. She grabbed stuff from a cupboard – two thick jackets, a first-aid kit.

<Sandy-Ava partial return to settlement.>

Ava looked at Sandy, subdued tones across their body. They looked exhausted. <Sandy, how many humans can you carry inside your body?>

<Unclear. Low energy.>

'Let's just get onto the ice,' Niviaq said, looking at the rising water. 'We can work it out there.'

She climbed onto the rail at the port side, held out her hand and helped Ava across from the bobbing wreck to the ice floe, then jumped across herself. Sandy and Heather slid easily from one to the other.

Ava and Niviaq threw on the heavy coats and watched as the boat listed and tipped, its nose poking up as the transom disappeared below the water line, then the whole thing vanished under the surface.

A brutal wind swept across the ice. Ava put her hood up and shivered.

Niviaq was staring at Sandy. <Thank you. You saved my life.>

Sandy flashed turquoise and brown. <Simple communication. Sandy-bear partial given different mindset.>

Ava looked around. The small patch of water where the boat had sunk was closing up, ice creaking as large slabs pushed together. She thought of Chloe down there under millions of tons of water.

<What now?> This was Heather in her mind. She was moving along the edge of the ice, agitated flickers up and down her tentacles.

Niviaq looked at Ava. <You need to get back to Chloe.>

Ava realised what this meant. Maybe Sandy could take her back to the settlement, but Heather couldn't carry Niviaq, she didn't have that power. So they would be abandoning Niviaq on the ice. The weather was closing in, the wind stronger now, stinging rain in their faces.

'It's OK,' Niviaq said. 'Go.'

'No way.'

'I can survive on the ice.' She sounded confident.

'There's a storm coming.'

Niviaq looked at the dark skies, then over to the land in the distance. 'I know where I am, there's a hunting hut not too far. There are lots of old shelters along the coast, for when you get caught out by the weather.'

<I can stay with her,> Heather sent.

Niviaq shook her head. <I don't need a babysitter.>

The wind whipped around them ferociously.

Ava touched Niviaq's shoulder. 'We can't just leave you here.'

'We Greenlanders are used to this, we know how to survive. Trust me.'

<Hello?>

Ava jumped at the new voice in her head – Vonnie's.

<Lennox, Ava, anyone?>

Ava scanned the horizon. <Where are you?>

# 46
# VONNIE

Vonnie grinned at Ava's voice in her head, a warm blanket against the wind. <Ava, thank fuck, where are you?>

Vonnie looked around. Rain smacked against the cockpit window, creeping fog reducing visibility. She'd been steering the boat away from Sedna, heading along the coast as best she could, sea ice growing as she travelled.

<It's hard to say,> Ava sent. <Where are you?>

<I'm on a boat.>

<With Lennox?>

<No.> Some things were too complicated to explain over telepathy, you needed body language.

<We're on the ice,> Ava sent. <We must be close if we can hear each other.>

Vonnie killed the engine, the boat bobbing on the currents. She lifted binoculars and ducked out of the cockpit for a better look, rain stinging her face. She gripped the handrail and looked through the glasses. Just ice and sea, then looming mountains peeking between swathes of fog.

<There's ice everywhere. I can't see you.> She could hear the hammering of rain on the deck, the slap and gloop of water against the hull, the distant creak of the patchwork ice. <Ava?>

<Wait, Sandy's going to try something.>

A few moments of quiet, Vonnie feeling small and alone.

<OK, do you have binoculars?> Ava asked.

<Yeah.>

<Look along the ice on your landward side.>

Vonnie spread her feet against the rocking boat and used both hands to steady the glasses as she scanned the horizon. After a few seconds, the binoculars swept past something and she looked back. A large ball shape flashing black and red, fast as a strobe, like a weird emo lighthouse against the white.

<I see something. What is it?>

<It's Sandy.> There was amusement in Ava's voice.

Vonnie ran back inside and started the engine, chugged the boat towards the beacon. The ice grew thicker as she went. She thudded into a couple of larger blocks but kept going. The ice was beginning to close in behind her. She looked through the glasses, saw the beacon, now recognisably an inflated octopus shape. Other figures alongside, two people and another octopus.

<Ava, I can't get any closer because of the ice.>

A few more moments of quiet, then Ava spoke.

<We see you. We'll come to you, wait there.>

Vonnie cut the engine and watched through the glasses. She saw two figures running, the other two scuttling across the ice. Eventually they were as close as the broken edges of ice would allow.

Vonnie waved and all four of them waved back. They talked amongst themselves for a moment then Sandy wrapped Ava in a hug, enveloping her. They jumped in the water and swam to the boat, then clambered over the side and squeezed Ava from their body. She looked dazed as Sandy went back for Niviaq, did the same, this time Heather joining them in the water. In the boat, Niviaq slid out of Sandy's body and sat on the deck looking freaked out.

Ava clocked Vonnie's Sedna jacket, the same logo on the side of the boat. 'What's going on?'

Vonnie blurted out everything that had happened since Ava had taken Chloe to the settlement. Her voice shook as she told them about Britt shooting Karl and blaming them, then she felt tears in her eyes as she explained about Lennox being separated from her and beaten, then taken to a mining station somewhere. She tried to calm her breathing as she explained how Thelma and Per helped her escape.

Niviaq sucked her teeth and shook her head in disbelief.

Heather scuttled anxiously around the deck, her body flashing in alarm.

'Oh my God,' Ava said, wrapping Vonnie in a big hug. 'What a nightmare. Are you OK?'

Vonnie felt the woman's warmth, wanted to stay there forever. Eventually she breathed deeply and pulled away. 'I will be.'

'This changes everything,' Ava said. 'What the hell are they planning?'

They'd all seen first-hand what humans could do.

The rain was still coming down and Vonnie had to raise her voice over the sound of it. 'It won't be good.'

Ava looked at Sandy and Heather, then Niviaq. 'It was too good to be true that they were interested in the Enceladons in a positive way.'

'I think Karl was genuine,' Vonnie said.

Ava shook her head. 'What about Lennox and this mining station?'

Vonnie felt tears in her eyes and lowered her head. Ava wrapped her in a hug, which made her cry more.

'He'll be fine,' Ava said softly. 'Lennox can look after himself.'

<I know about the mining.> This was Heather in Vonnie's head. She told them what she'd seen. <They must have a base on land.>

Vonnie straightened her shoulders. <Could you find the place in the ocean you saw the mining machine again?>

Heather flashed blue. <I think so, but they'll have moved by now.>

<We should go there anyway. Maybe we can find them, track them.>

Ava touched Vonnie's shoulder. 'We have to warn the Enceladons first, they could be in danger. And I have to get Chloe back on land. Once we've done that, we can find Lennox.'

Vonnie frowned. 'What about me and Niviaq? Sandy can't take us all to the Enceladon settlement, and Heather can't do it.'

Niviaq took the binoculars from Vonnie and looked along the coast. The ice was still crunching next to them, bumping the hull. She lowered the glasses and pointed north.

'That's a serious storm, we need to shelter. Your alien friends can take Ava to get Chloe.' She glanced at Vonnie, then the lightweight boat. 'We need to get off the water.' She pointed to a promontory further down the coast. 'There's a hut not far, the shore looks ice-free. We can shelter there.' She raised her face to the rain and wind. 'But we have to go now.'

# 47
# LENNOX

The cell door opened and Gunnar filled the doorframe, rifle pointing at him. 'Come on.'

'Where?'

Gunnar cocked his head to the side. 'Are you hungry?'

Lennox imagined rushing him, overpowering him, hitting him in the face with his own rifle butt, pointing the barrel at him and pulling the trigger.

Gunnar spat on the ground. 'The boss has invited you to dinner.'

He lifted his head to indicate Lennox should move.

Lennox eased off the hard bed. His body hurt in too many places to count. His shoulders slumped as he passed Gunnar, who pointed him down the corridor.

Out of the window, Lennox could see the harbour. One ship coming in, pulling one of those machines behind it, attached to floats. The ship was low in the water, like it was carrying a heavy load. Another ship was heading out with a similar machine loaded on the back area. Something about the haziness of the skies made Lennox think it was late in the evening. A thin film of cloud stretched across the horizon, making the sea and the sky blend together. The world felt endless.

<Sandy? Vonnie?>

He didn't expect a reply and didn't get one. He felt more alone than he had for years. No one in his head, unconnected. Maybe Ole had beaten him so hard he didn't have that power anymore.

'Here.' Gunnar opened a door to a meeting room, Britt sitting at the head of the table with a plate of food in front of her, another plate to her side.

She smiled and pointed to the seat. 'Please.'

Lennox took her in. She was beautiful in an austere way with her hair down. Her smile changed her face, made her seem warm. He remembered her icy stare after she shot Karl, her fake emotion when she summoned the guards.

His stomach grumbled as he stared at the salmon on the plate.

He sat.

Britt nodded at Gunnar, who hesitated then left.

Britt had a handgun on the table next to her, on the opposite side from Lennox. He tried to work out his chances, if he could get to her before she reached it.

'Please eat,' Britt said.

There were glasses of white wine too. She sipped hers, Lennox didn't.

'What's the point of being in charge if you can't live well,' Britt said. 'Karl was so austere. The guy had billions of dollars, never drank or smoked or took drugs. Did yoga and meditation every morning, ran marathons for fun. What a waste.'

'Is that why you killed him, because he was no fun?'

The tone of Lennox's voice made Britt purse her lips. 'Come on. Eat.'

He tried the salmon, which was smoky and delicious. There were roast potatoes too, and he snaffled a few of them. Green beans, salty and buttery, some sauce that was acidic and fresh. It all tasted like a spring morning and he hated that he was gobbling it up.

'We got off on the wrong foot,' Britt said.

Lennox took a sip of wine. He didn't drink wine usually, but this was OK. 'When you framed me for Karl's murder or when you had me beaten half to death?'

'I'm sorry.' Britt put her cutlery down. 'Ole can get carried away.'

'This is not going to work,' Lennox said, waving his hand around the room.

'I just want to talk to you. You've had such an amazing experience with these creatures.'

'You couldn't care less about the Enceladons. What's really going on here?'

Britt took a drink of wine. 'I don't suppose it matters if I tell you.'

'Because you're going to kill me.'

Britt smiled with her mouth, but her eyes were cold. 'I knew you were smart.'

'You'll keep us alive as long as we're useful, but there's no way we live to tell anyone about this.'

Britt took a mouthful of salmon, chewed while she looked at him. 'Karl was so stupid. He was serious about wanting to contact the Enceladons, and he thought the board were letting him.'

Lennox waited for more.

Eventually, Britt obliged. 'At the same time as he was setting up Sedna, we had two real objectives out here in the middle of nowhere. Get human telepaths as experimental subjects, then use the files from New Broom to work out how that power works. Exploit it to make billions for KJI.'

Lennox glanced out of the window. 'And this place?'

Britt smiled, warmly this time. 'Just good fortune, really. Routine surveys detected remarkable amounts of rare-earth metals on the Arctic ocean floor. Trillions of dollars' worth just sitting there, waiting to be scooped up.'

'But doing so would destroy the ecosystem. And it's illegal.'

Britt shrugged. 'The law doesn't matter. Money talks, always. We do it first, then pay off whoever we need to afterwards. That's how the world has always worked.'

Lennox stared at her. 'Don't you care about anything?'

Britt cleared her throat. 'I care about being on the winning side. The world is divided into winners and losers. Those who take advantage of a situation and those who don't, and who suffer as a consequence. Karl had moved from one side to the other, so the board lost confidence in him.'

'And you were happy to step into his shoes.'

Britt angled her head in agreement. 'Someone has to, it might as well be me.'

Lennox shook his head. 'What about the Enceladons?' He looked her in the eyes for a long time and she didn't waver. 'You're going to destroy them.'

He put his knife and fork down, glanced at Britt's gun. Her hand inched towards it on the table but she didn't pick it up.

'You have no idea who you're dealing with,' Lennox said, shaking his head. 'The Enceladons destroyed New Broom, and it was just like this place.'

Britt didn't like that, ran a tongue around her teeth. 'They won't get the chance to do anything like that.'

'Why not?'

Britt lifted the gun and stood, went to the window and looked at the ocean.

'A torpedo boat is on its way.'

Lennox clenched his fists. 'What?'

'It should've been here already but it's coming from Canada, the storm has slowed them down.'

'You're going to blow up the settlement. What about Ava and Chloe?' Lennox closed his eyes. <Ava? Vonnie? Sandy?>

'What about them?'

'You saw them go with the Enceladons. They're there right now.'

'So?'

Lennox pushed out of his seat, ran towards her. He saw her lift the gun, but he reached her before she managed to pull the trigger, pain sweeping through his knee and his face as he rammed into her, grabbing for the gun, which she brought down on the back of his head. The pair of them tumbled over and he heard the door opening, and before he could even think Gunnar was dragging him away.

# 48
# NIVIAQ

They got lucky, the small harbour by the hut wasn't completely frozen. They navigated ice chunks carefully before climbing ashore and tying the boat up as securely as they could. It might still get damaged in the storm, but they'd done their best. Vonnie was strong for a thin girl, pulling the ropes tight on the boat. Niviaq smiled as she worked alongside.

Rain turned to snow, a blizzard around them. Niviaq pulled her hood tight and led Vonnie to the hut, yanking on the door which was stiff against the snow. They stumbled in and heaved the door closed behind them.

The silence was shocking compared to the chaos outside. The two women shook snow off their jackets and lowered their hoods. Niviaq looked around the hut. Bunkbeds were piled with seal skins and polar-bear furs. There was an old petroleum heater and a canister of fuel. On a low shelf were some dried fish and narwhal blubber, a *tsakeq* for cutting it. Niviaq was surprised. Someone must've forgotten the food, because leaving it in the hut was an invitation for a polar bear to come sniffing around.

The wind shook the walls, rattled the door, wet snow slapping on the roof.

'Are we safe?' Vonnie said.

'This place has been here a lot longer than us.'

'Whose is it?'

'It belongs to everyone. There is a string of them up the coast.' Niviaq looked at Vonnie. 'Take off your wet clothes, I'll start a fire.'

She filled the heater from the canister and got it going. There was an old clothes horse folded against a wall. She opened it, hung Vonnie's jeans, jumper, T-shirt and socks on it, placed it next to the heater. Took off her own clothes and hung them on the other side. She hung their puffa jackets on a nail in the wall. Took a bearskin from the bunk and threw it onto the floor, motioned for Vonnie to sit.

<Hungry?>

Vonnie smiled and pointed at their heads. <You're still getting used to this.>

Niviaq widened her eyes. <Don't know if I ever will.>

<You will.>

<Not sure I want to.> Niviaq cleared her throat. 'But what does it mean?'

'For us?'

Niviaq held her arms wide. 'For everyone.'

Vonnie made a face, like she was used to this idea. 'I don't know.'

<You never answered my first question.>

Vonnie smiled. <Starving.>

Niviaq wiped off the only plate on the shelf, put the fish and blubber on there with the cutting tool.

'What do we have?' Vonnie said.

'We call this *ammatsaat panerdu* – dried capelin.'

They were small fish, shrivelled bodies, glassy eyes looking up.

'And you eat the whole thing?'

Niviaq showed her, swallowing the head first.

Vonnie copied her, smiled. 'Better than sardines.' She pointed at the blubber. 'What's that?'

'*Aammarqaar* – whale blubber. This is narwhal.'

Vonnie made a face.

It looked like good, fresh *aammarqaar*. Niviaq took the *tsakeq* and rocked the curved blade, cutting the slab into small cubes. She offered some to Vonnie.

Vonnie hesitated. 'Are you OK with eating this?'

'It's our way of life.'

Vonnie shifted her weight and ran her fingers through the bearskin fur. 'Don't get me wrong, I support any indigenous way of life. But...'

Niviaq knew what Vonnie meant, she was conflicted too. 'I get it, honestly. But eating this is better than the processed, factory shit you get in the rest of the world. We've done it sustainably for thousands of years. We respect the animal, it's part of the ecosystem, same as us. But we know how smart whales are, in Greenland we've always known. I understand that animals have rights. But this creature gave its life to sustain us, here in this hut. And we disrespect it if we choose not to eat.'

Vonnie was still hesitant.

Niviaq bit off a couple of cubes, felt the familiar taste – salty and sweet, nutty. Full of fat and calories, exactly why the Inuit had eaten it for centuries, to keep them warm in these conditions.

She held it out again and Vonnie took it, bit some off and chewed. 'I'm still not sure, but it tastes great.'

They ate in silence, passing the plate back and forth, steam rising from their wet clothes, the wind whining outside, making Vonnie jumpy.

'How long will this last?' she said.

'Could be hours. We should get some sleep.'

Vonnie wiped grease from her chin and shook her head. 'I don't know if I can. I don't even know if Lennox is still alive.'

Niviaq touched her hand. 'He'll be OK, he's a tough kid.'

'You don't know him.'

'I saw enough. He's been through some stuff.'

'He has.'

Vonnie looked down at her bare midriff, her skin pallid against her black underwear. She touched her belly. <I'm pregnant.>

Her voice sounded neutral.

<Congratulations?> Niviaq sent.

Vonnie laughed. 'Thanks.' She shook her head. 'You know, it was easier saying that inside your head than out loud.'

'Why?'

Vonnie shrugged. 'I haven't told Lennox yet.'

'Why not?'

'I'm worried.' She tapped her forehead with a finger. <We can both do this. Which means the baby will be able to do it as well, I guess. You've seen how worried Ava is about Chloe, what else comes with this power. We don't know anything about it.>

'I'm sure Ava and Chloe are fine.' Niviaq was surprised at the amount of emotion in her voice. She'd only met these people a couple of days ago, but they felt like family.

Vonnie cricked her neck and got a sly look on her face. <You like her.>

Niviaq was shocked at how personal that felt, like someone had seen under her skin. 'What do you mean?'

'Ava.' <You *like* her.>

Niviaq swallowed. 'What makes you say that?'

'I've seen you look at her.'

'She's a strong woman.'

<And beautiful.> Vonnie was grinning.

Niviaq realised how young Vonnie was, just a kid really. But she couldn't deny how she'd felt since she first met Ava.

'Is she…?' Niviaq didn't want to finish that question.

'I honestly don't know. She *was* married to a terrible man.'

'She told me.'

'But that doesn't mean anything. She likes good people, and you're a good person.'

Niviaq was annoyed at the blush coming to her cheeks, the warmth from the heater filling the room.

Vonnie gave her a kind smile.

'We should get some sleep.' Niviaq turned away, but glanced back at Vonnie and shared a look. She wondered what Ava was doing right now.

# 49
# AVA

She was drowning in a viscous liquid, unable to breathe or move, her lungs filling up with the sticky substance until her chest burst and millions of tiny baby octopuses spilled out of her, spiralling and dancing into the distance, leaving her with just her heart thumping in an open ribcage, all alone.

Ava woke in a panic. She'd fallen asleep inside Xander again. She wondered if they'd secreted something into her with a soporific effect. She'd been sitting in Xander's body watching Chloe sleep, hoping these creatures had cured her, when she must've crashed out.

She got her bearings and saw Chloe playing with Sandy, both of them still inside Xander's body. Chloe was doing slow star jumps and giggling as Sandy danced, tentacles whirling like a Catherine wheel, body flashing yellow and red. Chloe tried to clap her hands together but the thick substance of Xander's body made it impossible.

<Chloe.>

Chloe grinned, half swam and half walked over to Ava, wrapping her arms around her neck. <Mummy!>

Ava wondered if the girl would remember this. Ava's earliest memory was from when she was four, her dad scolding her mum while Ava listened from the top of the stairs. But other events before then must've gone towards shaping her, even if she had no recollection of them.

She was still holding Chloe, didn't want to let go, didn't want to ever be separated again. She felt a glow of love from her daughter and was overwhelmed.

<Sandy-Ava-Chloe partial good energy.> Sandy wrapped their tentacles around mother and daughter.

Ava straightened her shoulders. <Xander, did it work? Did you all fix Chloe's brain?>

A long pause made Ava throw a worried look at Sandy, who was tickling Chloe under her chin.

<Xander-Chloe molecular manipulation achieved.> Xander's sonorous voice made Ava's stomach flip.

<What does that mean?> Ava watched Chloe and Sandy play. It was like watching her daughter play with their dog Sheba, the pure pleasure of another lifeform's presence. <Is she cured? No more brain tumour?>

<Xander-Chloe partial efficiency is full.>

Ava burst out crying, tears soaking into Xander's body. <She won't have another stroke? She won't have any problems?>

Another longer pause made Ava feel sick.

<Chloe-Xander partial now same energy as Ava-Xander partial. Equal efficiency.>

It was the closest to a straight answer Ava could hope for. <Oh my God, thank you, thank you so much. You don't know what this means to me, to us.> She turned to Sandy. <I need to get Chloe somewhere safe on land.>

Sandy spun three tentacles into a pretend knot and flashed orange and purple. <Sandy-Ava-Chloe partial visit hut?>

<Yes, thank you.> She looked around. <Where's Heather?>

Sandy was already stretching their skin to envelop Chloe and Ava, preparing to carry them out of Xander's body. Ava wondered about Sandy and Xander's relationship. Not parent and child, not siblings, not symbiotic partners, but something more. They were part of the same creature, all the Enceladons were part of the same super-organism. And it was bigger than that, because the Enceladons were now a part of the Arctic marine ecosystem, which was a big part of Earth's biome, a living, breathing entity.

<Heather-Sandy partial location unclear.>

Ava looked around. The settlement was teeming with life, hundreds of creatures moving individually but creating a feeling of togetherness.

<Heather?>

Nothing.

Eventually Sandy's voice in her mind. <Heather-Sandy partial interested in human machines.>

The mining Heather had talked about. Ava and Heather had warned the Enceladons when they arrived earlier, told them that the people from KJI were up to no good and couldn't be trusted. They'd suggested that the Enceladons evacuate their home and find somewhere safer further north. But Ava didn't think the creatures had taken their warnings seriously. There was no sign of it in the settlement at the moment.

She understood Heather's preoccupation with the mining operation and Sedna, but Ava's priority was Chloe, always would be.

<Come on,> Ava sent. <Let's go to Niviaq and Vonnie in the hut.>

Sandy flickered turquoise and magenta, stretched their body wide and subsumed them, then slid out of Xander's body and launched across the settlement.

Soon, they were away from the busy area and into dark water, lit by Sandy's body, two seals in the distance flipping over each other.

Sandy swam upward and Ava saw the underside of the ice blocks on the surface, like a ceiling on their water world. Sandy broke the surface between ice chunks, slithered across a block of ice, then back into the water. Chloe giggled and Ava grinned at Sandy's simple joy.

Judging by the light, it was morning now, and Ava wondered how long she'd slept. Maybe a new day meant new hope, despite the people at Sedna, despite what happened to Vonnie and Lennox. Despite what those morons were doing at the deep-sea mine. Today would be a good day. Ava looked at Chloe and felt it would be a good day.

# 50
# LENNOX

He lay on the bed with a knot in his stomach, partly from the physical pain and partly from anxiety, knowing what Britt was planning. The whole Enceladon species could be wiped out along with anyone else who happened to be there. It was obscene, but it was the logical end point of all this. If you were happy to destroy habitats and massacre animals, why not alien creatures too, or humans? Thinking you were more important than nature was the first step on a slippery slope. Once you thought of others as less than you, you had free reign to treat them as subhuman. This exceptionalism went hand in hand with capitalism. Both were about exploitation rather than living within your means. Taking and never giving, destroying rather than creating.

Lennox stood slowly. He'd crashed out at some point last night after spending hours trying to communicate with anyone. He'd woken from the pain, kept trying, but he was either out of range or too weak.

He had to get out of here and warn the others but his brain was too foggy with pain to think straight. He tried to remember the layout of the base he saw when he was flown in. There were ships at the harbour, but he could hardly steal a ship. The helicopter was maybe still on the landing pad, but he would crash it if he even got off the ground. But he'd seen snowmobiles parked on the edge of the inland ice. He might freeze to death, but at least he would be doing something.

His left knee was swollen and stiff but he could move it. His bruised eye was agony to touch. His ribs ached.

He had an idea, grabbed the bucket he'd been using to piss in, breathed through his mouth. Went to the door and banged on it. Waited to the side.

Nothing.

Waited some more, his heart thudding.

He banged on the door with his fist again. 'Hey! I need help.'

Waited.

Eventually he heard footsteps, the door unlocking. It swung out and Lennox's chest tightened. He waited to see the rifle and the hands holding it, then he swung the bucket with all his might into the space of the doorway. It connected with Ole's face and his head smacked against the doorframe as he swore in Norwegian.

Lennox brought the bucket down as hard as he could on Ole's hands, piss spraying from it as it clanged off the rifle. Ole dropped the gun, which skittered across the room. He swung an elbow into Lennox's neck, choking him. Lennox still had the bucket in his hands and heaved it into Ole's face, Ole raising his forearms to block it. Lennox kicked at Ole's knee and heard a crunch. The guard threw a fist at him but he dodged it and dumped the bucket with the remaining urine onto Ole's head and shoved him as hard as he could into the cell, before stepping out and locking Ole inside.

He heard Ole on his radio and banging the door, then the sound of a rifle shot. He jumped to the side and saw an emergency exit to his right, staggered to the door as fast as his knee would let him.

Freezing air smacked him in the face as he lurched towards the snowmobiles, hoping that some idiot had left keys in one of them. He didn't know how to drive one but he would learn fast.

An alarm started blaring behind him as he stumbled across rocks and snow. He didn't have a jacket, would definitely freeze on the ice but he didn't have a choice. He reached the first snowmobile and checked the ignition – no key. He heard shouts, glanced behind and saw a handful of guards, Gunnar and Ole at the front, guns raised. He ducked behind the first machine and tried the second. No key. Heard gunshots, a bullet hitting the ground to his left. Fuck.

He scuttled to the next snowmobile, his heart soaring when he saw the key in it. He turned it as more shots rang out, fizzing into nearby snow. The engine started and he slid onto the seat, keeping his head down. He gunned the throttle on the handlebar and almost fell off as it jumped forward. He sped up, heading away from the guards and onto the ice sheet, steering between larger rocks. He glanced back and saw the guards mounting the other snowmobiles. He had a decent head start but nowhere to hide in the whiteness and daylight, his tracks obvious behind him.

<Sandy? Vonnie?> Snow sprayed up in waves as he drove over deeper stuff, then he hit harder ice again, the engine growling. <Ava? Heather?> He prayed they could hear him somehow, even if he didn't get a response. <You have to get out of the settlement. A boat is coming, they're going to destroy the whole place and anyone in it. Do you hear me? You have to get everyone out.>

He heard the guards behind him, glanced back and they were gaining on him. Ahead, he spotted something moving on the whiteness. A large shape lumbering in his direction. He watched it for a few moments before realising what it was.

A polar bear running fast, its fur shaking as its thick legs pounded on the ice. It was heading straight for him. He steered the snowmobile away but the bear changed direction too.

Lennox couldn't turn back, the guards would get him, and a large rock face to his right meant he couldn't outrun the bear that way. He steered away but it was only fifty metres from him now, moving fast.

His snowmobile lurched into a drift of powdery snow and he was thrown off balance, righted himself and gunned the throttle, but the tracks were deep in the heavy snow. He hit a rock under the surface and the vehicle flipped, throwing him into the snow.

He sat up. The polar bear was almost on him, the guards two hundred metres away, slowing at the sight of the beast, Gunnar raising his rifle.

The bear stood on its hind legs and roared, Lennox's ribcage shuddering.

<Stop! Wait!> Lennox's inner voice screamed.

The bear hesitated, growling and panting, the heat from its body palpable.

It had heard him, that was the only explanation. Holy shit.

<Don't do this! I'm a friend, understand?> Lennox's mind raced. How was this possible? Maybe the bear had met Enceladons, or maybe Lennox's powers had grown. He didn't care, he only had one thought. <Do you know the Enceladons? Sandy?>

The bear dropped to all four legs, paced back and forth as it stared at Lennox.

The guards were closer now.

Lennox tried to think. <Sandy-bear partial? Enceladon-bear partial? Tell them. If you can understand me, tell Enceladon-bear partial they have to leave their home. Now. Everyone. Bad humans are going to kill them. They have to leave now.>

A shot rang out and the bear flinched then turned to the guards on their snowmobiles. It gave a monstrous roar then looked at Lennox and snorted. Then it lumbered away from the guards, growling as it ran behind the rock face, leaving Lennox alone in the snow, just the crunch of the guards' footsteps as they jumped off their vehicles and sprinted towards him.

## 51
# NIVIAQ

They'd been heading southwest long enough that she was in familiar waters now, had passed Kuummiit a while back, Kulusuk coming up ahead. She remembered being there a few days ago, picking up some strangers and taking them to Tasiilaq in the fog. That simple job changed everything.

<Hey.>

Niviaq's heart warmed at Ava's voice in her head.

Ava joined her in the cockpit, Chloe behind her playing with a pile of rope.

'Hi.' She spoke out loud – maybe she wasn't ready for the intimacy of telepathy with someone she liked. She thought back to last night, Vonnie had read her like a book. She was into Ava. In amongst all this madness, it was crazy to think about.

It was just the three of them on the boat now. When Sandy came back to the hut this morning carrying Ava and Chloe inside them, they'd discussed what to do next. Vonnie wanted to find Lennox whatever it took, so Sandy took Vonnie back to the Enceladon settlement to get Heather and find the mine. Ava's priority was to get Chloe somewhere safe, so Niviaq offered to take them back to her home.

They were close now, at the end of Ammassalik Fjord, past Kulusuk Island and heading for Tasiilaq Bay. She hadn't expected to be gone so long, and wondered what her family were thinking.

<Thank you for this,> Ava sent with a smile.

Niviaq looked at her, eyes bright, hair whipping around her face in the breeze. Niviaq touched her headband self-consciously. She hadn't washed or even looked in a mirror in days, but neither had Ava. Niviaq had been attacked by a polar bear, shipwrecked and caught in a storm, while Ava had been inside alien creatures, had spent time with them underwater. Considering all they'd been through, they both looked pretty good.

'What are you laughing at?' Ava said.

Niviaq eased the boat into the bay, caught a first sight of the town. 'I was just thinking what we've been through,' she said. 'There's no way I can explain any of it to the people here. I'm not sure I believe any of it is real.'

Ava glanced back at Chloe. 'It's real.'

They got closer to Tasiilaq. Niviaq used to hate this place, couldn't wait to get away. Then she'd stubbornly returned, only to feel trapped. Now, with everything she'd experienced, it felt like home again, somewhere reliable.

'We have to *try* to tell them,' Niviaq said, pointing at the houses. She could see her own home amongst them, the steps up to the back door. 'These people up the coast are going to destroy the ecosystem. We can't let that happen.'

Ava looked at Chloe again. 'I have to keep her safe.'

Niviaq reached out and took Ava's hand, and Ava didn't pull away.

<We will,> Niviaq sent. <We'll keep your daughter safe, you have my word. But we also have to stop them. We can't allow the ocean to be destroyed.> She brought the boat into the harbour. 'The ocean is our life, we can't survive without it. If we let giant ships take the fish, we'll die. If we let companies dig up the ocean floor, the environment will be wrecked, us with it.'

A bunch of kids were kicking a football up the hill, and they spotted her. Niviaq smiled and waved, and two boys ran round the corner to her house.

Ava watched them go. <There's a real sense of community here.>

Niviaq snorted. 'Not always for the best, trust me.'

<But it's nice to have a home. I'm envious.>

Niviaq heard the hurt in Ava's voice. <Yes, it is.>

She killed the engine, stepped out of the cockpit and tied the boat up. Ava took Chloe's hand and stepped onto dry land, then Niviaq followed. She saw Pipaluk running round the corner, Ivala just behind, both of them kicking up dirt on the path, smiling and waving. She waved back and braced herself for the love that was hurtling towards her.

# 52
# HEATHER

She was sure this was where she'd seen the mining vehicle before. Heather was scared of being in the deep ocean on her own, felt the pressure on her body. She spotted a faint light up ahead. She switched off her bioluminescence to make it out better and swam towards it. For a moment she thought it was another Enceladon, but as she got closer she saw it was a spotlight.

It was down to her left and she jetted towards it, letting her own light display fire up again, pink and orange mirroring her anxiety. It was definitely one of those machines. She got close and realised it wasn't moving, had been trashed. It lay on its side, treads buckled and broken, the blades on its underside smashed to pieces. The body was dented in some places and pulverised in others. Most of the lights had been smashed, just one spotlight remaining.

Heather swam around taking it in, saw that the tube connecting it to its surface ship had been severed, coiled in a heap on the sea floor. She looked up and saw the faint outline of a gathering of animals, couldn't make out what kind.

<Heather.>

She inflated her head and looked round. Saw Sandy approaching flashing red and black, the outline of a human inside their body. <Vonnie?>

<What happened?> Vonnie sent.

Sandy reached the mining vehicle and swam around it, Vonnie peering through their skin.

<Someone destroyed it,> Heather sent. <Why are you here?>

<I need to find Lennox. I wanted to follow one of the mining ships to their base.>

Sandy approached Heather so she could see Vonnie's face more clearly under their skin.

Heather waved a tentacle upward. <There's something happening up there.>

Vonnie looked. <Can Vonnie-Sandy partial go up?>

Sandy flickered down their body. <Sandy-Vonnie partial rise.>

Heather followed them, trying to keep up with Sandy. As they rose, she could see the outlines of animals becoming clearer, then the light spill from Sandy's body fell on a huge number of seals and dolphins, whales and fish. It was like the scene she'd witnessed with the fishing ship, and she felt her body tense up.

The animals were like a giant writhing nest of life, and as Heather approached she saw they were attacking the mining ship on the surface.

<What are they doing?> Vonnie sent.

<Fighting back.> Heather suddenly understood how much the Enceladons had changed, both themselves and the world around them. They'd realised how fucked up human behaviour was and had communicated it to other animals, who were doing something about it. She wondered if humans would ever be safe in the water again.

<Tell them to stop,> Vonnie sent.

<Why?> Heather sent.

<They'll kill the crew.>

<They have lifeboats.>

Sandy and Heather were swimming just below the maelstrom of animals. Heather saw that the ship had been damaged and was already sinking. Then she saw lifeboats hit the water, humans alongside like tiny corks floating in a pond.

<I need to find their base,> Vonnie sent, agitated. <I was going to follow the ship.>

Heather waved her tentacles. <That ship is only going one place, the bottom of the sea.>

They'd gradually been swimming upward and were now in the chaos. Seals and belugas, dolphins and narwhals, walruses near the surface. Sandy grabbed a passing dolphin, latched on with their tentacles and rode along as the creature slowed.

<What are you doing, Sandy?> This was Vonnie again.

Heather saw a seal approaching and stuck out three tentacles, her suckers sticking to the animal's fur. The seal wasn't bothered by her presence, so she tried something.

<Can you hear me?> She clung on as the seal swam through the crowd. Above them, the ship was sinking, people swimming towards lifeboats. <Why are you doing this?> She'd lost sight of Sandy and Vonnie. <My name is Heather. Can you understand?>

<Seals help. Animals help animals.> The voice was low and steady. If the Enceladons had communicated everything they knew to the animals, maybe they also somehow conveyed human language to them.

The seal arched its back and turned to face her. <Human-alien. Human bad.>

It shook its body so that she lost grip, and she watched it slip into the crowd. She felt sick at what the seal had said – she was part human, part bad.

She floated away from the crowd and watched the ship sink. She rose to the surface and saw people scrambling into lifeboats, shivering in shock.

She looked around. <Vonnie? Sandy?>

A creature came towards her fast, just a head above the water. She ducked under and realised it was a polar bear. It dived under the surface, stared at her, its black eyes piercing her heart. It thrust out a giant paw then another. She grabbed both with her tentacles, felt a shimmer of connection between them.

<Human-alien.> The bear's voice was clear. <Message from human. Alien home in danger. Humans kill all.>

The bear pushed at Heather's tentacles and she let go, watched as the beast swam towards the cluster of other animals, all fighting back against humanity.

# 53
# VONNIE

Vonnie had never seen anything swim as fast as Sandy. From inside their body, it was dizzying. Sandy and Vonnie had both heard the warning from the polar bear. By the time Vonnie realised that she'd understood a bear, Sandy was already on the move, the bear's message lighting a fire under them.

Vonnie turned and saw Heather trailing behind. <Are you OK?>

Heather flashed across her forehead. <Let's just get there and warn them.>

<The message came from Lennox, didn't it?>

<I don't know who else would be warning us.>

<How did he tell a bear? How did it find us?>

Heather was struggling to keep up. <There's shit happening here we have no understanding of.>

Vonnie wondered if Lennox was OK. How he'd managed to meet a fucking polar bear, communicate with it, and not be eaten. They were in a war now. She thought of the animals destroying the mining ship, the polar bear talking to Heather, the way the Enceladons communicated with the ocean creatures. They were all working together.

The sea floor rose to meet them as they reached the continental shelf. Vonnie saw crabs on the seabed as they flashed by. She sensed anxiety in Sandy. <Are you OK?>

No answer, just a nervous flicker across their tentacles.

<Don't worry, they'll be fine,> Vonnie sent, but her voice betrayed her concern.

She assumed that Sandy was trying to contact the Enceladons in the settlement, though she couldn't hear anything. There would always be an unbridgeable gap between humans and Enceladons. She glanced again at Heather and wondered how she felt about that. She'd given up being human, but did she feel Enceladon?

Vonnie saw a light in the distance.

Heather caught up. <Sandy, have you warned them?>

They were approaching fast and Vonnie saw activity, the octopoid Enceladons moving in a synchronised way around the larger jellyfish, all of them rising from the ocean floor together.

<They need to get out of there,> Vonnie sent.

She felt a whump behind her, a change in pressure. She heard a fizzing sound, then another whump, then two more. She twisted up to look through Sandy's skin at the surface, but couldn't make anything out. She suddenly realised there were no other sea animals around the settlement, they must've already left.

<Now, Sandy. They need to get out of there now.>

Then she saw them, four missiles scudding through the water above them, trails of bubbles in their wake as they aimed for the settlement.

<Get out!> Heather sent.

Vonnie felt trapped inside Sandy's body, still swimming at breakneck pace towards their home. She watched the torpedoes skimming through the ocean. A handful of Enceladons at the edge of the settlement looked their way and signalled to Sandy, then there was a blinding flash, another and another and another, and Vonnie had to turn away, her eyes burning. A moment later, the shockwave blasted Sandy's body, blowing it backward. They thumped onto the sea floor, Heather alongside, both of their light displays gone dark. The way Sandy was lying, Vonnie couldn't see what was happening at the settlement, but there were more whumps and fizzes and more torpedoes flying overhead.

<Sandy!> Maybe the blast had knocked them out. She looked to her side. <Heather? Are you OK?>

Heather slowly righted herself, kicking up mud, then there were more bright flashes and staggering shockwaves forcing Sandy, Vonnie and Heather back again, rolling across the floor and kicking up sand so that the water was cloudy around them.

<Sandy, please, we have to help them.>

Sandy flickered grey across their brow and righted themself. <Sandy-Vonnie-Heather partial help.>

They swam upward out of the cloudy water.

Vonnie felt sick. There was *no settlement*. The torpedoes had destroyed the whole place, the water full of rubble, sand and rocks. And bodies. Hundreds of bodies. Large and small Enceladons floating amongst the chaos, no light displays, lifeless. Sandy swam closer, Heather alongside, and Vonnie saw body parts, tentacles and tendrils, torn to pieces from the explosions and shockwaves, hundreds of dead. She felt Sandy's distress and wanted to die. Sandy approached carefully, bodies and body parts floating around them.

There was a buzzing noise above them and Vonnie spotted underwater drones, a dozen or more converging above the site. She watched them release objects from their undersides.

<Sandy, watch out!>

The bombs reached almost to the sea floor then exploded, sending Sandy and Heather tumbling again with the force of it, Vonnie dizzy inside Sandy. They stopped rolling with Sandy facing the carnage and there were more dead Enceladons, more parts of bodies floating out from the epicentre, chunks of lifeless flesh so shocking Vonnie didn't have words.

Some of the drones had left the site already but a few remained, and Vonnie saw cameras underneath recording the genocide.

A jellyfish Enceladon was floating near them, dull and lifeless. Sandy approached it.

<Xander,> Heather sent. <Sandy, are they alive?>

Sandy reached their tentacles to the top of Xander's head and stayed there for a long time, sunken and squashed into the larger creature's body. Sandy's light display flickered and flashed, slowly at first then more forcefully, but there was no corresponding signal from Xander.

<Sandy?> Vonnie wished she could do something, wished she could help.

Sandy's light display faded to grey then disappeared. <Xander returned to original energy state.> They looked around at the carnage that used to be their home. <Many Enceladons returned to original energy state. Human bad energy.>

# 54
# LENNOX

Locked up again. Lennox lay on the floor where he'd been dumped and touched his chest, his nose. Pain everywhere. Back on the ice, they'd bound his wrists and ankles and thrown him over the rear of a snowmobile like a hunted seal, brought him back to the station. Ole was furious, having been bested by a skinny kid in his escape, and was very keen on revenge. But Gunnar reminded him that Britt wanted Lennox alive. That hadn't stopped Ole delivering a few heavy kicks to Lennox's ribs.

Lennox thought about the bear. He had no way of knowing if it understood, if it could do anything. But it had clearly been able to hear him. He wondered about that. He pressed his cheek against the cold floor, closed his eyes and found himself dreaming, talking to a cow in a field about which of its cuts were the tastiest. Then three lambs ambled over, begged him to eat their shanks.

He woke to the sound of the door being unbolted.

Ole came in, followed by Gunnar. Ole looked ready to rip Lennox's head off but Gunnar had his game face on.

'Up, shithead.'

Lennox coughed out some blood and cleared his throat. 'I might need some help.'

Ole booted him in the back, Lennox's kidneys crying out.

'Dumb fuck.'

Lennox tried to think of a funny reply, came up blank.

Gunnar heaved him up then shoved him through the door towards the meeting room. Ole knocked and opened the door, pushed Lennox through, both guards following him in.

Britt was watching a large screen on the far wall. It was split into four different feeds, three of them underwater drones, by the look of it, the fourth one from the bridge of a ship.

She smiled at Lennox. 'Come and sit.'

Lennox stood by the table, one hand leaning on it to keep him upright. He thought he might pass out, his vision slipping in and out of focus. He felt a jab in his side from a rifle barrel and collapsed into a seat.

Britt seemed upbeat.

He turned to the screen.

'The torpedo boat,' he said eventually.

Britt nodded, then looked at him closely. 'You look like shit.'

'Thanks.'

'Maybe you shouldn't try to escape.'

'Maybe you shouldn't try to kill my friends.'

'There are no humans at the Enceladon settlement, we've checked.' Britt pointed at the fourth screen, the view from a ship.

Lennox could see the back of the captain's head, some instrumentation on the dashboard, the prow of the ship out the cockpit window ploughing through the water, a smattering of icebergs either side.

'Please don't.' Lennox's voice sounded pathetic. 'I'll do anything. I'll get them to leave Earth. Just please don't do this.'

'Why would they listen to you?'

'Sandy would.'

Britt shrugged. 'It doesn't matter, we can't let them live.'

Lennox slammed his bound fists on the table. 'You can't fucking do this.'

'Watch.' Britt's voice was calm but she glanced at Gunnar and Ole to make sure they were alert. Both guards stepped forward to flank Lennox in his seat.

Britt tapped a small earpiece in her ear. 'Go ahead, Captain.'

There was no audio from the video streams. On the three drone cameras, Lennox saw a bioluminescent display far below. He recognised it as the Enceladon settlement. The fourth camera showed two torpedoes being launched from somewhere beneath the ship's prow, skimming on the water's surface for a few moments then diving underneath. Then two more, quickly on their tail.

Nothing for a minute or two, the silence unbearable.

Then Lennox saw the missiles and their bubble trails on the drone cameras, heading straight for the light display. Then all three drone feeds flashed with the explosions, over and over.

Lennox looked away then had to turn back, had to see. The drones showed a mess of churned-up mud from the sea floor as they moved in closer. Then Lennox saw more drones dropping bombs, more flashes. He held his breath for a long time. Eventually, the drones' spotlights began picking out things amongst the debris and Lennox thought he would puke. Body parts and dead Enceladons floating in the water. Huge chunks of flesh shifting in the currents, tendrils and tentacles adrift like broken spiders' webs, hundreds of dead beings, creatures just trying to live peacefully.

Lennox searched through the footage looking for Sandy or Heather, or any of his human friends. Then he spotted a giant body that he recognised. Xander.

He looked at Britt, who was still staring at the screen. He watched her swallow hard and blink too many times, and wondered for a moment if the sight of the massacre she'd brought about had penetrated her façade.

'How does it feel to be a mass murderer?' he said.

Britt gave a tiny shake of the head, but she was still watching the carnage on screen. Eventually she turned to Lennox.

'It's not murder,' she said. 'They're animals. It's just business.'

Lennox held her gaze, tried to see into her. It sounded like she was trying to convince herself.

'You'll pay for this,' he said quietly.

Britt cleared her throat and seemed to pull herself together.

'No,' she said. 'I don't think I will.'

# 55
# NIVIAQ

The school hall was bustling with the chatter of a hundred townsfolk, kids playing football in one corner, elders gossiping at the far wall. Niviaq's mother and many other women had set up in the canteen across the room, serving up *suaasat* and coffee. You never had any kind of gathering in Tasiilaq without feeding everyone and making sure they were caffeinated. Niviaq had missed this in Copenhagen. Many of these people could be irritating, but they were her community.

She looked at the mural the schoolkids had painted last year – polar bears and seals, Arctic foxes and sled dogs. Mountains and icebergs, flowers in the valley in summer, the northern lights in autumn. A pretty neat summary of life here, at least until Ava and the others had crashed into Niviaq's world.

She looked at Ava now, spooning seal soup into her mouth, watching Chloe play with Pipaluk, peering between adults' legs and laughing. Niviaq's heart swelled as she considered what Ava had been through with her daughter, her husband. She thought about what Vonnie said to her in the hut.

'Hey there.'

She turned. Kuupik had addressed her in Tunumiisut, and she was enjoying being surrounded by her native tongue again. He looked more tired than the last time she saw him, his police uniform dishevelled. She hugged him and he looked surprised.

'Easy, girl.' He waved around the room. 'What's this about?'

Niviaq didn't know how she was going to explain everything but she had to try. 'I'll tell you all in a minute.'

'Is it to do with the guy you found on the ice?'

She remembered the logo on Per's jacket, hauling him into the boat. The helicopter that came for him. She should've known then they were no good. 'Kind of.'

Kuupik smiled. 'Hey, the Maqe boys turned up.' He nodded to the corner of the hall, and Niviaq saw Aqqalu and Nuka mucking about.

'What happened to them?' Niviaq dreaded the answer. If the Enceladons had done something to their boat, it would make it harder for her to get folk on side.

'They were thrown overboard by the wake of some giant fishing ship sailing too close. Couldn't get back to the boat because of the currents. Had to hide out in the old hut at Apusiaajik. Had no signal for a long time, but eventually got help from the airport workers at Kulusuk.' Kuupik sucked his teeth. 'I reported the ship, of course, but we both know nothing will happen.'

Niviaq thought about that. Maybe it was the same vessel Heather had spotted, destroyed by sea animals. As far as she knew, no animals had attacked Inuit boats, but they'd destroyed larger ships, fishing and mining. Like they knew the difference between reciprocity and exploitation. There was only one way they knew about that.

She looked around the room. Most people had finished their bowls of soup and were waiting for her to speak.

'I need to talk to everyone,' Niviaq said to Kuupik, then headed to the stage.

In front of the mic, she cleared her throat and waited for the noise to die down. She glanced at Ava.

'Good luck,' Ava mouthed to her across the crowded hall, and she wondered if she was blushing.

'Hey, everyone.' She spoke first in Tunumiisut, then switched to English to include Ava. She felt self-conscious as she tried to lay it out as simply as possible. She found herself disassociating from the person on stage as she went on. This story started with her meeting a telepathic octopus – she realised how ridiculous it sounded. But she knew these people would take her seriously. They had a different attitude towards the out-of-the-ordinary, and most readily accepted the supernatural. They'd grown up amongst the spirits and ghosts of their ancestors, with tales of mythical beasts from the ice and sea. When you lived this close to death every day, nothing surprised you. The Mother of the Sea, *dupilaat*, *qivittut*, strange creatures with magical powers – the Enceladons fitted right in.

She explained what happened with the fishing ship, what the people at Sedna Station had done. All outsiders, that made a difference. And she told them what she knew about the mining station, how they were destroying the ocean floor, how the whole ecosystem could be ruined. Their livelihood. And she spoke about the Enceladons, how they were in danger too, that they only wanted to live in peace.

'We've seen them.' This was Aqqalu Maqe from the back of the hall, nudging his brother, who shuffled his feet and nodded. 'While out hunting. Brightly coloured shapes on the ice, sometimes in the water.' Aqqalu looked around the room. 'Others have too.'

That created a murmur through the crowd, some evidence to back Niviaq up.

'We have to help them,' she pleaded. 'The Enceladons want to protect their home and they want to protect our livelihood, the whole ecosystem. These other people who have come here, they want to destroy everything. We have to stop them.'

It was one thing to get people grumbling in a town meeting about bad things on the horizon, it was another to motivate a whole town to go out and fight. And this was all really still just her say-so, Niviaq didn't have proper proof.

Kuupik put his hand up. 'Where are these creatures you speak about?'

Niviaq had known it was the weak link in her argument from the start. If she could've brought Sandy or Heather to show everyone, that would've made the difference. She looked around the hall, at

Kuupik and the others, then at her mother standing next to her big pot of soup. There was love in her eyes, but concern too. Pipaluk was staring at her too, and Niviaq felt foolish.

Ava shrugged and tapped her temple. <If only you could show them this.>

The sound of a metal ladle clattering on the floor made Niviaq jump. She turned back to her mother, who was staring at Ava wide-eyed.

<I heard that.> This was unmistakably Ivala's voice in Niviaq's head.

There were gasps of shock around the hall, followed by murmurs.

<Mum, you can hear me?>

More gasps and exclamations from others in the room.

Then Kuupik's voice in her head. <I can hear too.> He gazed at Niviaq and Ava, then around the room, got nods of assent. <We all can.>

Niviaq couldn't understand what was happening. She turned to Ava. <How is this possible?>

Ava shook her head and looked at her empty bowl, confused. <I don't know.>

## 56
## HEATHER

She'd slipped into survival mode, the only way to cope with the carnage. The massacre. Genocide. She felt like a mother again, taking charge and checking on all the Enceladons. More of them were alive than she could've hoped for, she counted fifty-seven in total, many of them injured, all of them in shock.

She swam from creature to creature trying not to notice the dismembered bodies sinking to the bottom. The mud of the sea floor had settled, leaving a vision of hell like an old religious painting of God's wrath. She felt nauseous.

Amongst the dead were Jodie and some of the other converted humans. That hit Heather hard. These people had chosen this way of life and been punished for it. How could anyone do this? But she knew the simple truth, people did stuff like this all the time. They'd faced this before at New Broom and Heather had thought it was over, but it was back and a hundred times worse. This wasn't some military campaign, this was just the way the world worked. Heather hated it more than she could express.

Yolanda was still alive. They floated alongside Xander's dead body, displaying a swirling brown pattern that echoed the sand in the water around them. Sandy was there too, tentacles spread over part of Xander's head.

Heather watched Xander for a long time, hoping for some miracle to bring them and the others back to life. But for all the Enceladons' positive energy, for all their collective strength, they were powerless against missiles and bombs. Humans had spent millennia perfecting the art of violence, the destruction of the world.

Heather was so sick of still living through this.

She shook herself and went back to organising the survivors, trying to guide them away from the settlement. For all she knew there were more missiles coming.

But they wouldn't leave. The wounded Enceladons swam around their dead compatriots. It was like the site of a war crime, survivors lost and confused, unable to imagine a world where this was allowed to happen.

She kept pulling at octopuses and trying to shift the jellyfish. She looked back to where the missiles had come from, but didn't see anything. Forming a ring at a respectful distance were hundreds of sea mammals and fish – cod and capelin shifting in nervous shoals, seals tumbling over each other in an anxious ball, beluga and narwhals chattering, the sea filled with their mournful moans.

Heather couldn't fucking stand it, but she had to get the Enceladons away from here. She spoke to Sandy, still clinging to Xander's body.

<Sandy, we have to get the survivors out of here.>

No response.

Vonnie was still inside their body, eyes red from crying.

<I can't get through to them,> she sent. <It's like they've died too.>

Heather understood. She felt the same when her daughter died, like the biggest part of her was gone. But for the Enceladons, it must be even worse. Their sense of connection was so much stronger than humans'. They felt physical pain if separated from each other, and if kept alone in captivity, could sometimes die. But they had to move now, had to find somewhere safer.

<Sandy, please, more bombs might come.>

Nothing from Sandy.

Heather looked around. The other survivors were behaving the same as Sandy, refusing to leave their dead kin.

Heather approached Sandy and wrapped her tentacles around them, squeezing too hard. <Sandy, I know this feels impossible, but

it's not. It could get much worse. Look around – there are dozens of survivors, Enceladons who can live on. You owe it to the dead. Would Xander-Sandy partial want you to die? To revert to original energy state? You have to get to safety.>

Vonnie was anxious in Heather's mind. <Where can they go?>

<Tasiilaq. We need to find Ava and Niviaq. We need to tell people there what's going on. They can protect them.>

<You think?>

Heather honestly wasn't sure. She looked around again. The Enceladons were refugees on Earth, only to suffer this evil in their new home. History was full of massacres and genocides, maybe this was just the way the universe worked. But Heather refused to accept that. The Enceladons pointed the way towards a different way of life and she had to protect them.

<I need to get Lennox,> Vonnie sent, worry on her face. <I need to go to the mining station.>

Heather flickered red across her head. <That's crazy. You've seen their firepower, you know what they're capable of.>

Sandy flashed black and grey, the first time they'd shown any awareness since Xander's death.

<Sandy?> Heather sent.

<Sandy-Vonnie partial will find Lennox-Sandy-Vonnie partial.>

<No, it's too dangerous.>

Vonnie held her hands in a prayer. <Thank you.>

Heather didn't like it. <You can't.>

<Simple task for Sandy-Vonnie partial.> Their voice was full of despair, but something else too, a steel Heather hadn't heard before.

She pointed behind her. <What about the others?>

<Heather-Enceladon partial go to Ava-Niviaq partial. Safe.>

It sounded as if Sandy was already determined. And at least this way they were doing something, getting out of here.

<OK,> Heather sent, but she could hear the doubt in her own voice.

# 57
# VONNIE

She felt as helpless as a baby. Inside Sandy's body, Vonnie was safe from the freezing-cold water and the high pressure, but if Sandy died, she died too. She thought about her baby, safe inside her for now. She wondered how it was possible to be a good mother. She thought about Chloe, born with special powers but also a curse. She wondered what kind of world her baby and Chloe would grow up in, what kind of future they had.

She had no idea where they were. What if Sandy was tricking her or lying to her? What if they had decided that all humans were bad energy, including this one hitching a ride inside them?

<Sandy, I'm so sorry. Please talk to me.>

They swam past a shoal of fish, Vonnie couldn't make out what kind in the dark. Sandy had no light display, and that scared her more than the silence. She'd never known them to go dark like this.

<Sandy?>

More silence, then their voice. <Vonnie-Sandy partial mistake?>

Vonnie frowned. She moved her hand to her face but couldn't see anything without light. <I don't understand. I don't think I made a mistake.>

<Vonnie-Sandy partial said sorry.>

Vonnie thought about how to answer. <I meant sorry for your loss. I'm sorry that terrible thing happened.>

<Sorrow is pain.>

Vonnie felt a jolt at those words. <Yes. Bad energy.>

They swam downward and Sandy began flickering light across their body, sombre blues and greens, slow ripples. Vonnie saw different creatures around them – a knobbly black fish, something orange. The faint outline of a larger animal shifting in the gloom.

<Vonnie-Lennox-Sandy good energy?> The tone of Sandy's voice made it a question.

<Yes, Vonnie-Lennox-Sandy good energy. Always.>

She spotted a light up ahead. It was the destroyed mining machine they'd found earlier. Sandy swam past it to another wreck on the ocean floor, this was the destroyed ship. Sandy investigated it with their tentacles. Vonnie wondered if there were bodies inside. She thought about the dead Enceladons at the settlement. So much fucking death.

Sandy swam away from the wreck, renewed purpose in their movement.

<Do you know where Lennox is, Sandy?>

<Can taste ship route to shore. Vonnie-Lennox-Sandy partial together soon. Not stretched.>

<It won't be easy, there are people there keeping him captive. They'll try to kill us.>

Sandy swam faster. <No.>

The bluntness of Sandy's reply surprised Vonnie. <What?>

<Vonnie-Lennox-Sandy partial will not return to original energy state.>

Sandy sounded very sure of themself. Vonnie worried what that might lead to.

They raced through the water, deep currents replaced by shallower waves.

They broke the surface and Vonnie looked around. It took her a moment to get her bearings after so long in the ocean. But she saw it clearly enough on the nearby coast. A heavily secured compound, razor wire and armed guards, mining ships in the harbour alongside.

They were here.

# 58
# AVA

A hundred shocked and confused voices in her head, and she opened her mind to all of it. She felt disoriented but she wanted to be a part of this. She looked at Chloe. Pipaluk had joined the adults in looking gobsmacked at their newfound powers. They were all talking with their mouths too, frazzled excitement filling the air.

Ava focused on Niviaq, who'd stepped down from the stage. <Are you OK?>

Niviaq walked over and hugged her tight, and Ava felt a thrill through her body.

Eventually Niviaq pulled back, but they still held hands. <How is this happening?>

<I'm not sure,> Ava sent, holding up her empty soup bowl. <But everyone has eaten some of this, right? Maybe if the seal was telepathic, everyone who ate some is telepathic now too.>

It was a crazy idea but no more crazy than everything else that'd happened since she first met Sandy.

<That can't be true,> Niviaq sent. <Can it?>

Ava was reminded of an old Monty Python comedy sketch her dad used to reference, when Death came to visit a dinner party and they all realised it was the salmon mousse that'd killed them.

She laughed and shrugged. <The Enceladons are all about connection, being an integral part of a bigger ecosystem. Maybe this is the logical conclusion. You are what you eat, I suppose.>

She watched a group of locals now examining the pot of seal soup in fascination, some laughing, others very serious, all of them amazed.

She turned to Niviaq. <We're changing.> She'd tuned out the

other voices but could still hear them in the background, like the murmur of conversation at a party. <All of us.>

They were still holding hands and Ava didn't want to stop.

Niviaq looked at her mother and was clearly sending a message to her. Then to Pipaluk, who grinned and nodded, ran over and hugged Niviaq.

Chloe toddled over and Ava picked her up. <How are you, baby?>

<I hear Pipaluk,> Chloe sent.

<I know, honey, it's exciting.>

But she was thinking of the implications. If they could all hear each other's thoughts just from eating a single telepathic creature, the repercussions were revolutionary. Maybe the Enceladons had communicated with everything in the sea – fish, crabs and starfish, even plankton and krill. Once this power moved through the food chain, everyone would have it. Everything and everyone on the planet would be able to communicate telepathically, would suddenly be privy to the thoughts of other people, animals too. And who knows, maybe plants, fungi, bacteria – where did it stop? To the Enceladons this was as natural as breathing, but they'd changed Earth forever. This was beyond good or bad, it was profound, and Ava couldn't get her head around what it might mean for the future.

'Everyone, hey.' This was Kuupik at the back of the hall, standing at the open door. He waved his hands to get attention and the noise quietened. Ava noticed that the background murmur of voices in her head continued. 'Come and see.'

Something in Kuupik's voice made everyone obey. He left the building and they followed. Ava and Niviaq were near the back of the crowd, Ava carrying Chloe and Niviaq holding Pipaluk's hand as they left the school. In front of them, people were stopping abruptly in their tracks and Ava heard gasps of shock. She glanced over the crowd's heads and realised why.

Down in the bay, around fifty Enceladons were either floating in the water or sitting on ice. She looked amongst the smaller octopoid ones for Sandy or Heather, but couldn't spot them. There were just a few giant jellyfish, one hovering in the air by the shore. It was Yolanda, something about their light patterns that Ava recognised.

The crowd was standing in the street slack-jawed at the spectacle, even though it was only a fraction of the Enceladon community. They were flickering and swirling patterns that seemed to pass from one body to the next, sombre and demure colours and shapes, but it was still incredible.

'Why are they here?' Niviaq said.

It felt suddenly odd to hear her voice out loud, like they'd become less intimate.

'I don't know.'

Ava pushed through the crowd and walked to the shore, Niviaq with her. First the telepathy, now this – today would never be forgotten in Tasiilaq.

<Sandy? Heather?>

<Ava?> She recognised Heather's voice, looked amongst the creatures for her.

<Heather, where are you?>

Heather clambered out of the water at the shore then climbed over rocks to the path.

Ava glanced behind, the locals were carefully making their way down the hill. <Why are you here, what happened?>

Heather flashed yellow then threw herself into a hug with Ava and Chloe, who played with a tentacle. The icy wet of the embrace made Ava flinch, and she sensed anguish. <What is it?>

Heather pulled away and kicked up dirt with her tentacles, head expanding and contracting. <It was awful, Ava. They attacked the settlement.>

<What do you mean?>

<They destroyed it. With torpedoes and bombs.>

Ava's eyes widened. <What the fuck?>

Heather waved her tentacles at the Enceladons. <This is all that are left.>

<But there were hundreds.>

<They killed them all, slaughtered them in cold blood.>

Niviaq and Pipaluk were with them now and Niviaq shook her head. <That's mass murder.>

Ava looked around. <Where's Sandy? And Vonnie?>

Behind her, people were getting closer.

<They're OK,> Heather sent. <They've gone to find Lennox.>

Ava looked at the remaining Enceladons, turned back to Heather. <Where's Xander?>

Heather's tentacles fell and her bioluminescence flickered out. <Dead.>

<Oh my God.> Ava felt tears welling up and struggled to breathe. <I can't believe it.> She hugged Heather again, squeezed her body tight. <How could they do this?>

Heather pulsed red. <It was...> Her voice in Ava's mind was broken.

Ava breathed carefully as tears rolled down her cheeks. <How's Sandy taking it?>

<Not good. Not good at all.> Heather pulled away and slumped her body, looking forlorn. <I'm so, so sick of this, Ava. All of it. I don't...> She raised a tentacle then dropped it again.

Niviaq looked at the Enceladons then glanced back at the others from the town. <You need protection.>

Heather waved a tentacle. <We have nowhere else to go.>

Niviaq got nods from the crowd before she spoke. <You're welcome here. You're safe.>

# 59
# VONNIE

Vonnie flopped out of Sandy like a newborn foal, her legs giving way as she collapsed onto the stony shore. She'd been inside Sandy so long, her feet were briefly numb.

They were behind a cluster of boulders two hundred metres from the base. The connected buildings looked similar to Sedna, but there was also a giant warehouse or factory to the side, all of it surrounded by high fences and razor wire. Cameras at frequent intervals on the fenceposts, two tall lookout towers with armed guards, two more guards at the front gate. More fencing and guards at the dock.

<Lennox? Can you hear me?>

Silence for a moment, then a voice that made her heart sing. <Vonnie? Where are you?>

Sandy flickered blue and green, threw two tentacles in the air.

Vonnie watched the guards chatting at the gate. <I'm here with Sandy, outside the base.>

<It's so good to hear your voice. But you shouldn't be here, it's too dangerous. Don't try to get me out.>

Vonnie looked at Sandy, their head crinkling above their eyes. <Don't be stupid, that's why we're here.>

A moment of silence. <Vonnie, something terrible has happened.>

Vonnie watched Sandy's head deflate.

<We know,> she sent. <The settlement. We were there.>

<My God.>

Vonnie breathed deeply. <Ava and Chloe are fine, they weren't there. Niviaq took them back to Tasiilaq. Heather is OK too, she survived. But most didn't.>

<Xander?>

Vonnie looked at Sandy. <No.>

Sandy was clinging to the rock, watching the guards.

<Sandy, I'm so sorry.> Lennox sounded like he was crying.

A long silence.

<Sandy-Lennox-Vonnie partial will be reunited. Not stretched.>

Vonnie wondered what was going through Sandy's head. Seeing your family killed was unthinkable. Unbearable.

<How many...?>

Vonnie assumed Lennox meant how many were killed. <Maybe fifty survived. They've gone to Tasiilaq for protection.>

<Britt is determined to destroy them.> Lennox sounded exhausted.

Vonnie was about to reply when Sandy darted from behind the rocks and ran low to the ground on all five tentacles towards the main gate, camouflaging their body against the surroundings.

<Sandy, wait!>

<What's happening?> Lennox sent.

<Sandy's heading for the guards. Where are you?>

<Shit. I'm in a cell at the back of the main building. But it's guarded. Vonnie, please don't do anything stupid.>

<Would I?> Vonnie crouch-ran after Sandy, aware of the cameras and guards ahead.

Sandy reached the guard hut without being noticed and launched themself at the first guard, smothering him with their body, wrapping two tentacles around his neck, using another two to grab the second guard's rifle and toss it into the snow. The first guard slumped to the ground and Sandy jumped onto the second, performed the same choking manoeuvre then slid to the ground as the second guard toppled.

<Wait!> Vonnie was catching up as Sandy bustled towards the door of the first building. The sound of gunfire from the watchtowers made Vonnie jump and swerve.

The door of the building opened and two more guards came out pointing guns, but Sandy was already on them, wrapping one tentacle around the first guard's feet and whipping him off balance into the dirt, lashing the other across the face with a sparking tentacle that left a burn mark, then rolling another tentacle into a ball that unleashed into his guts, doubling him over.

<Vonnie, what's happening?>

<Fuck.> Vonnie raced after Sandy. She stepped over the guards and into the building, saw Sandy down a corridor pulling doors open as they went. They seemed in a rage. Vonnie had never seen them this way before, barely contained fury.

She ran down the corridor then heard a door behind her, a man shouting, then felt a blinding pain in her shoulder and span round, smacking her head off the wall as she dropped like a stone and passed out.

She was one of a set of Russian nesting dolls, somewhere in the middle. They stood in a row. She looked one way, and the dolls just got bigger and older until she could only see their wrinkled feet, their bodies disappearing in the mist. In the other direction, the dolls got smaller and younger so that there was a teenage version of her, then a seven year old, a toddler, a baby, a foetus. Then just an egg, a single molecule, an atom, a neutron, then other subatomic dolls she knew were there even though she couldn't see them.

Her shoulder roared with pain and she bolted upright, hands on her stomach.

'Von.' Lennox was on the bed next to her, his face covered in bruises and cuts, one eye swollen. She reached for his cheek and he flinched.

'What happened?'

Lennox shrugged. 'Local hospitality.'

The way he was breathing, Vonnie knew he had other injuries but she didn't ask. She looked at her shoulder. Her sweatshirt had been cut away and a basic field bandage wrapped around it. Blood was soaking through the material.

'The guards shot you.'

Vonnie looked around the windowless room. 'Where's Sandy?'

Lennox shook his head. 'I've tried contacting them but I can't get anything.'

Vonnie felt a tightness in her stomach. 'You think they're dead?'

Lennox ran his tongue around his teeth. 'I don't know.'

Heat rushed up Vonnie's throat then she burst into tears. Lennox hugged her and she smelled his hair, his sweat, and more tears came to her eyes.

They stayed like that a long time, her shoulder throbbing. Her breathing slowly returned to normal as she felt his body next to hers. Eventually she pulled away and wiped her tears.

<Lennox, I'm pregnant.>

He looked at her with his big eyes wide, and straightened his shoulders.

<Really?>

She nodded, sniffing back more tears.

He took her hands and glanced at her stomach, then back in her eyes. <Von, that's amazing.> He grinned and touched her cheek, then kissed her, and she kissed him back and wondered why she'd taken so long to tell him.

She looked down at her stomach and imagined the tiny person in there, no bigger than a fingertip, hanging on, just like they all were.

Lennox touched her belly. <You're growing a new life. Our kid. That's incredible.>

Vonnie laughed. 'It's crazy, look at us.'

Lennox shook his head. <It's the most beautiful thing in the world.>

The clunk of the bolt sliding made her jump, then the door opened. Britt appeared with the two guards she'd seen back at Sedna.

'Where's Sandy?' Vonnie said.

Britt ignored her. 'Come on, I want you to see this.'

Vonnie stood. 'What did you do to Sandy?'

Britt rolled her eyes. 'It's fine, it's already on board.'

'On board what?'

'The torpedo ship.' Britt angled her head. 'The drones spotted survivors heading for Tasiilaq. We're going to finish them off. You both get front-row seats.'

## 60
# NIVIAQ

The northern lights were a sign. They were rare in the summer, and you couldn't make them out well against the midnight sky, but Niviaq hoped that everyone in town would take it as a message from the spirits that they were doing the right thing.

She looked at the Enceladons in the water and on the ice. They were still in shock. Niviaq wasn't surprised, given what had happened. She was part of a community who didn't suffer genocide as badly as some indigenous peoples of the world, but they'd still been attacked and assimilated, their culture destroyed beyond recognition. The only thing that had prevented complete annihilation was the climate. The Inuit could survive the harsh winters, their imperial colonists couldn't. But they were still colonised, made to settle in towns instead of their nomadic existence. Sent to Christian church and made to wear western clothes, forced to speak Danish and English over their own language, told to forget their heritage, give up everything it meant to be Inuit. So Niviaq wasn't surprised that some corporation wanted to destroy the Enceladons.

She looked over the bay. She'd spent her life here, played on the frozen ice as a kid, cheered the first supply ship as it sounded its horn on arrival in late spring, raced dogsleds, hunted seals. It was home to the people of Tasiilaq and now it would be home to the Enceladons.

On the beach, some locals were shaking their heads at the supernatural display in front of them. But it wasn't supernatural, it was just natural, just what their world *was* now.

Niviaq thought about the seal soup. It was mad they'd picked up telepathy from something they ate, but it had colossal implications. Surely it was only a matter of time until it spread around the world.

<Hey.>

Niviaq jumped at Kuupik's voice in her head. She turned and he was grinning at her, tapping his temple. 'Still getting used to it.' He waved his hand to take in the town, the bay, the mountains across the water. <This is crazy, eh?>

<Crazy.>

He touched the police radio on his waist. 'I have someone on here trying to get in touch with you. Calls himself Per Nordström.'

From Sedna, shit. Niviaq took the radio and pressed the button. 'Hello?'

'Thank God.' Per sounded stressed. 'Are you OK?'

Niviaq watched Ava and Chloe playing with Pipaluk and Ivala near the shore.

'We know about the attack on the settlement, I thought maybe you were there.'

Niviaq had to think. Vonnie had said that Per and Thelma helped her escape, but she still had to be cautious. 'Where are you?'

'At Sedna,' he said, 'but things are changing.'

'How?'

'Since Britt went to the Ikusik mining station, Thelma and I have been speaking to the others about what happened to Karl, what Britt is doing in the name of KJI.'

Niviaq shook her head. They'd named the mining station after a terrifying mythical Inuit monster. But 'Ikusik' was the West Greenlandic name, here they called it Ererqortsordor. These people had never given a damn about this place.

'You trust the others at your base?' she said.

'No one here wants what she's doing, believe me. We're scientists. She ran the attack on the settlement from Ikusik for a reason. She took the guards with her when she went up there.'

Something nagged at the back of Niviaq's mind. 'Why were you out on the ice when I found you? Did the Enceladons attack your ship?'

'No, it was whales and seals, walruses. Britt knew, but she wanted to blame the Enceladons. Listen, we're abandoning Sedna. We've destroyed all the research data on the Enceladons, in case it can be used against the survivors. We're going to torch the base and sail a research ship to Nuuk. Try to fly home from there, if KJI goons don't stop us.'

Niviaq didn't know what to think. It was easy to run. 'What makes you think there are survivors?'

'We hacked into the drone footage, saw them heading towards you. That's why I'm calling. Britt knows there are Enceladons still alive. She knows they're in Tasiilaq with you. She's coming to get them.'

'What do you mean?'

'She's bringing the torpedo ship to finish the job.'

'And you're just running away.'

'What else can we do?' Per's voice was strained.

'Stay and fight.'

'We're scientists, not soldiers.'

Niviaq looked at the kids playing down the slope. 'We're not soldiers either.'

'That's why you have to get out of there. Get to safety.'

'No,' she said. 'We're not running. Not anymore.'

She ended the call and spat in the dirt, turned to Kuupik.

'I heard,' Kuupik said. 'Let's get everyone together.'

## 61
# LENNOX

The ship was smaller and faster than he expected. Wind whipped his face as he looked ahead from the raised deck. He could see occasional huts amongst the craggy landscape either side of the fjord, chunks of ice on the water.

<Anything yet?>

This was Vonnie in his mind. He looked at her and shook his head. He'd been trying to send a message to Ava or Heather. He had no idea how far it was to Tasiilaq, how far he could transmit.

The guard Ole was standing behind him and Vonnie, gun in hand. They had their wrists bound behind their backs but they weren't tied down – where would they run to?

Lennox turned to Sandy, who was squeezed into a small Perspex box. <Anything?>

<Sandy-Enceladon whole stretched thin.>

Britt said she'd read everything about what happened at New Broom, but they didn't have the EM cages that the military there used to subdue Enceladons and their telepathic comms. Maybe they just didn't care.

Sandy had already been in their box when Lennox and Vonnie were pushed onto the ship. The fact that Sandy had hurt or maybe killed several guards trying to bust Lennox out made him wary. But if Sandy was different since the attack, Lennox didn't blame them.

The ship had a crew of a dozen, half of them armed guards. Britt was behind them on the deck, talking with a security guard in a thick jacket and black beanie. Drones were parked on a platform and

Lennox could see explosive devices underneath each one. They'd already launched two drones without bombs for recon.

In the distance, Lennox saw smoke billowing into the air, and he thought for a moment it was Tasiilaq, that they'd sent bombs ahead without him realising. But as they drew closer, he saw it was Sedna Station on fire.

Britt came to the side of the ship and looked through binoculars for a long time, her hands gripping tight. Eventually she lowered them and took the guard's radio, spoke into it. She tried again and again but got no reply. She slammed the radio back into the guard's hand and looked again at the smoking wreckage of the science station.

Lennox looked at Vonnie. <You think it was the Enceladons?>

Vonnie shook her head. <They were so shellshocked by the attack they could hardly move.>

Britt walked to the armoured drones, watched as two guards finished prepping them. Another two men were sitting at screens to the side, piloting the recon drones. On the screens, Lennox could see mountains that he thought he recognised.

<Heather, Ava, anyone. You have to get out of Tasiilaq, you're in danger.>

No reply.

He spotted movement on the horizon. First to his right in the water, then some shapes against the white of an iceberg. Then more shapes moving towards the ship. He narrowed his eyes against the glare. It was the middle of the night but the sky was bright, green and blue aurora dancing in the east.

He glanced at Vonnie, who'd also spotted the movements.

<What is it?>

Vonnie stared out to sea. <Polar bears.>

Lennox focused on one shape in the water, realised it was a bear swimming towards the ship. Several more bears ran across the nearest iceberg and dived into the water. Now that he was attuned to them, Lennox saw loads more in the water around the ship.

A guard spotted them too, ran to the side and shaded his eyes. 'Hey.' He turned and shouted louder. 'Hey!'

Britt and Gunnar ran to the starboard side. Ole watched them but kept his gun on Lennox and Vonnie.

Lennox turned to Sandy. <Did you do this?>

Sandy flashed maroon and green. <Sandy-bear partials will help Enceladon-good-human whole. Good-energy creatures.>

Vonnie shook her head. 'What the fuck?'

The bears were closing in. Gunnar sounded the alarm and guards assembled along the railing. The bears slipped through the water on course to intercept them. And not just on the starboard side either, Lennox saw more swimming in the sea to their left.

The gunfire made him jump and he turned to see guards shooting into the water or aiming at the few bears still on icebergs. But the first bears were almost at the ship already. Shots cracked in the air as the guards continued to aim at the bears in the sea. Ole had joined Gunnar at the side. The ship rocked. There were thuds from down below. The bears must be pushing at the hull.

Lennox saw the face of a polar bear emerge over the prow of the ship. It had gone unnoticed by the guards looking down the sides, but then a shout went out. A guard turned just as the bear roared in his face then swiped at his arm with a giant paw and clawed it off in a ragged mess of blood and flesh and bone. The bear lunged and ripped the guard's throat out, dropping the body onto the deck.

More bears were over the side now, guards panicking and shooting. A bear came up to Sandy in their box, pressed its nose against the Perspex then open its jaws and cracked the plastic carefully with its teeth until the box was in pieces. Sandy leapt out and hugged the bear, which stood on its hind legs and roared.

Bullets were flying across deck as guards shot here and there, but they were getting destroyed by the bears.

Sandy scuttled over and placed a tentacle on Lennox's wrist

restraints, then Vonnie's. Lennox smelled melting plastic then his restraints snapped.

The bear that had freed Sandy approached them. <Bears help.>

Lennox was sure this was the same bear he'd met before, the one he'd given the message to.

'Lennox.'

He turned. Vonnie was pointing into the sea behind them. Lennox ran to the side and saw Britt, Gunnar and Ole in a small speedboat heading for shore.

'Maybe we leave them,' he said. He waved a hand around the ship. The deck was a mess of dead guards, swimming in their own blood. Dozens of polar bears stood around, some roaring on hind legs, others sniffing the corpses, licking the blood. 'We've got the ship. The Enceladons are not in danger anymore.'

Sandy darted to the side, saw the speedboat then turned to Lennox. <Enceladons not safe until bad human energy returned to original energy state.>

<Sandy, come on.>

But Sandy stood on two tentacles and expanded their body until it engulfed Lennox and Vonnie. They held them tight inside their body and leapt over the side of the ship into the sea.

# 62
# AVA

She wiped tears from her eyes as she stood at the prow of the boat. It was the small Sedna vessel that Vonnie had escaped in, now refuelled and heading back into open water, maybe into battle. Ava looked back at Tasiilaq in the distance. She didn't know if she could actually hear Chloe's cries in her mind, or if it was just an echo of her cries when they separated. She felt sick, wrenched from her little girl after everything they'd been through. But she had to come with Niviaq and Heather, with the locals, and this was no place for her daughter.

After Niviaq got that call from Per, the people of the town quickly agreed to take the fight to the enemy. Every able-bodied person had collected their hunting rifles, spears and harpoons, and gone to their boats. Older people and kids were left behind on the shore, Ivala holding a squirming Chloe in her arms, Pipaluk trying to distract her with a cuddly polar bear.

Ava looked around now as they headed up the fjord, surrounded by endless freckles of ice. There were around thirty small boats, each of them packed with people, guns pointing into the air, lookouts with binoculars searching for any approaching ship.

After everything they'd been through, it came down to this – putting themselves in the firing line for something they believed in. A way of life, a way of looking at the world. Ava looked at the other boats. She didn't know these people, had only met a couple of them. And they didn't know the Enceladons, had only just met them. But it had been clear from the moment the Enceladons turned up in Tasiilaq that the Inuit would help them.

Ava had wondered if some of the Enceladons would come and

fight, but the people of Tasiilaq never asked, and the Enceladons were so shocked at what had happened to them that they were barely functioning.

So it was down to these ordinary people.

'Hey.' Niviaq put her arm around Ava. Ava briefly leaned her head on the other woman's shoulder, felt the warmth of her breath. She imagined Niviaq's heart beating under her jacket, pictured both of their hearts beating in synch. She straightened up but Niviaq kept her arm around her. 'You OK?'

<Sure.> Ava wanted to be inside Niviaq's mind.

Niviaq looked up the fjord. <Are you ready for this?>

<No.>

Niviaq laughed. She looked at Kuupik at the helm, then at the neighbouring boats. 'These people know how to fight, how to survive.'

'I believe it.' Ava meant everyone, but especially Niviaq, who seemed like the strongest person she'd ever met.

Niviaq glanced behind them. <Chloe will be fine. My mother will look after her.>

<I know.>

<And I think Pipaluk has a new best friend.>

They both smiled, then Ava thought about everything that had happened, the lives lost, and her smile faded.

<Ava.> This was Heather, leaping out of the water and onto the prow of the boat. <Something's happening.>

<What do you mean?>

Heather shifted orange across her skin and pointed two tentacles at the sea. <They're gathering.>

Ava looked at the surface of the ocean and spotted something, bodies shimmering underwater. <Who?>

Heather gave an octopus equivalent of a shrug. <Everyone.>

Two dolphins broke the water's surface and leapt into the air alongside the boat then dived back in graceful arcs. Then more dolphins followed suit. Ava saw the tusks of narwhals, ten or more, pointing through the waves like daggers. And the domed heads of belugas now swimming at the surface, larger whales in the distance, humpbacks and bowheads. She looked around and the seas were alive, their flotilla accompanied by hundreds of animals. In between the dolphins and whales were thousands of fish, shimmying in schools, silverly pinpricks amongst the waves, darting around and under chunks of ice, the ocean alive with them. And seals, hundreds of their shiny grey bodies darting forward, their snub noses and whiskers appearing and disappearing as they dovetailed each other.

Ava looked at Niviaq, who was grinning. 'We seem to have increased our numbers.'

'It looks like it.' <Heather, what's happening?>

<They just want to help.>

It was the most amazing display of life Ava had ever seen. She was mesmerised by it, just like when she'd first set eyes on the Enceladons. The joy of life being lived.

'Hey.' This was Kuupik at the controls. He was nodding ahead, binoculars at his face. 'Something coming up.'

Ava's chest tightened as they approached a ship. In the other boats, some people had their rifles raised. In the water, seals had raced ahead, dolphins spreading out to surround the vessel.

Ava squinted in the brightness. There were just a few traces of aurora in the sky now, faint shimmers of blue and red. She looked for activity on the ship's deck, but what she saw didn't make sense.

She heard Niviaq in her mind. <Is that what I think it is?>

They were closer now, Kuupik slowing the boat. Men and women in the other boats were having the same conversation by the look of it.

<It can't be,> Ava sent.

She saw the torpedo ports in the hull, guns mounted on the prow, the raised control room. And the deck, populated by polar bears, some wandering around, others roaring and stretching, a few feeding on something, ripping flesh apart with red teeth and bloody snouts.

'Yep,' Ava said, wanting to hear the words out loud. 'That's a ship full of polar bears.'

# 63
# VONNIE

She stood on the rocky shore with Lennox and Sandy. Britt's speedboat was beached to their right, two hunting huts beyond it above the high-tide line. Surely Britt, Gunnar and Ole must be in there.

Vonnie had deep reservations. She'd just witnessed polar bears kill a bunch of people, for fuck's sake. And now that the immediate threat to the Enceladons was dealt with, why were they chasing Britt? But maybe Sandy was right, while Britt and people like her were still alive, still in control, the Enceladons would never be safe. But something about Sandy's attitude made Vonnie scared.

She looked at Lennox. They'd both effectively been abducted by Sandy and brought here. She compared that to the first time she met them, when they asked for permission before communicating with her. Such a gentle soul back then, but it felt like they'd been hardened by all this. Maybe that was the price of resistance, victims had to become like their persecutors to survive.

Sandy was waving their tentacles above their head, tasting the air, trying to catch the scent. They scuttled up the beach towards the first hut.

Vonnie took Lennox's hand as they followed.

<This is all wrong,> she sent. <This doesn't feel like Sandy.>

<They just saw their family murdered in front of their eyes.>

Vonnie dropped Lennox's hand and stopped. 'I know that, I was fucking there.'

'Hey, I didn't mean anything.'

She pictured the torpedoes fizzing through the water, the blinding light. Felt the shockwaves.

<Hey.> Lennox's voice in her head was apologetic. <I'm sorry, OK? But we need to make sure Sandy doesn't do anything stupid.>

Vonnie eventually nodded in agreement.

An engine roared into life ahead of them somewhere, then a moment later a large snowmobile burst out from behind the huts, bumping over the patchy ice until it reached the thick stuff. Gunnar was steering, Britt in the middle, Ole facing backward at the rear, gun pointing in their direction.

'Shit,' Vonnie said.

The crack of gunfire made them duck for shelter behind the first hut. After a few moments, Vonnie looked round and the snowmobile was already in the distance. There were no other vehicles nearby. Maybe this was the answer, they couldn't give chase, so it was over.

Sandy stood weirdly on one tentacle, the other four waving in different directions, flashing spirals of orange and blue across their head.

<Sandy, what are you doing?> Vonnie sent.

She heard splashing, then roars that shook her ribcage.

She turned and saw three polar bears shaking water from their fur at the shore.

<Sandy-bear partial help reach bad human energy.>

Vonnie assumed Britt and the others were heading back to Ikusik Station. With Sedna up in smoke there was nowhere else for them.

Lennox shook his head. <Sandy, we need to let them go.>

<Many Enceladons returned to original energy state. Bad-energy humans kill.>

All the Enceladons had found on Earth was suffering and death. But Vonnie wanted to take a moment. She'd already seen two massacres – the Enceladons, then the crew of the torpedo ship. If they followed Britt, nothing good would happen. But what was the alternative – go back to Tasiilaq and wait for another attack?

Sandy ran to the first polar bear, who lowered its head and crouched on its haunches. Sandy touched its forehead with two tentacles, glistening bright blue, then grabbed the animal's fur and climbed onto its back.

The other two polar bears walked to Lennox and Vonnie and lowered themselves in similar fashion.

'Do we?' Lennox said.

Vonnie smelled the bear's breath, fish and blood. She touched its fur and felt its warmth. She held on for a long time then pulled herself up and onto its back. She watched as Lennox did the same.

The bears stood on four legs and Vonnie shifted her weight.

<Bear go.>

This was her bear in her head. She wondered what her old self would've made of this. The woman a week ago who'd just found out she was pregnant.

All three bears lumbered towards the ice sheet where the snowmobile had gone, gathering speed so that Vonnie's ears burned from the cold. They reached the ice sheet and she buried her face in the animal's neck, smelled its essential bearness, felt the weight underneath her, sensed the power and violence and freedom of the animal.

# 64
# NIVIAQ

The deck of the ship was covered in blood and human innards, severed limbs and entrails strewn about the place. The polar bears watched them climb on board, Heather first, Niviaq close behind, then Ava and Kuupik bringing up the rear. He carried his rifle but the barrel pointed down. A single gun was useless against all these bears anyway. If the bears wanted to kill them all, they would've done it already.

Niviaq looked around the ship. She'd seen plenty of blood in her time, every hunt she'd been on. But she'd never seen this much *human* blood, she doubted any of them had. She felt sick, but also something else. This was victory for the bears, the people of Tasiilaq and the Enceladons.

Kuupik checked some of the bodies, shaking his head and spitting on the deck. 'This is not how bears behave. They did this deliberately. For us.'

'Yes.' It was unbelievable, but Niviaq didn't know what that word meant anymore. Telepathic humans, aliens sheltering in the bay, collaborating polar bears and sea life. If someone had told her any of this a week ago she would've called them insane. Yet here she was.

Kuupik went to the starboard side and signalled to the other boats. Niviaq heard him in her mind explaining to the others what'd happened. She couldn't get her head around any of this.

Ava took Kuupik's binoculars and pointed them at the shore. Niviaq and Heather joined her, and she lowered the glasses and handed them over with a shocked look.

Niviaq lifted them and saw movement, took a moment to focus.

She saw Britt and two guards on a snowmobile, white spraying behind them. Then further back on the ice sheet, three polar bears chasing after them, Lennox, Vonnie and Sandy on their backs. She couldn't believe her eyes. She lowered the glasses and shook her head.

'They're riding bears.'

'They are,' Ava said.

Heather was agitated, flashing pink and white down her tentacles. <The bears want to help. They say this isn't over.> She waved at the horizon, then at the corpses on the ship. <They have to finish it.>

Niviaq thought about that. <At the mining station?>

<Yes.>

Niviaq looked at the bears, all sniffing the air.

<They'll do it with or without us,> Heather sent.

Niviaq didn't like it. This was starting a war, or maybe trying to end one. But she knew that more people would come, more machines, bigger guns. They wouldn't stop until the Enceladons were dead, until the landscape was destroyed.

She looked at Ava, who nodded.

Kuupik was already heading for the bridge. 'I'm on it.'

The engine started up and the ship began to turn. The bears got excited, walking to the side and staring at the shore.

They picked up speed, their own little Sedna boat bumping along behind, tied to the aft of the torpedo ship.

Niviaq wondered what was waiting at Ikusik Station. If Britt's team had one torpedo ship, maybe they had others. More powerful weaponry. They could be sailing into a trap. But Niviaq looked at the flotilla of boats around them, could sense the willingness to fight.

Ava rubbed her back.

<It'll be OK,> Ava said in her mind.

<Will it?>

<As long as we stick together.>

Niviaq watched dolphins leap alongside the boat, bowhead whales easing through the water between icebergs. The bears crowding at the prow of the ship now.

After a while, Kuupik started shouting and pointing from the bridge. Niviaq saw the buildings of the mining station surrounded by high fencing.

The bears began roaring and pacing up and down, then they leapt into the water, making the ship rock. There were more bears already on shore. What the hell? The sea around their ship was teeming with life. She imagined stepping across the backs of seals, whales and dolphins to the shore.

Ava glanced through the binoculars. 'I think they made it back to the station, I don't see the snowmobile anywhere. Lennox, Vonnie and Sandy are still coming.'

A thin whistle pierced the air, followed by another and another, and Niviaq turned to see three rockets climbing through the air from behind the station defences, heading for the ship.

## 65
## HEATHER

The first explosion knocked Heather off her tentacles and sent her sprawling, her head smacking the deck. Then more impacts, two more screaming crashes. She felt dizzy and sick. She untangled her tentacles and smelled the air, burning oil and flesh. She looked around, saw black smoke billowing from a ragged hole in the deck. The last few polar bears leapt into the water. She couldn't see anyone.

<Ava! Niviaq?>

She scurried to the port side, clambering over bodies of the crew, splashing through blood, oil and seawater, salty on her suckers.

<Ava, where are you?>

She saw movement through the smoke then Niviaq emerged, dragging Ava by her armpits. Heather ran over and lifted Ava's legs as they took her to the aft of the ship. The deck was lurching underneath them. The whistle of more rockets made her look up. Two flew over them and exploded amongst the flotilla, upending a boat and spilling people into the water. Another whistle and fizz, then a blinding flash and the bridge of their ship vanished in smoke and fire.

Niviaq looked up. 'Kuupik?'

Ava was coming round, blinking heavily.

<Ava, are you OK?> Heather stroked her face with one tentacle, pressed two more on her back to help her sit up. The ship lurched again, the aft dropping close to the waterline.

Niviaq stood unsteadily. <Kuupik?>

<Here.> He staggered out of the smoke, coughing and retching, then grabbed the handrail.

'We need to get out of here,' Niviaq said, pointing at the boat still tied behind them.

Heather helped Ava stand then wrapped herself around her as best she could and slid over the side into the water. She felt Ava's shock at the cold, she wasn't protecting her like Sandy could, but she was doing her best. She heard splashes behind her, Niviaq and Kuupik in the water, then she heaved her body with Ava inside her onto the deck of the small boat.

She released Ava and went to help the others aboard.

Kuupik didn't waste time, shivering as he untied the boat from the sinking ship. He went to the cockpit and started the engine.

Niviaq crouched next to Ava. <Are you OK?>

Ava nodded as they headed for shore.

Heather saw Lennox, Vonnie and Sandy standing with three polar bears in a rocky cove near the station.

Other boats were heading for shore as well, rockets still launching from behind the station fences. One exploded close behind their boat, throwing the stern up so that they all lost balance. The water around them was churning with boats and explosions, a maelstrom of chaos.

Then Heather heard gunshots, first from the station then from the flotilla, the Inuit returning fire. Guards in the watchtowers were spraying bullets into the water and along the shore, aiming at anything that moved.

Another rocket exploded next to them, drenching them in seawater, their hull shuddering. Kuupik struggled to steer the boat to the cove.

Niviaq helped Ava to her feet as Heather looked around – everyone was helping everyone else, humans, animals and aliens.

Kuupik drove the boat onto the stony beach, lurching to a stop, then jumped out and helped the others onto dry land.

Lennox ran over and hugged Ava, Vonnie grabbing Niviaq in an embrace. Heather watched for a moment from the boat, then levered herself over the side and onto shore.

More gunfire ripped through the air, making them all flinch and duck. Heather looked out to sea. Three more boats had been sunk and people in neighbouring vessels were helping grab survivors out of the water amongst the choppy waves. And animals were helping too – Heather was amazed to see two young men on the back of a bowhead whale, which carefully swam alongside a boat so they could be dragged on board.

Rockets were still coming down in the water around them, their piercing screams followed by shocking thumps as they exploded. Then Heather spotted two rockets heading towards them on the shore. <Watch out!>

Everyone ducked but the missiles sailed over their heads, exploding along the beach in a shower of gravel and ice. Too close for comfort.

Heather heard other noises beneath the gunshots, the guttural roar of polar bears, the spouting of narwhals and whales, the chattering of belugas. Inland on the ice sheet were over a hundred bears running towards Ikusik. Bullets thudded into the snow and ice around them, ricocheted off rocks, occasionally lodging in a bear's thick hide, which hardly slowed it.

The bears reached the station perimeter and began climbing the fences, tearing at the razor wire, roaring and grunting as they launched over the other side. A dozen bears headed for the front gate, heads down, and bulldozed into it, roaring loudly, tangling up in it to begin with, bullets flying around them, then they powered over and through, lifting guards off their feet and hurling them into the air like ragdolls, some of them attacking machinery within the station. Inside the station's defences, a handful of bears were climbing a watchtower, the guards trying to shoot them off. The other tower swayed as six bears pushed against its legs. It toppled, two guards leaping from it only to be trampled by the bears where they landed. The soldiers with the rocket launchers were now getting mauled, Heather heard their screams as they were ripped apart in a spray of blood and gore.

This was all going on without them. There was no need for humans or aliens, the bears had taken over.

<Sandy, what should we do?> This was Lennox.

Heather looked at him, remembered the shy boy she'd met years ago, thought of how they'd both changed.

Sandy didn't answer, just took off for the destroyed front gate, scuttling across the snow and rocks, lights flickering up and down their body.

<Sandy?> Heather sent.

<Bad-energy humans must return to original energy state.>

Lennox raised his eyebrows at Vonnie then they followed Sandy into the bloody chaos of the mining station. Heather watched Ava, Niviaq and Kuupik go too, then eventually she followed.

There were no guards left alive inside the fences. Some dead bodies weren't in uniform, so presumably they were mine workers. It was indiscriminate, the animals had killed them all. All the mining equipment was destroyed, some of the buildings damaged, doors and walls buckled, windows smashed in. Bears roamed around the courtyard, some walking into the building complex. Sandy was at the main door, easing themself in, the humans close behind.

Heather felt like a war correspondent, like she was an outside observer of all this, trying to take it in. She wasn't an animal, wasn't an alien, wasn't really human.

She followed the trail of destruction into what looked like a control room, big screens on the walls, lots of computer terminals. Half a dozen dead bodies in here, savaged by bears, throats ripped out, guts spreading over the floor.

On the screens were feeds from cameras all over the site, so much death and destruction. What had they done?

One screen showed the mining boats in the harbour being destroyed by bears from above and whales and dolphins in the water. They were ripping them apart, smashing the hulls until they were holed, the ships already partially submerged.

'Look,' said Lennox, pointing at another screen.

Britt and her two guards were climbing onto another snowmobile at the back of the site, panic in their body language, then they were off onto the ice sheet.

<Come on.> This was Sandy in Heather's head, but they didn't sound Enceladon, they sounded human.

## 66
## AVA

Sandy scurried out of a door at the back of the control room. The others all looked at each other for a moment.

Lennox shook his head. <I have to go with them.>

He got a nod from Vonnie and a flash of agreement from Heather, and they left through the same door.

Ava hesitated and looked at Niviaq. <I have to go too.>

<Of course,> Niviaq sent. She looked at Kuupik, who was checking for survivors amongst the bodies.

'Go,' Kuupik said.

Ava and Niviaq ran out of the door and along a corridor past a storage area, then out an exit at the back of the building. Ava squinted against the snow glare.

Snowmobiles were parked in a row, half a dozen more bodies out here, blood splattered against the ice. Six polar bears were standing around growling, two of them nudging at bodies on the ground. The tang of blood caught in Ava's throat.

She made herself look at the dead men and women on the ground. These were ordinary people with lives of their own – they had families, friends, maybe children. No one deserved this. The world was fucked up but this wasn't the answer. Killing your enemies was exactly the bullshit human attitude she hated. It had once felt like Sandy was the antidote to that, the Enceladons the way forward, but not like this.

Sandy was already on a snowmobile looking back at Lennox. Ava didn't hear the conversation between them. Lennox hesitated, looked at Vonnie, then they both walked to the snowmobile and got on.

Lennox threw a look over his shoulder then started the engine, and they were off across the ice.

<We have to go with them,> Heather said in Ava's mind.

Ava stared at the bodies on the ground. <Do we?>

Heather clambered onto a snowmobile.

Ava looked at Niviaq. <Maybe I have to see this through.>

She waited a long moment, then walked over and mounted the snowmobile, and Niviaq followed suit.

On the ice, the wind was freezing. Ava shook from the cold and adrenaline. She could see Britt's vehicle in the distance, then Lennox's.

Gunshots popped and bullets whizzed past her, fired by the guard on the back of Britt's vehicle.

Ava spotted something in the distance, two polar bears running fast across the ice towards them all.

The guard began shooting at the bears, who ran on regardless, breath billowing behind them like steam engines.

Ava was trying to navigate across the snow, watching for rocks. They were close behind Lennox's snowmobile but still a distance from Britt. She'd steered her vehicle away from the bears but they were closing fast.

They caught up with her, and the bear in front leapt and landed on the back of the snowmobile, slashing at one guard with its claws, tipping the vehicle over in a spray of snow, throwing them all clear. The second bear reached the other guard on the snow and pounced on him, pounding on his chest and chewing his neck.

The bears finished with the guards then approached Britt lying on the snow. They stopped and turned to look at the others approaching.

Ava looked at Sandy in the other snowmobile, someone had communicated with the bears, told them to hold off.

They reached the toppled snowmobile and stopped, then jumped off onto the ice. Sandy went to check the two dead guards, tentacles touching their necks. Ava remembered how Sandy had saved humans in the past.

The rest of them walked towards Britt, sitting upright now, the polar bears standing over her. She pulled a gun from her jacket pocket but the closest bear swiped it away easily, slicing her palm with its claws. She gasped and held her hand, breathed heavily. She stared at the bears, then at Sandy and Heather, then the others.

'This won't make a difference,' she said.

No one replied.

'All of this,' she said, waving her bloody hand at Ikusik Station. 'It's all backed up. All the information is with KJI. They'll come again. They want the riches of the ocean, and they want the Enceladons dead.'

'It's too late,' Niviaq said.

Ava was surprised to hear her voice and turned to her.

Britt frowned. 'You were just the boat driver. How the hell are you involved in all this?'

Niviaq waved towards the fjord. 'My people are custodians of this land. We live here in harmony, with respect.'

'Romantic bullshit, no one *really* lives in harmony.' Britt stared at Niviaq. 'What did you mean, it's too late?'

Niviaq looked at Ava then the others. <She doesn't know that we can all do this.>

Britt narrowed her eyes. 'Are you talking to each other?'

Niviaq gave her a pitying look. 'All of us. It's spreading, it can't be stopped.'

Britt looked at everyone standing over her – humans, bears, aliens. She sighed. 'At least I won't go out alone.' She opened her jacket and took out a second pistol. The humans all straightened their shoulders. The bears and Sandy didn't flinch.

<Bad energy.> Sandy's words clear in Ava's mind. <Return to original energy state.>

Britt looked around at the faces watching her. 'What's it saying?'

'They want to kill you,' Ava said.

Britt smiled. 'Good. It's finally learned how to be human.'

She pointed the gun at Sandy. Sandy lifted a tentacle in the air and stepped forward. But Heather pushed in front of them and leapt for Britt's hand, tentacles wrapping around her wrist, another at her throat, Heather's body pushing into her face, her skin billowing and enveloping Britt's body and for a moment there was only silence, then the crack of a gunshot, another and another. Each bang made Heather's body shudder and deflate. Three more shots in quick succession saw Heather fall away from Britt onto the ice.

Ava ran over to them. Britt's dead eyes were wide, her neck red with strangulation marks. Heather's body was slumped and full of leaking bullet holes, no light on her skin, no life in her eyes.

# 67
# VONNIE

The heaviest silence filled her mind as the wind across the ice made her shiver. She watched Lennox run to Heather and hold her, tears on his face.

Vonnie's eyes welled up as she looked around. Ava and Niviaq were holding each other as they watched Lennox, Sandy to the side, the bears still standing there.

Lennox looked up. <Sandy, do something.>

Sandy didn't move, a subdued green display across their head.

<Sandy, please.>

They'd been here before, but they all knew Sandy couldn't do anything if someone was dead. Some things couldn't be reversed.

<Sandy, this is Heather, come on!>

Sandy stepped closer. <Sandy-Heather partial wanted to return to original energy state. Was not happy.>

Vonnie burst out crying at those words.

Lennox shifted his weight, held Heather's head tighter. <No, you have to do something.>

Vonnie couldn't stand this. <Lennox.>

He turned to her. <She can't die.>

Ava let go of Niviaq's hand and stepped forward. <Lennox, she's gone.>

Vonnie looked towards Ikusik, smoke billowing into the crisp, blue air. She turned back and Lennox was still sitting there crying with his head touching Heather's.

'She did this for us.' Vonnie didn't know what to say. She'd spoken out loud just to hear her own voice, make sure she still existed.

Niviaq was at Britt's body, checking for a pulse. She shook her head.

Vonnie thought about what Britt said, that everything from Ikusik and Sedna was backed up, KJI had it. Maybe they were coming right now, sailing up the fjord for revenge. 'Lennox, we have to get out of here.'

Lennox didn't move, so Vonnie went over and crouched next to him. 'We need to leave. Heather would want us to be safe.'

She touched his face and he looked at her. She saw emptiness and loneliness in his eyes. She wanted to change that, hug him forever, but people would always be separate from each other no matter how much they tried.

She felt numb with shock at the carnage of Ikusik. Dead bodies and blood everywhere, smoke blossoming from buildings, bears stalking around, whales and dolphins in the harbour, leaping out of the waves.

The people from Tasiilaq had gathered on the shore next to Ikusik and in the boats that survived the onslaught. Niviaq drove her snowmobile over to check on them, Ava riding on the back. Lennox and Vonnie dismounted from their vehicle at the edge of the gathering, Lennox holding Heather's body in his arms, hands and face red with cold. Over his shoulder the sun was rising. It never got dark, but it was a new day anyway.

Sandy arrived clinging to the fur of one of the bears, then slid from its body and stood with their head next to the bear's face for a moment. Sandy seemed so different to the creature Vonnie had first met in Loch Broom. But they were all different now. She looked at Niviaq, Ava and the Greenlanders with new powers. And she looked at all the animals, on land and in the water. They were different now, too.

She thought about the new life growing inside her. She had no idea what to expect, but the baby was her focus now, and it gave her a sense of calm, a confidence she hadn't felt before. She looked at the ruins of Ikusik, a manmade blip in the vast expanse of the natural world. Grey mountains, white snow and ice, blue seas and a piercing sky with a cold sun rising.

'Come on,' she said to Lennox. 'Let's go.'

# 68
# NIVIAQ

She looked at their depleted flotilla and felt her heart surge with pride. Incredibly, they'd lost boats but no people. The survivors of the sunken boats were cold and wet, and some were in shock, but they were all still alive to tell the story of a lifetime, of the animals fighting back. Niviaq felt a deep guilt in her gut about the deaths at Ikusik, and was sure she would never be without it. But the animals had done what was necessary to protect themselves and the ecosystem, including the Enceladons. That's why the Inuit had sailed up the fjord – for land and sea and sky. For the future. She kept telling herself that but would picture the dead on the ship and at the station, think of their families back home, their grief and distress. Her shoulders slumped.

They were back on the old Sedna boat, packed with refugees from the sunken vessels, some wrapped in blankets. Kuupik was at the wheel. Niviaq closed her eyes, felt how tired she was. It was already tomorrow and no one had slept, strung out on adrenaline.

They were close to Tasiilaq now, Kulusuk on the left. That's where this had started for her, picking up a handful of strangers stranded by fog and taking them home. And Tasiilaq *was* her home, she knew that now. She'd resented living here for so long, but she didn't feel at home anywhere else. Maybe that's all home was, somewhere you felt least alone and lost.

Ava touched her back, and she turned and shared a smile. They gazed at each other for a long time, then held hands and looked forward as the boat came into the bay, Tasiilaq on the left. The sight of those colourful houses made Niviaq choke up with emotion.

Kuupik had radioed ahead and Niviaq saw people standing at the harbour. She tried to pick out Ivala, Pipaluk and Chloe, but they were still too far away. Some Enceladons were floating in the water amongst the icebergs, flickering sombre colours.

She turned to look at the people in her boat, Lennox and Vonnie in the back with Heather's body. Heather had been the first alien creature Niviaq had encountered, even if she was only half alien, and Niviaq would never forget her. She looked into the water for Sandy, but couldn't see them. There were still some animals dipping in and out of the waves alongside the flotilla, a few seals and a pair of beluga. The others had left Ikusik with them but gradually slipped away into the depths.

Ava squeezed her hand. <Are you OK?>

Niviaq looked at her beautiful eyes, tired but full of compassion. <No, but I will be.> She spotted Pipaluk and Chloe. 'Look.'

Ava clasped her hands together and narrowed her eyes, sending a message to her daughter. They were not far now, and Niviaq could hear the hubbub from the harbour. Pipaluk helped Chloe find her mum by pointing and waving, and Chloe clapped her hands. They reached the harbour and climbed ashore as Kuupik tied the boat up, the other vessels following suit alongside.

Niviaq hugged her mother, grabbed Pipaluk and watched Ava squeeze her daughter. The atmosphere on the dock was relief and celebration, though the people who'd stayed behind were more upbeat than the ones who'd gone.

Maybe they weren't safe here – humans, animals or Enceladons. Maybe the future was coming for them. But for now they were alive and together, that was all that mattered.

She looked at the people hugging with relief and burst into tears, crying for everything she had, everything she was.

# 69
# AVA

She wished that Heather could've had her human body back for this.

Most of the locals were watching from up the hill, in the winding lanes and spreading slopes. In the harbour water, all the remaining Enceladons were floating in a semi-circle, mostly octopuses, a handful of jellyfish. They were sending a flickering ribbon pattern from one body to the next along the row.

Heather lay on the ground at the edge of the harbour. Ava could still make out the small vestiges of her face, a ghostly presence under the skin. Sandy was right, Heather hadn't been happy since her daughter died. When she first met Sandy she was trying to kill herself, and that feeling never truly left her. When Sandy cured her cancer, she put on the façade of living, taking care of others, purpose in her found family. But deep in her heart she hadn't bought into it. That was why she tried being Enceladon. Maybe it worked for a while, but the darkness never left her. Ava wasn't surprised when she stepped in front of Britt's gun, took bullets to save others.

Tears ran down Ava's cheeks as she stared at her friend's body. Chloe next to her squeezed her leg and Ava ran a hand through her daughter's hair. What was Chloe going to become? The Enceladons claimed they'd fixed her brain, but Heather's cancer came back. Ava would forever be looking for signs – a moment of dizziness, a queasy headache. But that was the same as any mother. That was the job, to fret about your kids forever.

'Anyone want to say something?' Lennox said. He stood a few steps away from her, Vonnie at his side.

Niviaq had her arm looped through Ava's, whose heart ached at the idea she and Chloe might have to leave soon, that she might never see Niviaq again. She wiped away tears and Niviaq squeezed her arm.

Lennox cleared his throat. 'Heather was the best of us.' His voice faltered. 'I know that's a cliché, but she was.' He glanced at Ava. 'When we met her in hospital, I knew straight away she was someone I could rely on. I hadn't had that in my life. Heather was a rock.'

He looked around the harbour at the Enceladons, ran a hand through his hair, shook his head. Vonnie rubbed his back.

He turned to Ava. 'Everything we've been through. I couldn't have done any of it without Heather. She saved my life more than once. It's another cliché, but she was the mum I never had.'

Ava knew why Lennox was saying this out loud instead of using telepathy. This needed to be declared to the world. They should be screaming it from the highest mountain.

Ava picked up Chloe and hugged her.

<Sad.>

Ava sobbed. <Yes, Mummy is sad.>

She wondered what all this was going to do to Chloe in the long term. Maybe she was too young to remember. Chloe wriggled out of her arms and walked over to Heather's body, bent down and gave her a hug, then stood back.

'She died saving our lives,' Lennox said. 'She was always looking out for others, more concerned about us than herself. She fought for what was right, always. She knew Sandy and the others were important. We all did, but she felt it in her heart. She suffered so much, but she was always kind.'

He was crying now, and turned his face into Vonnie's shoulder.

They stood there for a long time in silence.

<Sandy-Heather partial broken.> Sandy's voice was mournful in Ava's mind. <Good energy, now original energy state. Live on in human and Enceladon whole.>

They scuttled forward and enveloped Heather's body in an

embrace, flashing blue and green up and down their tentacles, billowing waves of melancholic colours across their head.

Eventually they moved away and sat on the edge of the harbour. The nearest Enceladon in the water nudged a slab of ice to the harbour edge.

Ava and Lennox stepped forward and lifted Heather's body. She was wet and cold in Ava's hands. Ava had a tightness in her chest as they placed the body on the ice.

The Enceladons in the water pushed the slab into the bay. Heather's body was soon just a dark smudge against the white, all of it dwarfed by the giant skies.

They all watched it for a long time. Ava cried, not just for Heather but for all of them, the massacred Enceladons, the dead animals, the people on the torpedo ship and at Ikusik. She wiped her eyes and looked at the Enceladons, everyone at the harbour, the people of Tasiilaq behind them. Maybe it was time for a new way of life.

Niviaq hugged her and Chloe, and a thought crystallised in Ava's mind. It had been lurking inside her for a while but she finally recognised it.

She looked into Niviaq's big eyes. 'I don't think Chloe and I are quite ready to head back to Scotland yet. I was hoping maybe we could stay here for a while. With you.'

Niviaq grinned. 'I was hoping you'd ask.'

# 70
# LENNOX

The others left the harbour, but Lennox stayed and watched Heather's block of ice until it was lost in a low haze coming down from the mountains. Maybe the bears would eat her, or she'd tip off the ice in a wave, sink to the bottom of the ocean, become food for tiny organisms or an ancient Greenland shark. She was part of the world now in a way she hadn't felt when she was alive. Lennox was warmed by that, even as he tried to get his breathing regular and his shoulders to relax.

All the Enceladons except Sandy had disappeared into the bay. Vonnie and the other humans were back at Niviaq's house drinking coffee. There was to be another gathering in the school hall soon. The people wanted to protect the Enceladons.

Lennox thought about what Britt said. The company had all the information about the Enceladons and the deep-sea mining. They'd be back.

But the animals were communicating and collaborating now because of the Enceladons. If they organised and fought back like today, what did that mean for the future? If anyone or anything became telepathic by eating another telepathic creature, soon the whole planet would be like this. Land animals ate fish and sea creatures, it would reach factory farming. Humans would have to face up to what they were doing, the torture of billions of creatures, the destruction of the land. Or maybe they would just keep doing it. More death, more economic growth, whatever that meant, using up resources and getting rich until there was nothing left.

He watched Sandy in the harbour water now. He'd felt so close to them when they first met. He'd wanted to be reunited so badly at the start of this, but it wasn't the same. Sandy wasn't the same and neither was Lennox. He had Vonnie and now a baby on the way. He wasn't ready for that, but no one ever was. Every parent worried about what kind of world they were bringing their kid into, but Lennox couldn't begin to fathom what the world would be like in a year, or ten or fifty.

<What are you thinking, Sandy?> Lennox tried to keep his voice light.

Sandy clambered out of the water and up the harbour wall to sit alongside him. He grinned at their flickering skin and big eyes, their shifting body, always moving.

<Enceladon-human whole is change.>

Lennox laughed. <Yes, Enceladon-*Earth* whole is change.>

<Sandy-Lennox partial is change.>

<How do you mean?>

They shimmered yellow in the sunshine and Lennox wondered what that meant. He would never properly understand Enceladon body language. Sandy's head expanded then contracted, like taking a deep breath.

<Sandy-Enceladon partial now understand anger, hate. Kill.>

What had they done to these creatures? Lennox put a hand out and took one of Sandy's tentacles. <But humans are changed as well. Me and the others, everyone here. We're good energy. And there will be many more. You've done something amazing, Sandy. You've changed things.>

<Sandy-Enceladon partial not good energy.>

There was nothing Lennox could say. There was a cost for what they'd done. Britt was right, Sandy had wanted to kill her, there was no going back from that.

<But we're together,> Lennox sent. <We can look after each other.>

Sandy squeezed his hand then let go. Flashes of orange and purple ran up and down their head. <Sandy-Lennox partial good energy.>

Lennox leaned his forehead against Sandy's. <Good energy.>

Sandy slipped into the water and disappeared under the surface. Lennox watched the ripples until they were gone, lost in the waves.

He looked across the bay then stood and walked up the hill to Niviaq's house. He waited a moment before stepping inside, then was met by a ruckus of noise, both in his ears and his mind. Everyone talking over each other, excited and tense, nervous and full of life.

Vonnie spotted him and got up from the sofa, hugged and kissed him, held his face. 'You OK?'

'Yeah.' He glanced at her stomach. <You two?>

She grinned. <We're good.>

Lennox took in the room. Ava and Niviaq were talking closely, Chloe and Pipaluk playing, Niviaq's mother refilling coffee cups and offering biscuits.

'Niviaq says we can stay as long as we want,' Vonnie said. 'Ava and Chloe are hanging around. Do you want to?'

Lennox smiled. 'That would be great.'

A cloud came over Vonnie's face. <What about what Britt said? What's going to happen?>

Lennox thought about the Enceladons in the bay, the animals up and down the coast, in the water. The people of Tasiilaq. His friends. He didn't have an answer, but that didn't matter.

<Good question.>

## ACKNOWLEDGEMENTS

The biggest thanks go to Karen Sullivan for her unwavering support over the years. Likewise, huge thanks to everyone else at Orenda Books for all their commitment and hard work. Thanks to Phil Patterson and all at Marjacq for always fighting my corner. For this book in particular thanks to Suzy Aspley, Ian Dawson and Line Kristiansen, who put me in touch with Jaakusaaq Sørensen. Eternal thanks to Jaakusaaq for his feedback on elements of East Greenlandic life, culture, geography, weather and so much more. Any remaining inaccuracies are mine alone. I am forever in debt to everyone who has read my books, thank you so much. Finally, all my love to Tricia, Aidan and Amber.